The Tin Cravat

The Tin Cravat

a novel by

J A C K D . H U N T E R

HARPER & ROW, PUBLISHERS, New York
Cambridge, Philadelphia, San Francisco,
London, Mexico City, São Paulo, Sydney

1817

Grateful thanks to Neal W. O'Connor and
Cornelius B. Tyson for their valuable counsel.

FIRST EDITION

Designed by Mary Blanchard

Library of Congress Cataloging in Publication Data

Hunter, Jack D
    The tin cravat.

    1. World War, 1939–1945—Fiction.   I. Title.
PS3558. U48T5   1981   813'.54   81-47356
ISBN 0-06-038004-7

81 82 83 84 85 10 9 8 7 6 5 4 3 2 1

To Tommie—
die ewige Elfi.

"When the tyrant has disposed of foreign enemies by conquest or treaty, and there is nothing to fear from them, then he is always stirring up some war or other, in order that the people may require a leader."

—PLATO, 427–347 B.C.

CAST OF CHARACTERS

Ludwig Auer	Disabled army veteran
Maria Benner	Business secretary
Hans Berger	SS Sturmbannführer
Martin Bormann	Politician
Fritz Dunkel	Gestapo agent
Trudi Eberhardt	Schoolgirl
Thomas Finnegan	Crew chief, U.S. Army Air Corps
Alex Gautzsch	SS Brigadeführer
Hermann Göring	Politician
Dieter Hansen	Feldwebel, documents expert
Elfi Heidemann	Nurse (Aliases: Inge Stolz, Luisa Nagele)
Heinrich Himmler	Politician
Oswald Kaspar	Gestapo informant
Klugschnacker	Wiseguy
Gordon Koscoe	U.S. Department of State
Ludwig, the Baron von und zu Lemmerhof	German General Staff member
Anna Leopold	Farm wife
Polly Loomis	OSS case officer
Max	Gestapo letter drop, Bern
Harold Radmer	Corporal, U.S. Army
Ernst Randelmann	Major, Luftwaffe (Alias: Karl Denzinger)
Alden Riggles	Flight Officer, Royal Air Force
Karl Schroeder	U.S. Intelligence agent, Bern
Emilie Stachel	Widow, mother
Bruno Stachel	Generalmajor, Luftwaffe (Aliases: Pastor Emil Ritter; SS Standartenführer Franz von Kistner; Alfred Knabe, tax accountant; Hans Braunek, city building inspector)
Egbert Steiger	Feldwebel, Luftwaffe crew chief
Amos Tarbell	Colonel, U.S. Army Air Corps (Alias: Karl Folger)
Robert Thompson	Attaché, U.S. Embassy, Bern
Oskar Vestner	Agent, Secret Field Police
Huey Vought	Counterintelligence officer, OSS
Pieter Weigand	SS Obersturmführer
Siegfried Weiss	Major, German Army

GLOSSARY

Abwehr	Intelligence branch
Ami	American (German slang)
Amtchef	Office chief
CE	Counterespionage
DF	Direction finder
Deutscher	German
Feldgrau	Field gray (German uniform)
Feldwebel	Master sergeant
Frau	Woman, Mrs.
Fräulein	Young woman, Miss
Führer	Leader
G-2	U.S. Army intelligence
GFP	Secret Field Police
Gasthof	Inn
Gebietsführer	District leader, Nazi party
Gefreiter	Corporal
Generalmajor	Brigadier general
Gestapo	Secret State Police
Hauptmann	Captain
Herr	Gentleman, Mr.
Hipo	Hilfspolizei, or auxiliary police
Hitler Jugend	Hitler Youth (HJ)
Home Plate	OSS headquarters, England
Ingenieur	Engineer
Joan-Eleanor	Radio set
Kennkarte	Identification card
Landser	American equivalent: GI
Leutnant	Lieutenant
Luftwaffe	Air Force
Marschall	Marshal
Marschbefehle	Travel orders
MI-5	British counterintelligence
NSDAP	Nazi party
Oberbayern	Upper Bavaria
Oberleutnant	First lieutenant
OKL	Luftwaffe High Command
OKW	Wehrmacht High Command

OSS	Office of Strategic Services (U.S.A.)
Panzer	Tank
Peter-Panning	Airlifting
Quatsch	Nonsense (American equivalent: baloney)
Reich	Empire, nation
Reichsjugendführung	National Youth Leadership
Reichsleiter	National leader
SI	Secret Intelligence
SS	Schütz Staffel, Elite Guard
Sicherheitsdienst	Security Service
Soldatenheim	Rest house for troops
Unteroffizier	Sergeant
V-2	German rocket weapon
VW recon	German jeep
Wehrmacht	Armed services
Weltschmerz	World-weariness
W-T	Wireless telegraphy
X-2	Counterintelligence branch, OSS

The Tin Cravat

P R O L O G U E

December 10, 1944

VON LEMMERHOF CAUGHT his first glimpse of Nebelburg as their car broke from the fir-forest twilight at the top of the eastern rim of hills. The village huddled in a cuplike valley, its cluster of faded Gasthöfe and pensions seemingly crestfallen over their failure to give the place some claim to elegance.

He was mildly consoled to find that there were still towns whose roofs held their tiles and windows their panes and where no yawning rubble pits gave off the stench of decay. On the flight from Berlin he had become increasingly depressed as the sores of the Fatherland's fatal gangrene passed below. Each shattered city, every smoldering factory and railhead had been clinical confirmation of—What had Kaspar snickered in one of his unguarded moments?—the terminal stage of Götterdämmerung. The pain of Berlin had been endurable because Berlin was the logical focus of the enemy's abrasions and could be expected to blister and become ugly and raw. But to soar over Germany and discover that the Berlin blister was only one in a hideous rash had been appalling. He had known, of course, what was happening to his homeland, but to know death exists and to see it occur are vastly different things.

"Checkpoint ahead, Herr General," Kaspar announced over his shoulder.

"A checkpoint in this godforsaken hole? Unbelievable."

Kaspar shook his head, exasperated. "Give a German the chance to stamp a pass, to punch a ticket, or to shuffle a pile of papers and he'll pass up a piece of tail."

The general made no further comment. The Mercedes slowed to a halt behind a hay wagon and a trio of VW recons, each piled high with unhappy army Landsers huddled together against the Alpine cold. The Hipo constable who had been swaggering along the tiny file of vehicles finally spotted the Luftwaffe command serial on the bumper of the big sedan and came quickly in the Laufschritt, concluding the quickstep with a crash of heels and the stiff-armed greeting.

"Heil Hitler. May I see your papers?"

Kaspar presented his trip ticket and Soldbuch, the small brown pocket folder carried by German soldiers as identification and history of service. "Make it fast, friend. We don't want to keep the general waiting."

Von Lemmerhof leaned forward. Through the window he said, "Which one of those buildings is the Nebelhof?"

The Hipo man's eyes, small and yellow, settled on the Knight's Cross hanging from the general's throat. "The one with the blue shutters, Herr General." With a fawning smile, the man added, "You are the second important visitor to arrive this evening. There is also an SS Brigadeführer putting up for the night. Our village is doubly honored."

"I suggest," the general grated, "that you pay more attention to security and less to the welcoming-committee ebullience. From now on you will make no further mention of my presence in this rotten little place. Understood?"

The man's smile disappeared. "Yes, Herr General. I'll clear the way at once."

Von Lemmerhof sank back into the warmth of his greatcoat, watching as the Hipo man bullied the other vehicles into shifting, backfiring activity. Strange, he thought bitterly in the spirit of Kaspar's earlier outburst, how so many of his countrymen cherished authority for authority's sake. From trolley-car conductors to SS chieftains, they doted on badges that would endow their arrogance with official respectability.

It was no good to brood about such things, he told himself in silent reproval. For days now, since receiving the mysterious summons to Nebelburg, he'd had to exert an extraordinary effort to sublimate his sense of guilt. During his months in Berlin he had been able to restrain a gathering inner conviction that he, personally, had caused Germany's ruin. Actually, he had welcomed the bureaucratic madness—the mountains of orders and counterorders, the dispatches, cables, inventories, morning reports, intelligence analyses that had to be processed to make room for the mountains to come—because it gave him little time to wander the haunted halls of conscience. But the call from Gautzsch had broken his carefully built dams, and his mind had been flooded anew with nameless anxieties.

The inn was a medieval half-timber structure with narrow windows and angular roof lines, and, as the car pulled up to the door, Lemmerhof could smell cooking fat and ancient manure. Flipping up his collar, he stepped out, blinking against the sleety snow that had begun to swirl out of the oncoming night.

A tall, squarish man in a Brigadeführer's uniform stood at the far end of the entrance hallway. He brought himself together in a polite suggestion of attention. "Good evening, Herr General. Would you step this way, please?"

"You're Gautzsch?" Lemmerhof asked, pulling off his gloves and removing his cap.

"Yes, General. Would you like something to eat before we chat?" Gautzsch's voice was a rumbling basso.

"No. Let's get on with it. Are we alone here?"

"Of course. I have taken the entire building, and the innkeeper and his few people will be ushered out by my driver as soon as our needs have been met."

5

"Dismiss them, then. I'm exhausted from my day. I want a few hours' sleep."

Settled in a big chair in the sitting room, cigar carefully clipped and lighted, von Lemmerhof regarded Gautzsch with weary curiosity. "So then," he said, "the drama begins."

"He has lost the war," Gautzsch said bluntly.

Odd, Lemmerhof thought, how often today in Germany it was no longer der Führer, der Reichskanzler, der Mehrer, der Held, der Retter. No longer the Leader, the Chancellor, the Expander, the Hero, the Savior. Now, after—How many years? Twelve? Twelve hundred?—He was only He. Capitalized.

"I'm afraid so, Gautzsch."

"Klugschnacker says His plan to fight to the last German is absurd. Klugschnacker says He can die a hero's death in Berlin if He wants to, but the party—the Führer principle —must be kept alive. You and I will help Klugschnacker accomplish that noble aim."

"What does he want me to do?"

Gautzsch rested back in his chair and crossed his booted legs. "Klugschnacker has certain long-range plans for a clandestine organization in Bavaria, the Tyrol, and the underbelly of the Reich. It suffices at this stage to say that this secret structure will be designed to keep the NSDAP viable no matter which enemy army occupies German national territory. To cover these preparations and keep Hitler's loyalists in the dark, Klugschnacker wants you, General, to become chief of a Hitler Jugend Wehrmacht replacement pool here in the Nebelburg area."

"You mean the Werewolf thing?"

Gautzsch smirked. "Not exactly. The Werewolf idea, in which it was proposed to set up a guerrilla operation in the Austrian Alps, was rejected months ago by Him as defeatist. But General Eisenhower still worries about the concept, apparently. Our intelligence people tell us that Eisenhower has designed his overall strategy for the invasion of Germany and Central Europe so as to negate any plans we might have to carry through on the Werewolf. Which is fine. We welcome anything that keeps the Allied armed forces off balance, and that's why Klugschnacker wants you to contact Eisenhower and, pretending to be a turncoat Nazi, offer him the complete Werewolf operational plan."

"You are joking, of course."

"Do I look like a man who jokes, Herr General?"

"But I'm no traitor—"

"Of course not. We simply want Eisenhower to think you are."

"I see. What will I ask Eisenhower to do for me? I mean, every turncoat has his price."

"You will ask for amnesty. The Allies have decreed that all German officials above certain ranks will be, upon the Fatherland's defeat, automatically arrested and held on suspicion of so-called war crimes. You fall into such a category. In return for your, ah, delivery of Werewolf secrets, you will demand amnesty and a plane—an American plane —to fly you to sanctuary beyond Nazi retribution."

Von Lemmerhof sighed and dropped the ash of his cigar into a ceramic tray on the table beside him. "You told me an audacious plot was afoot, Gautzsch, but I had no idea it could be this audacious. But tell me—if the Werewolf thing is a red herring, what is Klugschnacker's real plan?"

"That's where Fuglein comes in. We'll go into all of that tomorrow. We both need a bath and some sleep right now."

"Very well." Lemmerhof paused, thinking. Then he asked, "This American plane—who will fly it for me? On a thing this delicate we'll have to be especially careful as to who knows how much."

"For an Ami airplane, an Ami crew is indicated," Gautzsch said. "But the pilot must speak fluent German. That's why you will specify Bruno Stachel."

7

Von Lemmerhof's eyes widened. "Stachel? He's still in America? Still flying?"

Gautzsch coughed dryly. "He's in America. But not flying. Since his defection in 1938 the Amis have engaged him as a civilian instructor at their War Department Intelligence Training Center in Maryland, near Washington. He teaches embryo intelligence officers Luftwaffe order of battle, Nazi party organization, and operational procedures of the Gestapo, Abwehr, and other security groups. Our agents tell us he has become a cantankerous malcontent."

"He was never anything else. He was on my staff in Berlin before he was awarded the Blood Order and elevated to sainthood by the Führer. And he was a cantankerous malcontent. Most of the time, that is. He can be a charming bastard when he wants to be." The general hesitated again. After a moment he said, "But why Stachel? There must be plenty of Ami pilots who speak German—"

"There are not, as a matter of fact. But aside from that, Klugschnacker has reasons of his own. And ours is not to question why, as the saying goes."

Von Lemmerhof puffed slowly on his cigar, remembering Stachel—the World War One ace who stemmed from the working class; who had fought his way to fame and the Blue Max, the Kaiser's highest award; who had married into one of the Fatherland's greatest fortunes and, after the war, destroyed the marriage by very nearly drinking himself to death; who had given early support to Hitler (and, in fact, had personally introduced General Ludwig, the Baron von und zu Lemmerhof, himself to the Führer one fine evening in Wannsee); and who had, in his eventual disenchantment with the Nazis, flown a planeload of Jews and dissident Christians into France and subsequent political asylum in the United States.

"Can we trust Stachel, Gautzsch?"

"Probably not. But Klugschnacker has designed a means of controlling him. I'll give you the details tomorrow. Mean-

8

while, I suggest we nap until midnight. It's been a long day and we both are about kaput."

Rising from his chair, the general brushed some ashes from his lapel and said, "What's the timetable on all this?"

"With the Amis approaching the Rhine and the Russians boring in from the east, Klugschnacker privately expects the war to be lost by next fall. To have his grand design in operation by then he must have all his planning completed in the next two weeks. Allowing time to assemble our resources here and in Munich, to brief and train Stachel and whatever crew members he brings along from the States, the exercise should be in its opening stage by April 1. Meantime, I'll be your liaison with Klugschnacker. I'll relay his orders to you in person. Secrecy must be absolute. You will speak of this to no one until I, personally, give you Klugschnacker's permission. Understood, Herr General?"

"Understood."

At the door, von Lemmerhof paused and looked back. "I'm especially curious about one thing, Gautzsch. Why me? Why have I been selected for this little exercise in deception?"

"Because, Herr General, He trusts you. You are the only General Staff officer He would readily permit to leave Berlin these days."

"I see. Tell me something else, Gautzsch. Will I, like Klugschnacker, have a code name?"

"Of course, Herr General. You will be known as Geflüster. 'Whisper,' to the Americans."

Von Lemmerhof nodded thoughtfully. "Well, it's rather fitting, I guess. I'll be whispering in Eisenhower's ear. And at least it isn't a silly slang term, like 'Klugschnacker.'"

"That's not so silly, either, when you think about it," Gautzsch said. "After all, Klugschnacker is indeed wise."

"But a wise *guy*? Isn't that sort of demeaning?" von Lemmerhof's lips suggested a smile.

"He is never demeaned by things that stand to benefit him, my dear General. And as Wiseguy, he expects to be the Führer of the Fourth Reich that will come out of Germany's ruins. Someday, Klugschnacker—Wiseguy—will be a revered name in the Fatherland's history."

"Maybe so, Gautzsch. But in the meantime, what—besides the self-satisfaction that comes from our, ah, indefatigable patriotism—can we expect for our part in Wiseguy's ambitious scheme?"

Gautzsch's craggy face accommodated a smile of its own. "That's the good part, Herr General. Wiseguy plans to take you and me with him, all the way to the top. You will not regret your—How did you put it?—patriotism."

"Well, then. Good night, Gautzsch."

"Sleep well, Herr Whisper. I'll rouse you"—Gautzsch glanced at his wristwatch—"in, say, five hours. You'll see then how you and I and Wiseguy will make complete fools of the Americans."

1

THE STINSON CAME from the southeast, flying low and fast through the advance spittle of a snow squall, and its blattering beat down on the field as it made its final turn into the wind.

Stachel hunched deeper into his overcoat and moved to the lee of the car, which stood cold and shapeless in the drift forming between the flight line and the service hangar. Snow, fine and gritty, stung his face and hurt his eyes, but he watched anyhow, alternating his admiration of the airplane with envy of whoever was at the controls. He hadn't flown in a long time, a condition that now touched him with the restlessness of the reformed smoker who smells a cigar nearby.

The roar dropped off to a clacking sigh as the Stinson sank, wings cocked, over the hot-dog stands and gas stations that smeared the far horizon. The plane snarled again briefly, fishtailed, then crumped to the turf, teetering and rumbling over the winter stubble and kicking up a plume of snow that followed it all the way to the far fence. It sat there for a time, its propeller ticking over in the insistent flurry; then it stirred briefly, rumbled through a tail-flicking turn, and flounced toward the transient-aircraft hangar, nose high and haughty.

Stachel let himself through the gate and, huddling against the wind, waited until the aircraft had fussed its way through its parking chores. Then he went to the tarmac, where he shifted from one foot to the other in the cold.

A young navy officer appeared in the Stinson's side hatch, then stepped to the ground to assist her as she emerged from the cabin shadows. She saw Stachel at once and came toward him, her mouth set in a polite smile.

"Hi, Bruno. Long time no see."

"Welcome to beautiful Hagerstown, Miss Loomis," he said without enthusiasm.

"Does beautiful Hagerstown have a coffeepot? I'm coming apart."

"There's a small eating place here. It's open, I think."

"That'll be fine." She glanced at the navy fellow, who stood in the wind, looking sincere. "My bag—would you take it to this gentleman's car? You do have a car, Bruno?"

"I borrowed a friend's. That Packard over there."

"You can save me a cab ride to Ritchie. I have a conference there tomorrow."

The wind was rising, and the snow danced across the field and made patterns on the somber scarps of the hangar area. Overhead, low-rolling clouds brought an early twilight that whispered of the bitter night to come. Stachel shivered, pulled his hat low, and, taking her arm, made for the diner, whose steamy windows glowed in the gloom beyond the fence.

Inside, the air was warm and thick with smells of toast and ancient cooking, and the greasy radio on the shelf delivered itself of some Tommy Dorsey. The man behind the counter, splashing a stack of dishes in the rinse sink, looked up, tongued the toothpick to the other corner of his mouth, and said, "Help you?"

"Two coffees."

"Aren't you going to spring for dinner, Bruno?"

"I don't have time for dinner. I've got to get home and check on my mother. She's been ill."

"Sorry to hear that. As I was sorry to hear about your dad."

"We all have to go sometime, as the saying has it."

"How did your mother take it?"

"Poorly. They were very close. And far from home."

She was unmoved by his irony, he saw. He wanted to make it clear that he had not forgotten the truth; he and his parents had been tossed into this sorry limbo due to her wretched little plots. It was not right that she sit there at the linoleum counter and act as if this were a class reunion. Watching her stir her coffee, he tried without much success to hate her. He considered the dark, downcast eyes; the narrow face, with its slightly parted, lascivious lips, the whiteness of her neck, arching below the careful disarray of her hair to join little-girl shoulders. These were the things that defined the entity known to him as Polly Loomis; these were the things he asked himself to hate because—obvious, touchable—they were proxies for all the indefinable forces that had combined to make her the world's most cunning woman.

"So what does America's Mata Hari want of me after all this time?"

"Dear Bruno—so blunt, so impatient."

"Don't be superior. You may be wearing a mink coat, but I remember you in Woolworth underwear."

"You're trying to make me mad, aren't you? It won't work, pal. I'm your old friend."

"You are trouble, Miss Loomis. Whenever you appear, there is trouble. The moment I read your telex I began looking over my shoulder."

She laughed, and he could sense her searching, chameleon-like, for the attitude that would play to his mood. "Let's take that booth in the far corner. The cook can't hear us there."

As they carried their coffee to the place by the windows he was aware of the stirring in the belly that accompanies the anticipation of danger. His mind went to the day, a thousand years ago, when he reported to his squadron in France and stood on the silent, snowswept airfield. He had known that day that he was on the rim of something dreadful, of course, but the feeling had surrendered to an adolescent's impatience to see how bad things could get. Now, as a Methuselah who appreciated how really bad things could get, his byword was caution. Granted, he might be dying of boredom, but (as his father had liked to say) it never paid to cure a headache by leaping off the Matterhorn.

"There," she breathed, settling at the table, "all nice and comfy." Calling to the cook then: "Turn up that terrific music, will you?"

Stachel sipped his coffee, self-conscious under her scrutiny.

"Your years as a schoolteacher have done wonders for your English, Bruno. It's still accented, of course. But your command of the American idiom is fantastic."

He shrugged.

"You're pale, though. You should get outdoors more often."

"I suppose."

She lit a cigarette with a silver-plated Zippo, inhaling with her eyes half closed. Blowing a stream of smoke at the ceiling, she said, with no suggestion of accusation, "I hear you have turned into Von Peck's Bad Boy. The people at Camp Ritchie say you spend much of your time haranguing the brass, intimidating your students, and making an all-round pain in the ass of yourself."

He stared into his cup, thinking about this. "Your information is good. I am exactly what you say."

"Unhappy, huh?"

"Six years as the Pentagon's specimen Nazi-who-has-seen-the-light does not amount to ecstasy, Miss Loomis."

"I guess not."

"Do you realize that it was only two months ago the FBI granted me permission to drive a car?"

"Well," Miss Loomis said, feigning sympathy, "things are tough all over. Actually, the FBI had to be sure that your anti-Nazi postures weren't mere cover fabricated by German intelligence. That you were really one of us good guys."

Unable to find words for his scorn, Stachel gazed out the window at the vacant lot across the alley, as if among the frozen weeds and pop bottles and Baby Ruth wrappers there lurked an explanation of how he had come to this sorry condition. Down the hangar line an airplane coughed, blared for a moment, then subsided in a balky idling, and he remembered clouds and far horizons.

I am, he thought, *a zero. Forty-five years old, and after all that time I have left no mark anywhere. Even in the sky, which I love more than anything, there are no signs of my having been there.*

* * *

Polly Loomis watched Stachel with unblinking eyes, feeling a peculiar melancholy.

In the beginning, during her tour with the United States Embassy in Berlin, Stachel, as a Luftwaffe bureaucrat, had been nothing more to her than a cat's paw to be used in the conduct of her intelligence mission. She had viewed him as a wary animal—elemental, intelligent, driven—and tried to manage him accordingly. But he'd proved to be another Bobby Liggett, the blond, blue-eyed kid in the seventh grade who had unwittingly lit her pilot light. Her school days in Chicago had been endured in a warren of dirty brick that echoed to a persistent wind and the sounds of illness and poverty. Then, one day, Bobby had ceased to be a bratty klutz at the next desk; his creamy skin, his faraway eyes, the pout on his pink lips had ignited some kind of flame in her belly—an irrational, liquid craving that caused her to rivet her gaze on him in class, to follow him home after school, to devise ridiculous schemes by which to engage him in conversation, and, at night, to lie in her cot and imagine him there with her. The city became beautiful; her loneliness gave way to cheer. Then Bobby's father, a seaman on an ore ship, had been lost in a storm off Duluth, and Bobby and his mother had gone to live with relatives in Buffalo. For months afterward, she would alternately pine and curse the little bastard for leaving her with this ungodly fire in her, and even years later, when in bed with some man of the moment, she would remember Bobby as her means of enduring the night.

Until Stachel.

Stachel was the only human being on the face of the earth ever to affect her as Bobby had.

The son of a bitch.

She cleared her throat, a soft sound. "I've missed you, Bruno."

"That's nonsense, Miss Loomis."

"We once had a good thing going."

He gave her a quick glance, full of impatience. "What are you getting at? If it's a return to old times, forget it. I had enough of your duplicity long ago."

It never got any easier, his rejection. But, being as she was, she absorbed the impact of this latest, then, behind a deliberately formed smile, went on to business.

"I need your help," she said, projecting confidentiality.

"You? The—How did you sign your telex?—Deputy Director, Operations, X-2 Division, Office of Strategic Services?"

She ignored his sarcasm. "As a former German intelligence officer, there is something you can do for your country."

"Which country, Miss Loomis? Germany or the United States? I belong to neither." He was in one of his famous stubborn moods now—immovable, implacable, and full of righteousness. But she smiled and winked, letting him see that she appreciated irony as his special brand of humor.

"I want you to return to Germany, Bruno."

"You're mad."

"I'm serious. There's something you can do there."

"You can't force me to do anything, Miss Loomis. I'm no lawyer, but I am what you Yankees call an enemy alien. And the Geneva Convention forbids a belligerent to compel an

16

enemy prisoner—or detainee—to serve against his own nation."

God, but his eyes are blue, she thought.

"I'm not trying to compel you to do anything, Bruno. I want you to volunteer. I want you to go willingly into Germany on a mission that will guarantee the peace to come." She knew she sounded like a recruitment brochure, but all war was extravagant, even its rhetoric, so to hell with it.

"You are being ridiculous."

"The war is almost over. The peace is yet to be secured."

"You sound like a recruitment brochure."

"Clichés are clichés because they are true, as somebody once said."

"I'd be recognized in an instant."

"Your fame, you mean?"

"Put it any way you like. But the Gestapo still considers me a traitor. There are formal charges. A return to Germany would be suicide, because there are a lot of people there who remember me—from Hitler to my postman."

She sipped her coffee, only to find it cold. She considered calling for a fresh cup, but it would aggravate an already deteriorating situation. Her sadness persisted, and she longed for an end to his domination of her life. "We have thought of all that," she said coolly. "We would apply the rule of reasonable expectation."

He gave her another irritable look. "My English isn't good enough for that. What does it mean?"

"Nobody sees what he doesn't expect to see. You could put a white hat and an apron on Bing Crosby and set him to selling peanuts at a baseball game and only one in ten in the crowd would give him a second glance. And the one who gave him a second glance would dismiss the idea at once, because Bing Crosby is not about to be selling peanuts at a baseball game. Right? Bing Crosby is in Hollywood, making movies and living the life of a billionaire."

Stachel gave a sigh of exasperation, pushed clear of the

table, stood up, and put on his hat. At the cash register he handed the toothpick chewer a quarter, then turned to regard her across the aisle with noncommittal eyes. "Come on," he said, "I'll drive you out to Ritchie."

Outside, the snow was falling heavily and there was a miserable, penetrating dampness. The car started complainingly, deep in its own winter misery. Stachel backed it around and directed it through the freezing ruts to the highway. He drove in silence until they had cleared town and were climbing the eastern hills.

"Why should I help you Yankees?" he said, almost as if to himself.

"Why shouldn't you?" Polly said dryly, feeling the weight of years and unfulfillment. "Elfi Heidemann is."

She felt his eyes on her, a sidelong glance that lingered. "Elfi? Elfi Heidemann is returning to Germany?"

"She volunteered last week."

"On this same matter? The one you have in mind for me?"

"None other, pal." She kept her eyes on the road, trying to deal with her depression. *So it goes,* she thought. *A word or two, and the whole bloody world falls apart.*

*   *   *

They showed their ID cards at the camp's main gate, where a blue-faced military policeman, a mountain of olive drab and shining brass, waved them through. The Packard grumbled its way around the frozen lake, its headlights dimmed by the white swirling, its tire chains clacking a forlorn rhythm. Stachel braked to a sliding halt at the entrance to the VIP quarters, then sat, staring ahead at the snow.

After a time he said, "You know I'll go, don't you?"

"I never had the slightest doubt, Bruno dear."

"I have only one condition."

"Which is?"

"If things don't go well, my mother must continue to receive the fifty dollars a week I receive from the War

Department. As long as she lives."

"Done. And we'll take out the standard ten-thousand-dollar life-insurance policy the government provides for service-men. O.K.?"

"O.K."

2

THE HOUSE WAS a pile of tan clapboard, porches, and stained glass that stood in Victorian aloofness on a side street in Blue Ridge Summit, an infinitesimal dot on the world that had had the misfortune to be adjacent to Camp Ritchie and its olive-drab impositions. Stachel had been able to lease the place six months after his arrival in Maryland, when the commandant had put in a word for him with Mrs. Abercrombie, the melon-shaped president of Women for Christian Tolerance who doubled as landlady and social arbiter for Summit, Highfield, Pen Mar, and Sabillasville and all God's territory thereabouts. The news that Stachel and his parents had escaped the Nazis while smuggling dissident Lutherans to France clinched the matter, and Mrs. Abercrombie had shown her appreciation by reducing the rent from outrageous to exorbitant.

His mother was in the kitchen, presiding over a steam that smelled of coffee and frying potatoes. When she smiled at him he regretted once again having to leave her alone during the day. She had never truly recovered from his father's death, remaining in the shallows of what Reverend Mueller, the American minister, called "the slough of despond." But there had been no choice; his War Department stipend simply wasn't enough to provide her with a companion, while for him to stay home with her would have been to guarantee poverty and madness for them both.

It was nothing new for them, this living on the rim of desperation. In his boyhood, in the days of the Kaiser's empire and the compulsory military service that kept a half-million men constantly under arms, gaps in the menial work force had been filled by women. He had seen them toiling in the fields, digging ditches, sawing lumber, cleaning streets, scrubbing railroad depots, shoveling coal, carrying bricks—all the time bearing children and keeping house and thanking God for their blessings. His mother, although better off than most women (thanks to an innkeeper husband who loved her and sheltered her as best he could from a society rooted in male dominance), had been as hard put to create a home as any of them. She had worked herself to exhaustion in the bowels of the Gasthof, despite a touch of education in Switzerland that might have, in another marriage, made her mistress of a fine household in some fine city. Even so, Mama's faith in her God was absolute, and Stachel had wondered then—as he wondered now—what kind of magic provides one with a sense of God, an unshakable loyalty to the idea of a God, and a day-by-day, nuts-and-bolts trust in an unseeable God, when all the time so many things were so irredeemably rotten.

Feeling a sudden rush of sentiment for this tiny woman with the selfless past, he said, "Are you all right, Mama?"

"Of course I'm all right. Supper will be ready in a moment."

"How was your day?"

"Irmgard Hassler called. She said she's heard from Elfi and Elfi plans to write us soon."

"Elfi is still in Nebraska, I take it."

"They've made her head nurse in a camp for Wehrmacht prisoners. Near a town called Hastings."

"Did she say how long she'd be there?"

"What do you mean?"

"Well, the Americans are always moving people around."

"It was my impression Elfi thinks she's got a permanent place there. At least, nothing else was said."

"She should have tried for that job at Walter Reed in Washington."

"Her English isn't good enough."

"Well, it's no skin off my nose."

She put a lid carefully atop a pot and turned to give him a mother's inspection. "Is there something wrong?"

"Why do you ask?" he sparred.

"I've been worried about you lately. You're peevish. Surly."

He sat at the table and poured himself a cup of coffee, not sure how to answer. She was very perceptive, so it was difficult to strike poses with her. "It's this sameness in all the days. This pretending to be a schoolmaster for a stream of children playing soldier. The Americans are so naïve and puffed with self-righteousness. I'd like to kick them all in their behinds."

"You have to understand them, Bruno. They are very unusual people. Unlike us in so many ways. They love to complain about their country, their customs, but they get angry when somebody else does. And they're open and generous. But most important, they saved our lives and gave us a home."

"They gave us nothing. They tricked us into leaving Germany without asking if we wanted to go."

"To have stayed in Germany would have been to die. To be killed by our own countrymen."

"So now I'm being killed by Americans and their little hypocrisies. They dragged me out of Germany, set me up as a freak in a military circus, and expect me to be grateful."

"When the Nazis are gone we will return to Germany."

"We won't be welcome there, either. The good ones who

21

survive will see us as spineless deserters. The Nazis who survive will see us as traitors. Be realistic for a change. We don't belong anywhere."

"Bruno, what's the matter with you?"

"You tell me, Mama."

He had spent the morning in another try at reassignment, and, as usual, the effort had won him no more than two hours on a hard chair outside the commandant's office. The base CO was a good fellow in ordinary conditions, given to amiable chitchat and recollections of the old days at Fort Sill; but on those occasions when Stachel sought to persuade him that schoolteaching was for old maids and Jesuits, the colonel would slam his door in absolute refusal to expose himself to another of Stachel's tirades. Giving up after four skimmings through the anteroom's primeval copies of *Artillery Journal*, Stachel had gone to lunch at the Officers' Club, heavy with anger and the dreary knowledge that the afternoon would begin still another lecture series for still another gaggle of satraps in uniform. There would be the eager young ones, bustling and crisp in their certainty that God was in his military heaven and would most naturally bless them with eventual glory; there would be a scattering of sullen timeservers, doing enough to protect their privileges as officers and not enough to acquire obligations; and there would be the older, stoical ones—light colonels and eagles with gray, frozen faces—each of whom repressed the pain of a side-tracked career and the understanding that there would be no marble statue of him in any town square, ever.

"I began a new course this afternoon," he said. "The students are all field-grade officers, most of them majors, some colonels. They watched me as I lectured. Not as students watching a teacher, but with curiosity. Condescension even. In the early days it would amuse me, this attitude of the Americans. But it's been difficult to handle recently. They've become smug, indulgent, superior. They patronize me—in the way a clergyman patronizes a reformed hoodlum.

"Today was the worst. A lieutenant colonel named Tarbell was in the class. A thin, bald man who acts as if he's the cleverest fellow anywhere. I saw right away that he would be the smart aleck, the opinion leader who would take over the class if I didn't put him in his place at once. I tried first to humor him, joke with him. But he kept looking down his nose at me, and once, when I was talking about Hitler and how he was the result of an unresolved World War One, this Tarbell said, 'It seems to me that you Krauts are chronic losers.' I'd been grumpy all morning, Mama, but that remark sent me up in a spiral. It made me angrier than I've been in a long time. It shouldn't have, because the man was right. But it did."

She nodded. "What did you do about it?"

"Nothing. That's what makes me the angriest. Tarbell was challenging me, and I didn't do anything about it. Do you realize that I haven't done anything about the Nazis, either? They're the reason you are here in this hole, when you should be spending your old age in your real home, surrounded by friends. They're the ones who have ruined things, and I helped them do it. And I haven't done a single damned thing to make amends."

She gave him another lingering scrutiny. "What are you trying to tell me, Bruno?"

"Tell you?"

"I've known you for a long time. I know everything about you. And I know when you're trying to tell me something and can't find the words."

"The Americans want me to go somewhere on a special assignment."

"Are you going?"

"I don't want to leave you alone."

"Does it have to do with fighting the Nazis?"

"Well, yes—"

"Then I insist you go."

"Mama—"

"Irmgard will help me while you're gone. And Mrs. Abercrombie likes me. She'll help, too."

"I—"

"Not another word, Bruno."

"May I say one more thing?"

"Well?"

"You're a first-class woman, Mama. And I thank you."

3

POLLY'S MOOD HAD not been helped by supper at the VIP mess, which amounted to two hours of unbearable blather from the school's assembled Pharisees; nor had it eased with her retreat into the silence of her borrowed office. Consigning Stachel to eventual destruction had simply been tougher than she had imagined it would be, and it hurt like sin, and that was that.

She sat in the swivel chair and made much of studying her notes, hoping to smother her unhappiness with concentration on the business at hand. She looked up from her papers when, after a ritual rapping, Tarbell appeared in the doorway.

"Come in," she said, summoning up her affable career woman's façade. "Sit down, Amos. You observed Stachel, as planned?"

"He's a doozy, that one."

"That's the word, all right."

"I tried to make him angry. But with no great success."

Amos Tarbell was the kind of man who could never readily accept the idea of women in positions of authority. This, coupled with his own secret sense of inadequacy, guaranteed a difficult session. In an attempt to compensate, he crossed his legs and lit a cigarette, deliberately neglecting to offer her one. "I'm told that the Adjutant General's Office has selected me as someone who might help you on something," he said smoothly, in what he hoped to be the manner of George Sanders, his favorite film star.

She consulted a folder lying open on her desk. "Your two-oh-one file says that, in addition to your many skills as a multiengine pilot, you speak German."

"Ich kann gerade genug um mich verständlich zu machen," he said glibly, feeling a small pleasure at this unexpected opportunity to score one-up on her.

Polly leaned back in her chair and gazed at the wretched night beyond the window. She decided that she didn't like Tarbell at all, seeing in him those self-satisfied prep-school types, full of country-club superiority and senior proms and snazzy roadsters and rambling white houses on elm-shaded lawns, and, therefore, as remote from her own origins as Bertie Wooster and Jeeves.

Switching to German, she said, "You sound fluent enough. But your accent is atrociously American. However, I'm not looking for an American who can pass as a German. I'm interested in your capabilities as a flier who can communicate with German fliers, both directly and via radio."

Tarbell's faint smile faded, his carefully shaven cheeks turning pink. Continuing in German, he said, "I can do that, I suppose."

"There's no 'suppose' in this business, pal. Either you know or you don't."

"Well, ah, yes," he said, the pink becoming crimson, "I can get along with German fliers. And I suppose you're including Stachel."

"We want you to give him B-17 training, among other things."

Tarbell took a thoughtful pull at his cigarette, then exhaled twin streams of smoke from his nose. "Well," he said evenly, "you represent a civilian agency, and I'm on full military active duty. This, plus my dislike of Stachel, is enough, I'm afraid, to cause me to decline your offer."

"That's not quite so," Polly amended. "You are most anxious to accept the offer, since your air corps commanding officer is most anxious that you accept the offer. Would you like to read the general's memo to that effect?"

Tarbell flushed again and remained silent, and so she returned to English and went on.

"To give you some background, I was assigned to the American Embassy in Berlin from the mid-twenties to 1939. I was ostensibly a secretary, but in fact I served as a case officer in the department's intelligence section. Stachel, a famous ace in the first war, befriended Hitler when Hitler was still a grubby red-necked ward politician spooking about Munich, looking for votes and respectability. Stachel helped Hitler come to power, then went on to regret it. Watching him, I saw disaffection setting in—disillusionment with the Nazis. I saw a chance to turn his anti-Nazi tendencies to our favor. I tipped the Gestapo to the fact that Stachel's parents were running a clandestine refugee escape chain. To save his folks from arrest, Stachel flew them and a planeful of refugees to France. We brought him to the States and put him on hold, where he's remained through the war. Until now. Now something rather keen has come up, and it's time to blow the dust off him. It's time for Stachel to give expression to his dislike of the Nazis."

Tarbell tapped the ash from his cigarette, trying to recover his initial aplomb. "Forgive my skepticism, but after looking him over in class today, it's my guess that no one was more unlikely to have flown anti-Nazi refugees from Germany than Stachel was. He's an arrogant, self-satisfied boor, and I'm willing to bet that, given a true choice, he would no more have flown those refugees into France than I would stroll naked through a DAR convention. Do we really know what caused Stachel to fly the coop? We like to think you exploited him. But did you exploit him, or did he exploit you? Who tricked whom?"

She shrugged, trying to hide her annoyance. "That, Colonel Tarbell, is for me to worry about. Meanwhile, you will concentrate on flying and making Bruno Stachel proficient as a pilot of the B-17 Flying Fortress."

"Am I allowed to know why?"

"To a point," she said, wanting now to complete the interview and be rid of this pompous fool for the night. "A member of the German General Staff has secretly informed OSS, via Allen Dulles in Geneva, that he has been ordered to set up a so-called Werewolf resistance force in the Tyrolean Alps. Object—to conduct guerrilla warfare if and when the German armies collapse and the Allies occupy the Reich. But this staff member knows that, as a result of the October 1943 establishment of the United Nations War Crimes Commission in London, all high-ranking Nazi officers are to be automatically arrested on suspicion of war crimes once Allied Military Government takes over in Germany. He's disenchanted with his Nazi bosses and sees a German defeat as inevitable. He wants no part of the automatic arrest, and so he will trade the Werewolf plans for his personal amnesty."

"Question."

"No questions. Just listen. General Eisenhower is deeply concerned about the possibility of resistance in the Alps. Guerrillas locked up in those mountains could keep the entire European continent unstable for months, even years, to come. He has shaped his entire strategy to preclude such an eventuality, and he takes this offer from a general staffer most seriously. He has asked OSS to 'exploit this opening and pursue it vigorously,' to use his own musty phrase. And so you and I and Stachel have been anointed as the pursuers."

She paused, selected a cigarette from the pack on her desk, lit it, and blew a cloud at Tarbell's necktie. "We can't afford the high risk that attends a paradrop, so Stachel and his team will fly along with a routine Eighth Air Force raid on Berlin. They will simulate a disablement by enemy fire and will crash-land at a carefully selected spot, from which they will proceed to a safe-house. There they will hold secret interviews with the general staffer. From there they will transmit their findings to an RAF Mosquito circling overhead, using a J-E combo. They will continue this radio activity twice a week for as long as it takes to assure General Eisenhower that he has checkmated the Nazi plan. Your function, Colonel Tarbell, is twofold—you will give Stachel his transition training in the B-17, and you will be in the Mosquito, on the other end of the J-E. You may now ask questions."

Tarbell blinked and coughed against a fist. "Well," he said, "why Stachel? Why not a German-speaking American who, protected by your, ah, general staffer, as you call him, could send more reliable stuff? I mean, well—"

"You mean you don't trust Stachel."

"About as far as I can throw that desk of yours."

"There are three reasons. First, General Eisenhower insists that the general staffer—whose code name is Whisper, incidentally—be supervised and controlled, on site, by a reliable American agent. Second, Whisper, a former associate of Stachel's, specifically requires that the supervisor be Stachel. Third, we are fresh out of B-17 pilots who can speak German like a German. And, as I've indicated, the B-17 is critical to the success of this mission."

"I have another question. What is a J-E?"

"It's a special two-way radio devised by OSS. In the first half of the war, when our agents were operating in German-occupied territories, we did very well with wireless sets moved frequently from safe-house to safe-house. It was possible then because most of the populations were hostile to the Germans and would help to conceal our agents, their relatively large W-T sets, their code books, aerials, power supply, and so on and so on. But Germany itself is another matter—there are few friends and safe-houses; the security is

28

god-awful; wireless signals are picked up almost at once due to efficient German direction-finding equipment and a close monitoring of electric power usage. Also, we lose too many sets—seven out of twenty-two dropped by one SI desk alone—when we paradrop W-Ts into Germany itself. So we developed the Joan-Eleanor, a four-pound beauty that operates on batteries and lets the agent have a two-way conversation with a plane circling at thirty thousand feet. The high frequency and vertical directivity make it practically impossible for the German DF units to locate the agent and his set. And, best of all, OSS reports that a J-E set can exchange as much data in twenty minutes as a W-T communication can handle in six days."

Tarbell nodded appreciatively, hoping to show that he was as ready as anyone to respect technical brilliance. It was a mannerism he had perfected in hundreds of staff meetings during his salad days as an ROTC instructor at snooty Eastern colleges (where he had eked out a BA on the side). "Very nice, when do we start?"

"Tomorrow, in Wilmington, Delaware. The Stachel team, code name Nightstick, will be made up of a woman named Elfrieda Heidemann and another former Luftwaffe pilot named Ernst Randelmann. Nightstick will be assembled and trained at Wilmington because there's an airfield large enough for B-17 work and because the team is already familiar enough with Germany and German folkways and mores to make comprehensive schooling at one of our regular OSS stations unnecessary. Since we already have a strong fix on their aptitudes, mentalities, emotional structures, and all that, we start from a very high plateau with these people. We know how they act under pressure. We know their job fitness.

"Anyhow, the air base has a section of BOQs isolated from the cadre units and transient troop barracks. You'll do your class work there, where the team lives. Stachel and Randelmann will be identified—for local consumption—as test

29

pilots from Wright-Patterson field. You will be represented as an aircraft systems specialist from Second Air Force at Colorado Springs. This will allow the three of you to fly together."

"Fly in what?"

"A B-17 brought in from Barksdale, ostensibly to be tested as a platform for new electronics. Actually you will be guiding Stachel and Randelmann through familiarization with the B-17 and basic U.S. military air procedures. You will be their check pilot. You will test their navigation. You will put heavy emphasis on night operations."

"Night? The B-17 is not used in night operations in the ETO. Why are—"

"We'll do everything we can to assure that Stachel and Randelmann are not apprised of that fact. Right? Right."

"Why?"

"That, Colonel Amos Tarbell, is beyond your province. It's rather none of your need-to-know."

He shrugged. "You'll have to admit it was a logical question." After a moment, he thought of something else. "How about base administration? What explanation's been given them for all of this?"

"No explanation. I've simply handed them top-secret priority requisitions for housing, hangar space, a crew chief and maintenance crew, two jeeps, and an outside phone line. Chow will be brought to the area three times daily by a truck from the officers' mess."

"The crew chief and maintenance crew—won't they see there's no new electronics on the plane?"

"The Barksdale people will have placed assorted dummy black boxes around the ship. The maintenance people will be forbidden to touch them." She paused. "Any other questions?"

"Only two."

"What's the first?"

"Who are Randelmann and Heidemann?"

"Randelmann is a former Luftwaffe major, demoted when he unwittingly got in the way of some officers who framed Stachel in a trumped up court-martial. Stachel finally broke clear of the trap and, as part of his revenge, he brought the discredited Randelmann back to the military mainstream. He has been slavishly grateful to Stachel ever since. Mrs. Heidemann is the widow of Stachel's former squadron commander. She and Stachel have the hots for each other, but they're both so full of crappy pride, it's my bet they never consummated. For my money, she's a royal pain in the ass."

Tarbell thought about that, deciding in the process that he'd heard the brittle sound of jealousy in Polly Loomis's voice. He filed the impression as a possible advantage to be exploited down the way.

"What's your second question, Amos?"

"When and how often do you want me to wee-wee?"

She laughed. It was the first sign of life she'd seen in this hunt-club prig, and she suddenly felt a little better about him.

4

THE NIGHT WAS clear and bright with starlight, and, from where he stood in the cockpit gloom, it seemed to Tarbell that Stachel and Randelmann could have made the entire flight with no more than an altimeter, an airspeed indicator, and a set of tachometers. The Atlantic's unbroken blackness to starboard and the little pools of light marking coastal towns off the left wing created a kind of highway even a dunce-first-class could follow.

Stachel and Randelmann were no dunces, though—Stachel

handled the 17 as if it were a gently cruising bicycle—a touch of fingers, a movement of a foot, casual amalgamations of deliberation and reflex—and Randelmann, perched in the right-hand seat, surveyed his copilot's world with the unruffled satisfaction God must have shown on the seventh day. At Turkey Point, across the Chesapeake Bay from Aberdeen Proving Ground, Stachel turned east along the canal with an almost indiscernible adjustment of the controls, his face serene in the glow of the instrument lights. Randelmann, lips pursed in a soundless whistle, began the little tinkerings that inaugurated the before-landing check, and, as the big ship wheeled over the darkness of the Delaware River, he glanced over his shoulder to show with his eyebrows that all was ready for the call-in.

Tarbell served as the airplane's radio voice, since he thought it would be a bad idea for a military test pilot to have a German accent. He called the Wilmington tower, confirming the altimeter setting and getting permission to enter the pattern for the north-south runway. Signing off, he watched Stachel and Randelmann go through the checklist ritual— autopilot off, booster pumps on, intercoolers off, carburetor filters on, landing gear down and locked—and he thought aberrantly of Tommy Harding, ace quarterback of the Reginald B. Lewiston Normal School's 1937 varsity, hunched over in the November flurries and barking the signals for the decisive play against Central Tech. Tommy had been blessed as the only son of Lane County's only rich merchant and as an athlete and uncontested champion cocksman, and it had been easy to hate him for his smooth self-assurance and classy clothes and superiority in all things. It occurred to him now that enough of this same resentment remained for Stachel—a kind of Teutonic version of Tommy Harding—and all the others in the world to whom success came easily, including that archetypal bitch Polly Loomis.

Little had come easily for Amos Tarbell. Even the army, which he loved more than anything.

For a farm boy on the run from the grinding poverty and boredom of twenty acres of dust, enlistment had represented sanctuary. And, when subsequently rounded out by three squares a day, and at ease in khakis his German-born mother would call "Prima," he had begun to feel a measure of gratitude that eventually became preoccupation with duty and loyalty and "the good of the service." His upbringing demanded that food, shelter, and hospitality be repaid; from this frontiersman's ethos had grown a kind of military religiosity, in which sanctimonious adherence to The Book would most surely bring about his elevation to the army's priesthood some fine day.

Not that his service had been without its trials. Like any sensible man, he had writhed under the petty tyrannies, loathed the sweat and grit of bivouacs and forced marches, retched while cleaning latrines and garbage cans. But with it all had come a sense of belonging; when all the pots had been scrubbed and all the chicken shit had been endured and he had been appointed an aviation cadet, he knew at last he did have a role in the world—he did amount to more than a squeezer of cow tits and a digger of spuds. His country thought enough of him to spend $25,000 to teach him to fly and which fork to use and what to say when introducing a lady. The fact that his country demanded his undeviating attention and expected him to be ready to die on cue was no more to him than the other half of a bargain: for having been given his life it was only natural that he might have to return it. It was therefore difficult for him to understand someone like Bruno Stachel. The least a man could do was earn his keep, master his trade, remain loyal at all costs. How a man could accept the rank and privileges of a general—in any army—and then run away to another country when things did not go well was beyond his comprehension. The sad truth was, he admitted to himself, he could have admired Stachel more as an unreconstructed Nazi sinner than as the turncoat repentant he was purported to be.

Ah, well . . . who ever said life was logical?

At a thousand feet they ran into some freezing rain, small patches of mist backlighted by the glowing crescent of the city, and Stachel ordered intercoolers on. They turned lazily above the murky suburban fringe, descending to 800 feet in the downwind leg at the prescribed 145 mph IAS and 2,100 rpm. Three miles south of New Castle, Stachel went to half flaps and entered his base leg, fingering the controls like a cathedral organist working some Bach.

"Full flaps."

"Check," Randelmann confirmed.

"Intercoolers off."

"Check."

"How come you use English and Randelmann answers in German, Stachel?"

"He's more comfortable answering in German. He is, after all, a German pilot." Stachel's voice hinted dry amusement.

The airplane touched down with a mild chirping of tires and Stachel let it roll over the dim-lit concrete for a long time before braking.

"You're going to have to do better than that," Tarbell said. "We'll be wanting an abbreviated landing out of you next time. We want the shortest possible takeoffs and landings."

"Why?"

Tarbell had himself wondered why, but Polly Loomis was keeping him, along with the others, under a strict rule of need-to-know. However, he was in no mood to reveal this to Stachel. "All in due time," he said. "Meanwhile, get me to the flight line. I'm cold, and I want something to eat."

Later, when the three of them were being jeeped to the BOQ, bouncing through the clammy drizzle, Stachel, only his eyes and nose showing above the sheepskin collar of his flying suit, turned to Tarbell. "How is it you're not flying in a bomber squadron, Colonel? You wear pilot's wings. You monitor my flying techniques like a sharp-nosed schoolmaster. You like airplanes, I think. Why this work?"

"None of your business, Stachel."

"General Stachel."

Tarbell ignored the sarcasm, staring ahead over the driver's shoulder and feeling alone and sad.

* * *

Elfi Heidemann was in the dayroom when Stachel walked in. She had been held up in Omaha for three days for some kind of FBI clearance, which hadn't really affected the Nightstick training schedule because the period had been given over exclusively to the aviation phase anyhow.

They shook hands formally, and Stachel said, "It's good to see you again."

"I've just arrived," she said, patting her hair in that way of hers he remembered. "It was a miserable trip, and I feel rather a mess."

"You look fine."

"Where are the others?"

He looked about awkwardly, as if the others might be hiding in the corners, or under the Ping-Pong table. "Miss Loomis hasn't arrived from Washington yet. I suppose Randelmann and Tarbell are cleaning up for supper."

"Who is Tarbell?"

"Our flight instructor. He's somewhat of an ass."

"Have you eaten yet?"

"No. As you see, I've just come in from flying. I'm looking for a letter from my mother, and I popped in to check the mail slot. Are you hungry?"

"Famished."

"Leave your bags here. I'll take you to the mess. It's not much, but the food's edible. We can wash up there."

* * *

During the meal Stachel endeavored to keep the conversation light and neutral. Tarbell had not joined them (thank God for small favors), explaining that he was needed in the mainte-nance hangar, where the crew chief was complaining that one

35

of the secret black boxes installed on Oh-Four-Niner was drastically affecting the airplane's autopilot. This had caused Randelmann to break into noisy laughter. Stachel explained the joke to Elfi, and she tried bravely to be amused, but it was apparent the whole thing mystified her. Even so, there was a subtle drawing together of the three members of Nightstick, the kind of intimacy one sees among strangers who discover they each have experienced Buffalo in winter.

Through it all, Stachel's mind seemed independently determined to rummage among memories: the night they met in the ancient war of '18, when he had taken her to dinner in her husband's official absence; the way she had glowed, clean and satiny in the candlelight; her strange forthrightness. She was still a compelling woman, his indirect, casual glances told him. Her green eyes were still level and cool and guileless. There was still a sensuousness in her face, with its unseamed skin and lips that curled at the corners, as if suggesting a sad smile to come. Her voice was still throaty and measured, her hands still ready to explore textures and surfaces. Once, while Randelmann soliloquized on the sad state of contemporary opera, Stachel caught her studying him, and she blushed and pretended new interest in her meal.

Polly Loomis arrived late for the briefing, swirling into the lecture room in a flurry of fur and excuses. It occurred to Stachel that she was gushing and excessive, like a schoolgirl competing for the attention of the stag line, and he saw by her manner that she retained her dislike of Elfi Heidemann. Tarbell was back with them now, and only he seemed ready to pretend that this corner of the world was singularly blessed to have Polly Loomis drop in.

"If everybody's comfortable," Miss Loomis purred, "we'll get right down to work. This is our first meeting together, and I'll simply hit the highlights, with detailed briefings coming later in the program as you demonstrate team capability."

She paused, trying for a bit of drama. Her audience appeared to miss the suggested suspense, slumping as they did in their aluminum and plastic lounge chairs, faces impassive. "As you've been told," she went on, "we have an opportunity to strike a telling blow against Hitler, provided Nightstick measures up to some rather demanding requirements. As of now, you've all been given top-secret clearance, and I'm authorized to reveal some specifics previously withheld from you. Bruno, you have a quizzical look. Is there a question already?"

"Well, I was wondering what happens if Nightstick doesn't measure up, as you put it. If you reveal some specifics, and we don't meet the requirements, what happens? A firing squad?"

She gave him one of her patient-teacher smiles. "Hardly. But in that unlikely event, you would be placed in security isolation in one of the cottages reserved at our OSS station in Virginia. A kind of nonpunitive house arrest."

"For how long?"

"Until the end of the war. Maybe later, depending on how this matter turns out."

"We have, then," Stachel observed coolly, "a choice. We risk either our necks in Germany or our sanity in Virginia."

"That's a fair statement, yes."

"Please continue, Miss Loomis,"

She reddened, annoyed by his regal condescension, the implication that it was he who was in charge here. "As I've told you all, General Eisenhower has decided it's absolutely imperative that we deny the Nazis any chance to set up a guerrilla operation in the Alpine region. He has charged Nightstick with seeing that such plans never take root." After a pause, she glanced at Stachel. "You remember General von Lemmerhof, of course."

"He was my superior at OKL in Berlin."

"After you, ah, fled Germany, he had a bad spell. There was considerable Gestapo interest in your case, naturally, and he was suspected of complicity in your dramatic rescue of so-called enemies of the Reich. It was widely known that he

37

was fond of you, and there were those who thought he might be involved in your transgressions."

"How delicately you put it, Miss Loomis."

She winked theatrically. "General von Lemmerhof has sent us a message. He has advised us that he is horrified by the ruin Hitler has brought down on Germany. He is remorseful over Nazi sins abroad. He repents, for the Kingdom of Eisenhower is at hand. To prove how sorry he is—and to avoid automatic arrest on war crimes charges, of course—he has offered, through our OSS branch in Geneva, to turncoat. In return for his presentation to us of the Reich Chancellery's plans for the Werewolf, he asks amnesty."

Stachel sniffed. "Von Lemmerhof can't lead guerrillas. He's a staff officer. He doesn't know one end of a rifle squad from the other."

Miss Loomis dismissed this objection. "Ah, but he has a more important qualification. He's one of the few general staffers Hitler still trusts. Hitler, and his deputy, Bormann, both call Von Lemmerhof 'Ehrlicher Erich.' Faithful Erich, however, bears a heavy cross—Is that a blasphemous metaphor, Frau Heidemann?—in that he secretly has lost his enthusiasm for Hitler's plan to fight to the last German and wants out. Thus his offer to us."

The members of Nightstick traded glances, already looking to each other, even for tacit support.

"We've told General Lemmerhof," Polly Loomis said in her mock pedantry, "that there's no deal unless we send a supervisor to work behind the scenes with him—to assure that things are as he reports and that he's not a Nazi double deliberately misleading us. The problem is, he will work with only one supervisor—Bruno Stachel."

Stachel humphed. "Why, for God's sake?"

"Lemmerhof says he knows you and respects your anti-Nazi stance and believes that you recognize he's no war criminal. As a German, he says, you understand Germans."

Stachel sighed, shaking his head in sour amusement. "The general is a pompous weather vane. I know for a fact how earnestly he sucked up to Hitler. I introduced him to the Führer after much insistence on his part. I do indeed understand him. He's like all human beings—greedy, ambitious, opportunistic, and self-righteous. He's like all Nazis —greedy, ambitious, opportunistic, and self-righteous."

"Well, saint or sinner, he knows something Eisenhower wants to know. Nightstick will go to Germany and get it. Stachel will be team leader. Randelmann, you will be the radioman. Tarbell will be the J-E man aloft. Mrs. Heidemann will be courier, sally agent, and supply master."

Elfi held up a hand. "Excuse me. What is this sally agent?"

"In the old days, when castles were under siege, parties would sneak out the sally ports to make raids, capture prisoners, gather information, and so on. Nightstick needs someone who can serve a roughly similar function. We've chosen you because women can move about present-day Germany with considerably more freedom than men can."

"I'll be expected to capture prisoners?" Elfi asked, seeming suddenly to be vulnerable and unhappy.

Miss Loomis gave her a patronizing smile. "I rather doubt that there'll be a need for prisoners."

There was an interval of silence, broken eventually by Randelmann, who said, "So how do we get into Germany? Parcel post?"

"Stachel will pilot a B-17 on a raid on Berlin. You will be his copilot-navigator. Mrs. Heidemann will make herself generally useful as a participating passenger. At specific coordinates, the bomber will be belly-landed, the team will proceed to a safe-house in the Wannsee area, and commence its supervision of von Lemmerhof." She paused, cleared her throat importantly, and nodded at Stachel to signal her readiness for his question.

"There's something you must consider," he said.

"Well?"

"I assume you have your reasons for such an elaborate scheme—sending us along on a raid, expending an airplane, and all that—but it's my guess that there's nothing that would do more to alert German security forces. Parachutes would be bad enough in the Berlin area, but every fallen aircraft is probably reached in minutes by the police, the Gestapo, the fire fighters, irate civilians—everybody."

"Of course," Polly said easily. "That's a logical assumption."

"They would be very curious about a belly-landed airplane whose crew of nine was nowhere to be found. You would have—What do your cowboy movies call it? A posse?—so hot and keen we three wouldn't get to the nearest road, let alone to Wannsee."

"Of course."

"Well, then."

"Your chances will be considerably improved by a landing in a highly inaccessible place. A place set aside for you and protected by General von Lemmerhof. A tract of unpopulated land ostensibly to be used for training Lemmerhof's Werewolf commanders."

"The Gestapo can go anywhere, Miss Loomis. No place is inaccessible to the Gestapo."

"To be sure. But we assume it to be highly unlikely that the Gestapo, or anybody else, for that matter, will be immediately interested in just another of perhaps scores of American planes that will sprinkle down on Germany during the raid. Germany is one huge junk pile these days. The landscape is littered every day by more and more plane wrecks. Who will especially want to investigate just one more wreck that's fallen in an area already presumed to be crawling with SS troopers?"

Stachel sank back in his chair, shaking his head slowly. "Somebody will want to count bodies. I assure you of that."

"Don't you," Polly drawled, "imagine General von Lemmerhof has also thought of that? After all, it's no difficult feat to come up with nine bodies in the Third Reich today. It's no big accomplishment to place nine bodies dressed in U.S. uniforms in a wrecked B-17, then touch a match to the gasoline. Eh?"

Elfi pushed out of her chair and went to the door, her face pale. She did not look back as she let herself out and disappeared down the hall, her heels tapping urgently.

Stachel glanced at Randelmann and Tarbell, but they sat, staring at nothing in particular and lost in thought.

Sighing again, Stachel said, "It's people like you, Miss Loomis, who give secret intelligence a bad name."

5

THE TRUCK LEFT them at a fork in a farm lane, just as dusk became night. A bitter north wind moved restlessly across the frozen land, making mournful sounds. Stachel stood for a time, examining the sky and its low-rolling clouds and holding up a hand that called for caution.

"Where are we?" Randelmann muttered.

"Listen," Stachel said. "Hear it? The sound of traffic. There. Over that rise. Beyond the trees."

"That doesn't tell us where we are," Elfi said, shivering.

"Hold the penlight on the map, Randelmann. We'll orient it with the compass. Then we'll make for the highway and find out where we are and which way to go."

"What are they trying to prove by this?" Elfi put in testily. "Why do we have to wander around in this godforsaken nowhere? Why didn't they just take us to the factory and let us figure out how to get in?"

"Miss Loomis wants to see how well we can locate ourselves and go on to an objective. In case we get disoriented or lost when we land in Germany."

"Miss Loomis is an idiot," she snapped.

"I won't argue that."

"What does the map tell you, Herr General?"

"Well, with Polaris behind the clouds and with our only references the highway, that creek down there, and the glow of that town on the horizon, I'd guess we're in the vicinity of Newtown Square, Pennsylvania, slightly west and south of the Springfield reservoir."

"You must be a wizard, Herr General, to tell all that from a single glance at a map and a compass on a cold, black night. Not a wizard, a bloody genius."

Stachel folded the map and placed it in the side pocket of his overcoat. During the break in their photo-interpretation class that afternoon he had left the latrine to see Corporal Radmer, the team driver, taking instructions from Miss Loomis in the shadows of Hangar C. She had been talking quietly, making little punctuation marks in the air with a forefinger while the corporal took notes. With nothing more than intuition to go on, Stachel had deemed the conversation important enough to warrant a peek at Radmer's notebook —made handily available when Radmer hung his jacket on a peg in the dayroom during a presupper Ping-Pong game with the B-17 crew chief, a porky sergeant named Finnegan. The notes specified time and place for Radmer's blind drop-off of the Nightstick team at the outset of the evening's cross-country march and penetration exercise.

"I am indeed a genius, Randelmann." He glanced at the radium dial of his watch. "You both have twenty-one-forty-six hours?"

They consulted their watches and nodded.

"I think you knew where they would drop us off," Randelmann said, amused accusation in his voice. "And that's not fair. Miss Loomis is testing our ability as secret agents. Having advance knowledge is no test."

"A successful secret agent is never interested in being fair, my friend. He's interested only in being successful. Because a successful secret agent is a live secret agent, eh?"

"Ha."

"Come on," Elfi said irritably. "Let's go. I'm freezing."

* * *

They moved across the winter-stubble fields, holding to the tree lines and gullies. Elfi had a time of it, since she had chosen to wear regular shoes with galoshes, a combination poorly suited to a nighttime trek. And Randelmann began to puff badly, a sign of the price he had paid for all those months behind a desk.

"Hurry," Stachel said at one point. "We're on a deadline."

"My feet are cold and my ankles hurt," she complained.

"This is precisely why Loomis is running this exercise. To find our weaknesses. To catch our mistakes. Next time you'll wear more sensible shoes."

She was silent, and Stachel could feel her anger.

"Here. Give me your hand. We'll be at the highway soon."

"Never mind. I'm all right."

"Will you take my hand, Herr General? I'm just a little boy, and I'm afraid of the dark."

"You're also out of shape, Randelmann."

"How terribly true, Herr General."

* * *

Stachel flagged down a bus at the intersection of what the map revealed to be highways numbered State 352 and U.S. Route 1. The bus, dimly lighted and reeking of diesel fumes, showed a sign proclaiming its destination to be CHESTER, PA. Besides

43

the driver, the only occupants were four silent, unhappy men, each holding a lunch pail on his lap, each swaying to the bus's rhythm.

Nightstick took three seats at the extreme rear.

"We're in luck," Elfi murmured. "This bus is going to the town where our target is."

"Not so loud," Randelmann warned. "They might hear your German."

Stachel checked his watch again. "No more talking at all, until I say so."

As they rode, Stachel watched Elfi Heidemann, who sat by the window, green eyes staring into the opaque night. A sense of all the years came to him, a kind of panoramic overview of the past, in which she was simultaneously the lost girl he had known in that other war, the one so long ago, and the anxious woman of Hitler's Berlin, and the matron of today, with her serious face and prim disapproval of the world around her. She was very good-looking, remote and cool, with ivory skin and a delicate cheekline; and the easy curves of her body, the suggestion of gracefulness in the set of her shoulders, held him, fascinated, as always. It was no good, he thought. She had no business being involved in this madness, and he searched his mind for ways to convince her—and himself—that she must withdraw at once.

Almost as if she had been touched by some current of his thoughts, she turned her face to give him a long and somber study. For a moment he thought she might speak, but something in his own face must have dissuaded her, because her gaze returned to the dark window and the inscrutable patterns of lights and blackness flickering beyond it.

He wondered again why she was here. What had caused her to abandon the security of central Nebraska for this suicidal plunge into a dying Germany? What was really in the mind behind those brooding eyes? Would she, like him, rather be dead than not belong anywhere?

Well, first things first.

44

She could be dealt with.

Meanwhile, there was the business at hand.

In the initial briefing yesterday, Loomis had given much emphasis to the riverside location of the Collins and Jamison Electrical Supply Co. The Delaware flowed directly behind the main plant, which made approach from the east virtually impossible, what with the coast guard patrols and dockside security measures that sealed off the nearby Sun Shipyards, the refineries, Baldwin Locomotive, and, farther upstream, Westinghouse. The objective was to enter the plant unassisted from one of its other three sides, steal a copy of the plant management-organization chart, and then withdraw undetected and unidentified. No one was to know of the exercise, Loomis had reminded them, except Nightstick and, of course, herself. If they were caught by plant security or other authorities, they would have to suffer the consequences.

"What consequences?" Stachel had demanded.

"Who knows? A night or two in jail, at least. Until I can find some way to extricate you without too much fuss."

"It seems to me that would cost us considerable training time. It would be a stupid waste."

"Yes, indeed. And that would require you to enter Germany with two or three days less experience as a team. A very serious matter. That's why I don't expect you to get caught."

"What if we simply say to hell with it, Miss Loomis? What if Randelmann and Frau Heidemann and I simply decide to sit in jail? Talk to all who might listen? Let you find somebody else to handle the Werewolf thing?"

"That's my gamble. I'm betting you won't."

"You drop us off a truck, blind, march us cross-country to a strange city, send us into a guarded factory to steal a list of names—not merely to test our ingenuity but also our determination. Our motivation. Our reliability. Is that it?"

"I don't think that's unreasonable, do you?"

"Why Frau Heidemann? Why a naïve woman on a mission to Germany?"

"I've told you—efficiency. Every able-bodied man is either in uniform or in some war-related work, and that means he's always accountable to somebody or something. Hitler's refusal to draft women works to our advantage here. Mrs. Heidemann could very well go places not readily accessible to you or Randelmann. She won't always have to explain herself to somebody."

"Elfi Heidemann isn't cut out for this kind of thing."

"Any better ideas, Bruno, dear?"

"Perhaps."

"I don't want you improvising. Our plan doesn't allow tinkering. It must come off precisely as laid out."

"That's debatable, since I still have no idea what exactly your plan is."

"It will be revealed to you piece by piece. You will be told only what you need to know at various stages."

"I still think Frau Heidemann won't make it. You saw her reaction to all your gabble about burning bodies."

Miss Loomis had avoided further discussion of the matter by glancing at her watch and then striding from the room. It was one of her favorite ploys, this pretense of remembering a more important duty elsewhere whenever a conversation failed to satisfy her.

* * *

The lights of Chester were wan and cheerless in the snow. As the driver began to stop at key intersections to pick up and drop off passengers, Stachel felt Randelmann and Frau Heidemann tensing. They would shoot little glances at the passing storefronts and the dimmed-out gasoline stations and the melancholy side streets lined with drab houses, and he could see that they were gathering themselves for the coming test.

Stachel consulted his street map again. They were traveling toward the river on Edgmont, and his plan had been to leave the bus at the railroad station and walk the eight blocks to the Collins and Jamison plant. But he waited until the bus slowed for a stoplight at what seemed to be the intersection with Market Street, then, leaning, he pressed Frau Heidemann's hand and peered into her eyes.

"Let me see your right foot," he said softly. "And don't say anything."

Confused, she stared down at her galoshes and watched silently as Stachel, reaching, lifted her right foot.

"So then," he said, "I think it's time you leave our little group and go back to nursing in Nebraska, eh?"

He pulled quickly and the galosh and shoe came off her foot. "Come, Randelmann, this is where we get off."

As he swung from the bus, Stachel's last glimpse of Elfi Heidemann showed her sitting stiffly in the gloom at the rear of the bus, still staring, mouth open in astonishment, at her stockinged right foot.

*　　*　　*

"Down this way, Randelmann. This street leads to the plant."

"Why did you do that? Leave Elfi, I mean. Taking her boot with you."

"I didn't want her to come with us."

"Why, in God's name?"

"She isn't suited to clandestine visits to Germany. She'd only get herself killed. And maybe us, too."

"We've left her with nowhere to go. She can't even get off the bus. She can't walk in this snow . . . She can't speak a word of English."

"It's my guess the bus driver will eventually turn her over to the police. After a day or two, our friend Loomis will obtain her release and send her back to the rest home in Virginia, or whatever."

"Loomis will raise pluperfect hell."

"No doubt."

47

"You've changed the whole character of the team without so much as a by-your-leave. Loomis told you not to tinker. You tinker anyway."

"I'm a rascal, all right."

"I'm not so sure I want to visit Germany now, Herr General. I'd never know when you might leave me on a trolley in my underwear."

"You, Randelmann? Nonsense. I would never leave you. I need you to carry my golfing bags."

"You are indeed a rascal, Herr General. In fact, I might add—if I have the Herr General's permission—that the Herr General is the most sneaky frigging rascal I've ever known."

"Don't try to butter me up, Randelmann."

*   *   *

The truth lurks in jest, Stachel reminded himself sourly. It was the schemer in him, a propensity for connivance often verging on addiction, that seemed always to result in some measure of ruin for those around him. Yet the world was askew with unfairness and hypocrisy, and this tormented him—like a picture hanging crooked on a wall—and from his early days he had run about in a rage to straighten up the listing universe. Thwarted, disillusioned, he had tried to make the surrounding imperfection tolerable by drinking himself beyond caring. But even that, too, had become intolerable, itself an abrasion of his maddening perfectionism, and so he had become what he was today—a cranky abstainer, not only from the grape but from society and its genteel outrages as well. He was a rascal, first, because it was pragmatic—the only way to get things done—and, next, because it was the only satisfactory barrier between him and terminal heartbreak.

Striding through the snowy streets, he conceded to himself that Elfi Heidemann had posed a threat, not so much to the mission, but to his laboriously fabricated insulation against her. Their going to Germany together would have wrecked the work of years. And her virtually guaranteed capture and death would have tilted every picture on every wall he had ever managed to build. It was as simple as that.

* * *

The Collins and Jamison plant was even less attractive than the photos had shown it to be. It sat in brick and corrugated iron dejection on a prairie of frozen reeds and cinders, its fences pierced only by the entrance gate and a single-track spur from the railroad to the west. Across the street from the gatehouse was a low palisade of faded frame buildings, each seeming to lean on its neighbor. The only sign of life among them was a bar, which stood, blinking neon invitations, beside the darkened Texaco station at the end of the block.

"We'll never get in without being seen, Herr General."

"It doesn't look promising, to be sure."

"Armed guards at the gate, barbed wire on top of the fences. I'll bet those fences are electrified, too."

"Maybe."

"Well, what should we do? We can't stand here beside this gas station all night. We'll freeze to death."

"Try that window beside you, Randelmann."

"This one? Why?"

"I want to enter the gas station, that's why. I think I see a pay phone in there. On the wall. And if we're lucky, we won't have to enter the Collins and Jamison plant at all."

"The window's locked."

"Then break the glass and unlock it."

"That makes us burglars, you know," Randelmann warned theatrically.

"Ah, my friend, but we're not going to steal anything."

The place was frigid, and the smell of gasoline and rubber seemed to make the dampness even more oppressive. Stachel dropped a coin in the slot and was relieved to hear the dial tone.

"So far so good," he said, dialing. Randelmann said nothing.

49

"Collins and Jamison," a man's voice rasped.

Stachel folded his handkerchief over the mouthpiece and said, "Zurich, Switzerland, calling for the manager of the Collins and Jamison Company in Chester, Pennsylvania, U.S.A."

"Switzerland?" The man's voice was full of surprise. "Who's calling? I mean, I'm only captain of the security force. The management ain't here. It's after hours, and I'm on the switchboard."

"One moment, please." Stachel tapped the phone with a pencil several times, then removed the handkerchief. "Hello. Hello." he said. "I must speak with the manager regarding an order. Will you connect me, please?"

"Sorry," the captain said uncertainly, "but Mr. Reynolds —he's the plant manager—ain't here. It's real late, and he's home."

"Reynolds? Which is that? My correspondence has not involved a Reynolds—"

"Mr. John M. Reynolds. He's the plant manager."

Stachel covered the mouthpiece with a hand and whispered, "Write this down, Randelmann—the plant manager is John M. Reynolds." Then into the phone, he said, "Ah. I see. Well, then, who is in charge, please? Who would speak to me of an order? An assistant, perhaps?"

"Well, gee, I don't know. Al Sigmund, the assistant plant manager's home, too. The area superintendent and shift supervisor are out in the plant—"

"Who are they, please?"

"Sam Mills is the super, and the shift supervisor is, let's see, Bill Dooley."

"No. I recognize neither." Stachel relayed the names to Randelmann, and after the pause he said, "My correspondence was about an order of considerable size and value, mostly with your Chicago office. However, it has not come through, and I've been advised to inquire at your factory in Chester, Pennsylvania. I have done so, but I recognize no one among those you have suggested. Are you connected with the billing department, perhaps?"

"No, sir. Like I say, the plant's on shift, and all the office people ain't here. They work days. Eight to four-thirty."

"I am most disturbed. The order is valued at many thousands. To whom might I speak in the morning?"

"Golly, let me look at the chart. Just a sec'."

In the interval Stachel said, "Take the names as I say them, Randelmann."

"Hello? Switzerland?" The captain felt long-distance required shouting.

"Yes, yes. On the line."

"You might want to talk to Mr. H. A. Lang. He's the service superintendent. The mail room's his baby."

"H. A. Lang, service superintendent."

"Or maybe Mr. Fred Deemer, the control manager?"

"Fred Deemer, control manager."

"I doubt you'd want Ollie Riegelmeyer. He's the production manager. He don't get into orders, and like that."

"Ollie Riegelmeyer, production manager. No, I think not."

"There's engineering and design. Boss there is Dr. Mario Rinaldi. He's been to Europe, couple times."

"Dr. Mario Rinaldi. He's manager of engineering and design?"

"That's right."

"No. It's not he, I'm afraid. Anyone else, perhaps, sir?"

"Only Dr. Saul Steinberg, director of R. and D. Research and development, that means."

"I see. Dr. Saul Steinberg, director of R. and D. Could there be a shipping department?"

"Well, Traffic is handled by Chuck Bolinski. But he reports to Fred Deemer, at Control. You'd do better by calling Fred, I'd say."

"I see. Well, sir, you have been most helpful. And I thank you. I shall call Mr. Deemer at ten o'clock, your time."

"Okie-doke. I didn't get your name—"

Stachel rapped the phone with the pencil again. "—so —and—it is very—my company—"

He hung up.

Turning in the gloom, he said, "The customer is always right, Randelmann. Let's get out of this icebox, shall we?"

"I didn't know you could call the United States from Switzerland in wartime."

"I don't know, either. What counts is that our obliging friend, the Collins and Jamison security captain, thinks you can."

"Where now, Herr General?"

"To Wilmington, of course. There's a train at ten-twenty. And a bus from Wilmington to the airport."

Before he crawled through the window, Stachel hesitated. Pulling his billfold from his pocket, he held it to the reflected light of a streetlamp on the corner and selected a dollar bill. Placing the money on the grimy desk top, he glanced at Randelmann.

"For repairing the broken glass. Does that satisfy your Saxon sense of propriety, Randelmann?"

ƀ

AT FIRST, THE bus driver, a pasty man with drinker's eyes, had been gruff and resentful, in the manner of one who saw this as another of the world's plots to make his life miserable. She had ridden to the end of the line, using the time to quiet her panic and make some decisions; when at last the driver set the brakes and came to demand why she sat alone in the dark at the rear, she had been able to collect herself and play the role.

It had been interesting, in a way, to see the change in the man's attitude. Interesting, not unexpected. She had learned to appreciate the American vulnerability to the hurt and the lost: The Wehrmacht prison camp in Nebraska had represented an extraordinary paradox, in which the authorities could lavish creature comforts and elaborate courtesies on men who, only weeks before, would have killed them summarily. So, when she had batted her eyelashes and made the hopeless gestures of a dim-witted mute, the bus driver's transformation from truculent public servant to solicitous samaritan had come as no surprise—even when he'd used his own scarf to wrap her icy foot.

A policeman had put her in a car and taken her to a spartan office near the railroad station, a place presumably devoted to the assistance of travelers. Her English—beyond good morning and how do you do and please pass the salt and where is the toilet—was nonexistent, and it took a considerable amount of will to keep from breaking into tears of panic when a gray-haired woman, dressed in a kind of uniform, pressed her with gentle and entirely incomprehensible questions. But she'd held fast to her pose, answering in helpless mumbles.

The fact that she had twenty-two dollars in her pocket seemed to have made a difference; an amiable discussion between the policeman and the woman ended with the officer's departure and the woman's preoccupation with a telephone list, which she studied between obviously fruitless calls. Watching her, Elfi was moved by a memory of her mother, who, like the woman here, had pursed her lips just so when concentrating on one of her world's vexations. Mutti had represented her first and most meaningful encounter with the conflicting requirements of adulthood. Mutti had shown her, consistently and often unwittingly, that it was possible to meet cruelty without flinching and affection without conceit. Elfi had never been able to achieve a stability equal to her mother's, tyrannized as she was by a sense of inferiority and an anticipation of imminent doom, but at least she had been given a pattern against which to measure her own immaturity.

It had been considerable. Otto, her husband, had suffered from it the most, poor dear. As one of the early fliers, he had been a man divided by a love of the sky and a consuming need of his wife—a man tortured by the simple fact that when leading a squadron at three thousand meters, which God had designed him to do, he could not at the same time keep her near, which God had also designed him to do. Otto's personal conflict had been intensified by the contradictions in her own life: a desperate need for love, while living with a lovable man she didn't love. And when she drank to make the unendurable endurable, when she immersed herself in her nursing, it was not she who'd been helped but Otto who'd been hurt. Poor, dear man. What a relief it must have been for him to fall out of the sky and die in the grass.

She sat on the bench against the wall, her mind alternately racing with anxiety and drifting in nostalgia—zigzagging from herself to her mother, from Otto to Stachel, from expectations of calamity to anger and vengefulness and then around again.

I must concentrate. I must decide how to deal with this absurd situation. She gave herself little lectures, silent pep talks.

The woman seemed eventually to tire of the telephone business. She pushed back from her metal desk, stood up, patted her hair, and, after a few soft words, went down the corridor to disappear through a door marked WOMEN.

On the floor above, a mechanical voice began a thunderous monologue, the gist of which seemed to involve Wilmington, Delaware.

54

A train arrival.

That was it. Or was it?

Was the train arriving from Wilmington? Or was Wilmington its destination?

Her glance fell on the uniformed woman's galoshes, placed in careful parallel in the corner behind the desk. She hurried across the room, took the scarf from her foot, and quickly pulled on the overshoes. Placing two of her dollars on the woman's desk, she turned, looked about as if there were something important she was forgetting; then, realizing how silly this was, she went into the corridor, closed the door behind her, and awkwardly ran for the stairway and the clattering rumble of the incoming train.

She remembered the map. The railroad ran generally north and west of the river. If she were to stand on the high platform with the river behind her, southwest would be to her left. And, since the train appeared to be headed toward the left, it had to be en route to Wilmington.

Even so, she confirmed her judgment. She approached the man in the blue suit and brass buttons who stood beside the hissing cars, looking bored.

"Wilmington?"

The man nodded, wearied beyond words.

Unable to find a seat elsewhere, she stood in the bleakly lit vestibule of the rearmost car, sharing the space with two drowsy soldiers and an old man, who sat on a suitcase muttering to himself.

She leaned against the rattling steel, eyes half closed, watching the jagged lights and darks of the rushing night beyond the window. It was a cold, hard world of shadows and noise and malevolence, and she was suddenly overwhelmed with a sense of hopelessness and vulnerability. The trainman would not sell her a ticket; he would question her, demand things of her; he would not be kind, and there would be police and interrogations and custody and aloneness.

Goddamn Bruno Stachel.

How dare he do this to her.

The trainman was neither kind nor unkind. He simply glanced at her dully, and, when she'd said "Wilmington," took the ten-dollar bill from her, counted out some change, and returned it with a receipt.

* * *

She walked the five miles from the train station to the airport, partly because she was unable to identify the bus that might have taken her there, partly because a taxi would involve conversation with the driver, and partly because she feared she lacked the money to do either.

Trudging through the rutted snow, she leaned into the clammy wind and tried to ignore the pain of fatigue. She wanted no questioning of her stamina, her will to persist. There must be no reason for the others to doubt her ability to survive. But, more important, there must be no doubting her right to do what she was about to do.

* * *

She went directly to Stachel's quarters, marched through the unlocked door to his bedroom, pulled the blankets from the bed, and, when he sat up, blinking, struck him full in the face with a wide swing of an open hand.

"You swine."

She began another swing, but, awake now, he caught her arm.

"You swine. *Swine.*"

She was unable to halt the tears, and she heard herself sobbing with an anger that was an incandescence, roiling and molten, behind her eyes.

Stachel said nothing. With easy pressure, he turned her arm against itself, and she felt a collapsing, a surrender of body and will to a fatigue deeper than any she had ever known.

56

She awoke at dawn, and pale light came through the small window, a gentle rosiness in the board and tarpaper room.

He was sitting in the only chair, a robe around him, his eyes watching her.

"I tried to get your coat off," he said, "but you were too far gone. So I put blankets over you. It was the best I could do."

"I'm so cold."

"You've had a difficult night."

"You really are a swine, you know."

"Yes."

"You had no right to do what you did."

"I'm team captain. I do what I must."

"You always do what you want. Nothing stops you from doing what you want."

"That's not quite true. You still have your clothes on, don't you?"

"You're a swine."

"And you're quite a woman, Elfi Heidemann. Now, shut up and go back to sleep."

𝔷

POLLY LOVED WASHINGTON, especially in wartime. It hummed, it buzzed, it seethed with intrigue and debauchery, yet on occasion rose to greatness—even nobility. She loved it because she excelled at its games, and, as Gordon Koscoe, one of her admirers at State, said over martinis one afternoon, "You're a dirty rat, Polly Loomis, the dirtiest of all the rats I've known in my years in government, and that means I envy you more than anybody. Hell, you're even dirty enough to get elected to something. You ever thought of running for Congress?" They'd both laughed and later gone to the Mayflower for the night, mainly because she felt such adoration should be rewarded.

She thought of Gordon as the driver helped her from her car. She would have to call him one of these days. He was now in a very elevated post and ought to be cultivated, because she planned to stay in the agency once the war was done, and he could very well be her route to a key position. But not in counterespionage. CE was interesting, but it was limited in career potential, and, Gordon's joking nothwithstanding, there were many larger intelligence opportunities forming up. The X-2 branch of OSS—the vineyard in which she now was toiling—had two main CE functions: first, to place friendly agents in the enemy's intelligence apparatus to learn what skulduggery the enemy had in mind, and, second, to manipulate or neutralize the enemy's plans, be they espionage or open military operations. All of which was fine when you had a shooting enemy, but between times it was too narrow, too dull, too make-work. Deception was the name of the game, but there were more kicks in deceiving someone who was working to kill you.

She had come a long way, just since 1942. There had been a job in the Registry, that great, complex library of data on enemy intelligence personnel, enemy plans, organization, and international relationships; there had been a stint with liaison, the distribution center for CE gleanings that could be of interest to other military and government agencies; and, best of all, she had had in-depth experience in field operations —both in cooperative ventures with British MI-5 and as a case officer on some of the most sensitive theater-level undercover activities. Even General "Wild Bill" Donovan, the almighty emperor of OSS, had begun to make informal little visits to her office following her masterminding of Operation Jellyroll, a triple turn-around of Konrad Holzer, the Nazi agent who had penetrated the Pentagon's communications research center.

Donovan wasn't waiting in her office today, but Huey Vought was. Vought, a lanky, funereal former economist, was her direct boss, the only man between her and Wild Bill, and he was a worrier, the kind who always sounds as if he's wearing damp underwear.

"Ah," she said, shrugging off her coat, "you missed a good lunch. The chow at ONI is getting better all the time."

Vought sighed. "Somebody's got to run the war while you gallivant."

"Lou Domini was asking for you. He's back from Madrid."

Vought thought about that, as if wondering whether it was good news or bad. Deferring decision, he went to the window to watch the pigeons on the sill outside.

"What can I do for you, boss?" She sank into an easy chair and kicked off her overshoes.

Vought said, "How is Nightstick coming along? I've read your reports on Galahad, Rigmarole, and Big Dipper, but Nightstick wasn't there."

"It should be on your desk this evening. It's in typing right now."

He tapped on the windowpane, presumably in a kind of greeting to a large pigeon that stood in sober, puffed-chest pensiveness among its swirling brethren. "O.K." he said, "but give me a little fill-in. I'm due to see the general at two thirty, and he'll want to know."

"Nightstick is doing all right. There's a small problem, but I'm confident that I can iron it out."

"What means a small problem, Polly?"

"Stachel mainly. His independence. His tendency to play things his way, without checking first."

Vought turned to give her a pained glance. "That's a *small*

59

problem? It seems to me to be a very serious thing—a team captain who likes to ad-lib."

She arose from the chair and went to her desk, aware that the finely drawn perimeter of social-business had been crossed and they had now entered the hardball arena of business-business; the desk had ceased to be mere decor and had become her parapet, the sandbags behind which she would defend herself. "Well," she said coolly, "there's a question of predictability and initiative. You've got to decide which is more important—abject, single-minded adherence to orders from above or imagination, flexibility, adaptability, within the framework of the ultimate objective. Stachel is a rare German. He thinks for himself."

"Oh, come on, Polly—you sound like the employee relations manager of Smithereens, Incorporated. We're talking wartime counterintelligence, not recruitment for some girdle factory," Vought said petulantly.

"It's no problem, honest. I know Stachel. It's mainly this get-up-and-go aspect of his personality that made me choose him for Nightstick in the first place. After all, when you're dealing with a heavy cannon like Wiseguy, you need an angle shooter like Stachel, not some heel-clicking automaton."

"Wiseguy is very important to us. Nightstick is our route to him. Stachel must do what we tell him to do, or our chances of losing Wiseguy are just about a hundred percent."

"I know that as well as you do, Huey."

Vought's impatience was apparent. "What has Stachel been up to? What little problem has he caused?"

"Nothing really serious. He's claimed all along that he considers it a mistake to send the Heidemann woman in with Nightstick. Two nights ago, I gave Nightstick a field problem to work out—the usual exercise, breaking into a factory and so on. But in mid-exercise, Stachel abandoned Heidemann and set her adrift in a strange town. His idea was to have her picked up as an enemy alien, later rescued by me and put on a shelf in Virginia, hopelessly compromised as far as OSS ops are concerned."

"Did he get into the factory?" Vought sulked.

"Our observers at the plant didn't see hide nor hair of him. But when he returned to Wilmington, he had precisely what he was sent to get—a list of names."

"How did he manage that? Trainees always get caught on these exercises. They're supposed to be caught. It teaches them. Chastens them."

"Well, as I say. Stachel's different. He didn't even try to enter the plant. He simply called up the gatehouse and asked for the names."

To her surprise, Vought laughed—a soft, sucking sound. "So much for all our cloak-and-dagger planning, eh? Stachel just might have revolutionized the spy biz."

"You'll have to admit he's right for the Wiseguy thing."

"How about Heidemann? How did she enjoy being hung out to dry?"

"She didn't. But she fooled us all. She kept her head. She played a deaf mute, and the police took her to Travelers Aid at the Chester station. When she found the chance, she hopped a train to Wilmington, then walked to the airport and home base."

"You sound especially pleased by this."

"I want her to go on the mission. She has to go."

"And Stachel? How did he react to this?"

"Let's put it this way—Stachel now seems to regard Mrs. Heidemann with considerable respect. At least he's no longer grumping about her."

Vought nodded. "Well, that's one plus for us, I guess. How's Randelmann doing on the J-E?"

"Pretty good. He's quite familiar with radio procedures and technicalities anyhow, being a pilot. The Jean-Eleanor is just another set, the way he goes at it."

"He continues to get along well with Stachel?"

"Major Randelmann remains president of the Bruno Stachel fan club."

Vought sighed again. "I still wish we had a surer way to get Wiseguy out. I don't like all this cute stuff. I'm a direct-route guy, and this fancy-pantsy drill makes me nervous."

Everything makes you nervous, Polly thought tartly.

"Is Foreign Nationalities Section keeping us informed of Wiseguy's status and whereabouts?" Vought asked, watching the pigeons again.

"As best it can. Wiseguy is super security conscious—very careful about his contacts with us. The whole continent is a rat's nest of Nazi agents these days."

"We must keep absolutely current on Wiseguy."

"Mm. It's easier, with him at the top the way he is. Besides our own FNS, our British friends also have a very close watch on the comings and goings at the Reichs Chancellery."

"General Donovan will want to know of our progress on Nightstick arrangements overseas—"

Polly opened a folder on her desk and made a thing of checking her notes. It wasn't necessary, since her retention of data was keen and she could have recited the slightest details from memory; but Vought had a fondness for flipboards and charts and flow diagrams, being a former DuPont executive, and it paid dividends to play to his propensities. "The station at Harrington, England, is prepared to receive the team for final processing. Stachel and Randelmann will continue their flight drill, only there they will be familiarized with Eighth Air Force assembly and formation-flying procedures. Both will get further practice with the Jean-Eleanor transmitter-receiver set, while Heidemann will be briefed in depth on map reading, unit and vehicle identification, small arms use and maintenance, sabotage techniques, and document falsification. All three will be given a two-day bivouac, in which emphasis will be on forced night marches, obstacle courses under live fire, and combat-reactive tours through rigged buildings. Then they'll be flown to Dijon, France, for update documents, dressing, and fly-in."

Vought broke in. "How about parachute training?"

"It will be the last phase, and familiarization only. There's no time for practice jumps."

"When are you going over?"

"Tonight. There's an ATC Connie leaving Andrews just before midnight. It'll take me right to London. I'll spend an hour or two with Fred Delaney at SI headquarters there, then buzz on down to Harrington."

"You'll be in the ETO until this is over?" Vought ambled to the door, tired and seeming to care little about her answer.

"London, Harrington, Geneva for an update on Wiseguy, then to the ops office in Bern."

Vought nodded, said good-bye with an eyebrow, and went on to his meeting with the director. Polly spent the remainder of her day on the bureaucratic flotsam that had come to rest in her in-box. There were great wads of interpretive reports from the Foreign Nationalities branch. There were letters from MI-5, the Sûreté, and the Canadian Mounted Police, clippings from the foreign language press, and some ambiguous cables from State Department sources in Lisbon. There were bulletins, memos, reports, position papers, and crap, crap, crap.

As she worked, her mind insisted on presenting snapshots of Stachel and the olden-golden-bolden days in Berlin: Stachel with that pensive smile of his; Stachel somber and remote; Stachel asleep, in the dawn light.

To hell with him.

He was a dumb old memory.

Expendable.

8

 HE DAY HAD been very physical, with the entire
morning given to familiarization work with parachutes.
They had been given a long and tiresome lecture on risers and
canopies, chest packs, seat packs, pilot chutes, static lines,
and a catechism of proper techniques. Then they had
struggled in the wind with exasperatingly unmanageable silk
and tangled shroud lines, pulling and shoving, and, to Elfi
Heidemann's obvious disapproval, cursing. The worst,
though, was the falling off a platform, to be jerked upright by
a parachute harness, then cut loose for a teeth-clicking,
leg-crunching drop into a sawdust pit.

"Why, in the name of my Uncle Ludwig's piles, are we put
through this kind of nonsense?" Randelmann complained.
Staggering to his feet, spitting wood chips and wrestling with
harness straps, he coughed, "This can't be England. It simply
must be hades. You and I, Herr General, are dead and are
now in hell. Evenings, they keep us in a millionaire's manor
house. Days, they pull us through keyholes by our peckers."

Reflexively, Stachel, who was sprawled on a spectator
bench, glanced from his private discomforts to see if Elfi had
heard this. But if she had, she gave no sign. She stood by the
provision truck, sipping tea in weary solitude, stiff and pink
with the traces of her recent exertions. In her jump suit and
knit cap, she looked like an urchin, and he felt a pang of
sympathy for her.

"You're grumpy today, Randelmann. Don't you like your
work?"

"I adore it. The best part is crawling through snow drifts
and wading through frozen bogs. The rest is only half as
good."

Stachel, resuming his silence, thought he knew why the major was so testy this day. It was one thing to volunteer for a risky mission while enduring the tedium of wartime America, but England was close to the struggle's core, and treason, instead of an abstraction, was now a heavy presence only a few days and several hundreds of miles away. Randelmann, Stachel suspected, harbored a much larger capacity of humanism than his cynical façade would suggest. And, for the humanist, the betrayal of a political system lost its urgency and romanticism the nearer the betrayal and the clearer old faces and old memories.

"Did I ever tell you I once drank a lot, Randelmann?"

The major, slumped beside him, gave him a sidelong glance. "Well, no. But it was a rather well-known fact, Herr General. You cut a fancy figure in café society. The tabloids followed you quite closely."

"I don't drink now. I haven't for a long time. And do you know how I managed to keep from returning to the grape, so to speak?"

"I can't imagine. It must have been difficult, from what I hear about heavy drinking, and all."

"The first weeks were the worst. But I learned a useful trick—a device that would change my mind when I felt uneasy, shaky, ready to pack it in."

"Oh? What was that, Herr General?" Randelmann had become polite and uneasily attentive, in the manner of one who has just heard his priest confess a fondness for girls.

"I would think of the most rotten thing I ever did as a result of my drinking. I would remind myself of how I felt when I woke up after the stinkingest binge. Remembering took away the readiness to relive the so-called good times. I would get over the urge."

"That's very interesting, Herr General." Randelmann cleared his throat, puzzled and embarrassed. "But why do you tell me about this?"

"When you get qualms about what we're planning to do, Randelmann, when you feel guilt over our impending adventure, don't think of the good old days, the good old people. Think of the rotten trick those bastards played on you—kicking you down the military ladder, humiliating you, keeping you in obscurity for something you never did. Don't think of the mountains and the green lakes and the little white houses and the pink-cheeked farmers and the beautiful music and the splendid cities. Think of the jails and the piano-wire strangulations, the midnight raids and the beatings and the Catholics and Jews hanging by their balls from barn rafters. The tendency to accuse yourself of treason against the Fatherland dissipates quickly when you remember the bad things done by the bad people. We are not betraying our families and friends, my dear Randelmann, we are saving them from their hell."

"I'm not sure I understand, Herr General."

"Yes you do."

* * *

At dusk, Tarbell arrived in a jeep.

"Ha," Stachel said over the sound of the idling motor, "you are not expecting us to run to the manor house? You are offering us a ride for a change?"

"Climb in. We've a lot to do yet tonight."

"Ah, yes . . . we fly again. Still another problem in navigation for Randelmann, still another test of my flying ability."

"No flight exercise tonight. Tonight we talk."

Stachel waited for Elfi, then swung in to sit beside her on the rear seat. Randelmann sat beside Tarbell, his face blue with the cold. As they rode, bouncing along the darkening lane, Stachel said, "You did very well on the trap range today, Frau Heidemann."

"I hate guns."

"They're all right in their place. They have certain utility."

"The same could be said of a guillotine."

"You really ought to relax, Frau Heidemann. You're so—well—intense. Loosen up. Life's not so bad."

"Mind your own business, Generalmajor Stachel."

g

POLLY STOOD BEFORE the medieval fireplace, her back to the flickering logs, clasping her hands behind her and rocking on her heels. *Give her a pipe and a tweed suit,* Stachel thought dourly, *and she could be the inspector in a mystery film, about to reveal who had smitten Sir Reginald with the croquet mallet.*

"So then," Polly said, her gaze moving deliberately, first to Frau Heidemann, then to Randelmann, and finally to Stachel, "we have arrived at the point of commitment. Your team is established, functions with fair co-ordination, and is about as ready as we can make it in the time available. Are there any questions or comments?"

Stachel, as had become routine for him, set the mood. When he said nothing, Randelmann and Frau Heidemann sat impassively, listening to the crackling fire.

"What I'm saying," Polly put in softly, "is that this is your last chance to withdraw. If there is the slightest doubt, the slightest unwillingness to put it all on the line for the success of this mission, now is the time to make it known. The mission can fail, the whole team can be lost, if one among you falters."

"Miss Loomis," Stachel told the others, "is indulging her fondness for melodrama. She wonders if we are truly ready to save the world for generations yet unborn."

Randelmann sighed and rolled his eyes in stagey exasperation.

"How about you, Frau Heidemann? Anything you want to say to Miss Loomis?"

"Not now."

"Well, then." Polly, smugly professional, went to an easel and, pulling away the green cloth cover, revealed a map of Germany. "This is where you'll be operating," she said, attempting a small joke.

*   *   *

The plan, Polly assured, was relatively uncomplicated. She reviewed Eisenhower's apprehensions about the Werewolf concept. Sweeping a pointer stick from the Bodensee to Vienna, tapping it against the map in little bursts of emphasis, she said, "Organized harassment coming from this arc of mountains could destabilize Europe, perhaps the world political and economic scene, for decades to come. Your job will be to stifle the first attempt to set up such an organization."

She went over the von Lemmerhof disaffection, the decaying process in which a trusted subordinate was led to betray Adolf Hitler for the redemption of his own Feldgrau soul. Stachel's mind wandered. He had heard it all many times; besides, Lemmerhof, who had always bored him, was even more boring in the role of a whining tattletale. Instead of concentrating on Eisenhower's anxieties and Lemmerhof's cowardice, Stachel considered Elfi Heidemann's throat—a peach-colored construction of gentle curves and mysterious shadows that, it seemed to him, was absolutely the most erotic thing he'd ever laid eyes on. He had at times imagined her in the nude, but the resultant images had been about as stimulating as statuary in the Staatsmuseum; to study her throat this way, and to project its curves beyond the V of her collar, was to be a boy, steaming secretly over the maddeningly unattainable in the next pew.

"The code name for Lemmerhof is Whisper," Polly was

saying in her pedantic way. "We'll refer to him by that name henceforth. It will be that name we'll use for him in all radio or written communications. He's entirely useless to us if his cover is broken and he's lost to the Gestapo. He is, therefore, under the strictest orders from us to protect himself at all costs. We will, therefore, do the same. Whisper is his name, and that it will remain, until the case is declassified from its current top secret.

"As for Nightstick, Research and Development has provided carefully constructed covers for each of you. Censorship and Documents has provided the papers and material you will carry to justify the covers. You, Stachel, will be known as Pastor Emil Ritter, an apostolic minister who lost his church in the destruction of the village of Vogelheim, in Hesse. The town was leveled on the night of 21 September last, when a flight of British bombers, lost in a fog, jettisoned its bombs. Only eleven of the village's two hundred inhabitants survived —four are invalids in a Wiesbaden clinic, three are in the Wehrmacht on the Eastern Front, and four are children now living in a Frankfurt orphanage. The real Pastor Ritter was killed by a direct hit and his body was never found. C. and D., however, came into possession of a letter from the Apostolic Council in Augsburg, which names Pastor Ritter to a congregation in Lauderbach, a town of four hundred souls near Tegernsee, south of Munich. The council, it seems, was preparing to transfer Pastor Ritter, prior to his untimely departure for paradise"—Polly smiled again at her own drollery—"and the Bürger of Lauderbach have been awaiting him patiently. So the documents are all there, and your cover, Stachel, is that you are en route to your new charge at Lauderbach. The people who know the real Pastor Ritter are all beyond caring, and the people who await him have never seen him before. Moreover, according to our sources in Bern, the council hasn't the slightest idea that good old Pastor Ritter is now in the heavenly choir. You will carry a copy of the transfer letter, along with all the passes, permits, ration stamps, food cards, et cetera, et cetera, et cetera; together, your documents should protect you against Gestapo attention as you move about."

"Move about where?"

"I'm coming to that," Polly drawled. She stood for a time, examining the map in thoroughgoing enjoyment of her role as schoolmarm.

The Nightstick team exchanged looks, and Randelmann parodied her with a lugubrious, prissy expression on his face.

"Back to cover stories. Mrs. Heidemann will carry the papers of Inge Stolz, formerly a nurse at the Dietrich Clinic, which, before its destruction in a raid on Augsburg last summer, was a small and heavily endowed drying-out hospital for socially prominent Bavarians and UFA film actors who drink unsuccessfully. Since Fräulein Stolz was the only person—staff and patients alike—to survive the explosions and fire, she was unemployed; and, because she lost a few of her buttons in the horror of it all, the authorities are not likely to assign her to war-important work or military medicine. She has, therefore, been hired by Pastor Ritter—her brother-in-law—to assist in the church office in Lauderbach.

"As for Randelmann, he will carry the Soldbuch and related papers of Karl Denzinger, a Gefreiter of the 118th Motorized Infantry, a unit that was virtually wiped out in the fighting at Stalingrad. There are, in fact, several score alumni of the 118th, but they have been either hospitalized or reassigned to other Wehrmacht units. Randelmann will be one of the unsalvageables, completely addled but ambulatory, who has been placed on medical furlough and is now under the care of his hometown clergyman, Pastor Ritter. I might add, incidentally, that Mrs. Heidemann's effective use of the mental-defective gambit in Chester inspired us to adapt it to Nightstick."

Stachel glanced at Elfi. She blushed when Randelmann made an approving face and moved his hands in silent applause.

Polly Loomis turned to drop an acetate overlay across the map. A dotted red line made a zigzag from the Rhine above Strasbourg to a point southwest of Munich. "Here," she said, "you see the course to be followed in your mission. Takeoff point, Dijon, France. Landing pinpoint, four kilometers northeast of the village of Rott, south of Landsberg."

Stachel interrupted. "There's a question I think you ought to answer right now. Without any of your usual Quatsch."

"Well?" Her tone had become instantly wary.

"How is it, if we are supposed to supervise Whisper in Berlin, Nightstick is landing in Bavaria? That leaves us with a hell of a walk, I'd say."

Polly cleared her throat and managed a wry smile. "The plan has been altered somewhat, Bruno. Nightstick will not be sent to Berlin for its rendezvous with Whisper. Whisper is now located in Bavaria."

Stachel felt a sinking, a physical manifestation of the suspicion that had been plucking at him. "Why haven't you told us this before?"

"Security, Bruno. We haven't been sure, until now, that you three would be going anywhere, remember?"

"You're a very tiresome person, Miss Loomis."

"Perhaps. But careful, too."

"Any other surprises?"

"This is as good a moment as any to tell you, I suppose. The fact is, you will not be flying in. You will be going in by parachute."

"Why?" Stachel heard his mind: *I knew it. I knew it. I knew it.*

"Whisper can't guarantee good conditions for an aircraft landing."

"What can he guarantee?"

"Nothing, really. It's a whole new soccer match, now that he's been transferred to the southern Werewolf base."

"So we'll be jumping in blind?"

"Not entirely. We have a specially chosen pinpoint. Your

71

chances for an unobserved drop are excellent. Actually, this is better. We have taken control of your arrival. Before, we were putting too much reliance on Whisper's arrangements —on his promises. This way, we drop you where *we* think is best under circumstances and convenience *we* select."

"When and where, then?"

"Tomorrow afternoon, a C-47 takes you to Dijon. Tomorrow night, the plane will take you from Dijon—like so"—she swished the stick across the acetate—"in a feint to Schwäbisch Hall, where it will turn southeast for Munich. At a point due east of Augsburg—here"—the stick tapped—"you descend to a thousand feet and fly on a southwest heading until you reach this point—here—four kilometers northeast of Rott. There is a large, high meadow bounded on four sides by a state forest. It is bisected by a shallow ravine, lengthwise. Landing in this defilade, you should be screened from ground-level observation, and, since the area is thinly populated, you should have plenty of time to bury your parachutes and jump suits and helmets. You will proceed on foot to this road, a two-lane blacktop that leads to Weilheim. From there you will make your way to Königsberg, where Whisper will have placed a truck at the intersection of this road and Highway Eleven. You will help the driver change a tire. In gratitude, he will drive the three of you to Gmünd, at the north end of the Tegernsee. He will drop you off at an inn called the Herzoghof. You will wait there for further word from Whisper."

"And what will that word be?"

"Directions to the safe-house, where you will live and work."

Stachel sat for a time, absorbing the shock.

"Excuse me, Fräulein Loomis," Randelmann put in, "does that red line on the map wander around as much as I think it does?"

"Again it's a matter of security. The aircrew has exact coordinates for your drop point. Briefings on meterological conditions—wind and all that—will be held just prior to takeoff. The wandering around, as you put it, is to deny the Germans a clue as to where you pop out of the plane."

There was an awkward silence, an interval in which it was apparent that so much was being left to chance there was really no sense in trying to ask specific questions and expect specific answers.

Randelmann looked at Stachel. "Any comments, Herr General?"

"Let's put it this way," Stachel said. "I don't think any of us should make plans for old-age retirement."

10

RESTLESS, ELFI HAD postponed bed for some night air on the terrace. She huddled in her sheepskin jacket, the large air corps thing that was so warm, and, standing at the balustrade, breathed deeply of the wind and listened to the spidery trees clamoring in the darkness.

The meeting with the Loomis woman had left her feeling curiously empty, as if there should have been more than what had been delivered. She had learned long ago that Americans were generally guileless and straightforward. Moreover, they approached the war against Germany with the same superficiality of spirit and intent they gave to a game of football; she rather expected that when the Yanks entered Berlin they would look about for a goal post to knock down. But Miss Loomis was not the usual American, communicating as she did a slyness, a propensity for scheming. Coupled with the extraordinary alterations to the Nightstick plan, Loomis's indirection during this evening's meeting had been upsetting —even ominous.

Elfi was enough of a woman to discern Miss Loomis's real problem, trickery and conniving notwithstanding. Miss Loomis was trying to contain the steam of passion. Miss Loomis was, as the old Tyrolean saying had it, sitting on a sizzling.

And she was enough of a woman herself to acknowledge at last her own vulnerability. From their first encounter at dinner in Berlin, Bruno Stachel had been a silent, sometimes mocking part of her. There had never, in all the years of their acquaintance, been anything more physical than a shaking of hands, but she would now admit that he might very well have taken her to bed that first night, what with his unending presence within her mind—the insistent and lascivious imaginings he had bequeathed to her. Unaccustomed as she was to romance and its processes, she could not differentiate between sexual desire and the other-mindedness, the specific altruism, required of one who loves. Whatever the phenomenon, though, Stachel had somehow entered her with an absoluteness akin to anatomical penetration. When she thought of him, it was never with neutrality; either she raged with anger and accusation or she brooded, and melted, and surrendered to flooding daydreams. But whichever attitude of the seesaw prevailed, she knew—and accepted—that Stachel had become an unremovable part of her. (Why did God persist in teasing the humanity he was purported to love so much?)

She had overheard the bizarre little pep talk Stachel had given Randelmann at the parachute-training field, and it had been inexplicably moving—poignant—due, probably, to her own combat with alcohol in the early years. She had been there; she knew the frightfulness of the struggle; to hear Stachel articulating the unspeakable as a means to encourage a faltering friend was to love him in a way she'd not known before.

Annoyed with this new pain, she headed for the garden.

Because of the wind and the shifting shadows, she wasn't aware of his presence until she'd virtually walked into him.

"I'm sorry. I—"

"Ah. Inge Stolz. My old friend from Augsburg. What brings you out on a bitter night like this?"

He had thought he was alone, and to find that he was now expected to make small talk with Nightstick's resident prude was a real annoyance. Still, he made his manner light. "It's pretty late for a little spy like you to be wandering about."

There was a pause before she spoke. "I don't think that's an appropriate term, General Stachel. I am not a spy."

"I used the term deliberately, Frau Heidemann. It's time you face up to the fact you've been avoiding. You and Randelmann, too. You both have not permitted yourselves to think of yourselves as spies, because, if you do, you certify the treason we're about to commit." He knew he was being harsh, but it was the truth, and to hell with her.

To his surprise, she did not flare. She stood in silence for a long moment, as if considering his words. "I suppose you're right," she said. "I knew Randelmann was having a problem with it, but I wasn't really aware of my own."

"You don't need to have a problem."

"Because all I must do is forget the pretty little cottages and remember the Catholics hanging from rafters?"

"Oh. You heard me, then."

"I heard."

"Like it or not, Frau Heidemann, it's good advice."

She turned up her collar against the rawness, and her face was thoughtful in the dim light of the library's casements. The lamp glow made her look younger, he decided, and even prettier.

75

"Let me ask you a question," she said after an interval. "Do you ever get the feeling that you and I and Randelmann aren't being dealt with honestly?"

"Honestly?" He gave her a careful look. "What do you mean?"

"I have a hunch. It won't leave me. It tells me that Miss Loomis isn't letting us in on all that's going on. And her changing mind—first we will fly into Germany in daylight; now we parachute in at night. Then there's the elaborateness of the scheme—the—well—heavy-handedness, I guess you'd call it. It's Baroque. It's tacking a carpet with a pile driver."

He was compelled to smile. "I apologize for any doubts I might have had as to your suitability for this work."

"What is that supposed to mean?"

"I've had the same suspicion all along. And anybody who shares my opinions has to be a genius."

The indefinable tension between them broke. In the dimness he could see her answering smile. "What are you going to do about it?" she asked.

"Nothing."

"Well—" Her further questions hung in the air, as if she were groping for a thought just beyond reach.

"Do you remember the lecture we had from that air corps major last week? The major with the small head and the big behind?"

She nodded. "The man who instructed us on Luftwaffe combat procedures. What about him?"

"Remember what he said about the black B-17s?"

"The B-17s captured by Germany and flown by Luftwaffe pilots. Is that what you mean?"

"Right. They fly along with American formations and radio position, headings, altitude, and speed to the German fighter stations ahead. When the Americans reach Point X or Point Y, or whatever, there's a reception committee. But the Americans don't do much about their black outriders because the black outriders serve the valuable function of alerting them to impending attack. They know when to expect a reception committee. They get ready to fight wisely."

She nodded. "And that's what we shall do, I suppose? We shall carry on, doing nothing about Miss Loomis, getting ready to fight wisely."

"Well, I don't know if we'll have to fight. But it pays to be watchful."

"What a grubby business."

"Mm."

There was a moment in which they thought about this, and Stachel's memory took him to the night in France following their escape from their Nazi executioners. Elfi Heidemann and he had idled in a hospital restaurant, confronting the fact of their irreparable breach of the German law and their consignment to everlasting outness. They had talked bravely of a return to the Fatherland, of righting Hitler's wrongs, of bringing forgiveness and reconstruction to their addled countrymen. And now they were returning, not as righteous redeemers but as thieves in the night, trusting no one, not even the sponsors—the applauders—of their stealth and duplicity. Oh, God, what a grubby business indeed.

"Frau Heidemann, I must ask you something."

"What is it, General?"

"Why do you persist in this rotten scheme when you don't believe in it?"

She seemed to falter for a moment, in the manner of a trial witness who looks for ways to parry a potentially self-incriminating question. She said, "Essentially, for the same reason you persist, I suppose."

"How do you know what my reason is?"

"Randelmann has told me of your desire to atone for your support of Hitler in the early days." She paused again, then added uncomfortably, "I didn't support Hitler. But I didn't oppose him either. Which means I have amends of my own to make."

"Randelmann talks too much," Stachel said, feeling vaguely that his question had not been answered.

"Not really. He idolizes you, poor man."

"Then I can't be all bad, eh?" He felt his annoyance returning.

She studied him for a time, her eyes shadowed by the night, as the feeling in him gathered heat. Who was this bloody snob, to look down her Prussian nose? What had she ever done with her high-and-mighty self but marry some thickheaded Prussian prig and nearly drink herself to death on cooking wine because she couldn't face her mistakes?

"I've never for a moment thought you were all bad, General Stachel."

He pulled his scarf tighter about his throat and turned to make for the house. Looking back at her, he said dryly, "I admire your courage, your tenacity, and your perceptiveness, Frau Heidemann. You are, as I've said, an exceptional woman. But your patronizing, your long-suffering toleration of me as a country bumpkin has become a flaming pain in my ass. Now, if you'll excuse me, I'll go in to bed."

She reached out, an impulsive motion, for his sleeve, "Wait. I don't—"

"Good night, Frau Heidemann."

"You're the one who walked out on *me* in Chester, Herr General Smart Aleck," she snapped, her own anger forming. "Don't give *me* that air of injured righteousness."

"I walked out on you because I didn't want you to go to Germany."

"Why not, if I may be so bold?"

"Because I didn't want you to lose your hoity-toity neck, that's why," he said acidly.

"What's that to you, anyway?"

"None of your hoity-toity business, Frau Heidemann."

11

THERE WAS TALK among the dressers at Dijon of having Stachel shave his head and wear a mustache, but after his waspish objections and a telephone discussion with the commandant, the idea was dropped. The dressers most usually had their way, according to Tarbell, who had come along on the C-47 from Harrington and was only too ready to exhibit his extensive new knowledge of OSS operations. The dressers, he said, were often all that stood between an agent and a Gestapo interrogation, since it was they who provided the proper clothes with the proper weave and labels, the proper cigarettes and theater stubs, the proper Soldbücher and insignia, and the proper toilet paper, hairpins, underwear, shoe soles, toothpicks, and love letters that made a clandestine agent appear to be an honest, hardworking Deutscher or Hausfrau. The chief dresser made no secret of his concern that Stachel's fame might "pull the plug on Nightstick," and it was he who made the hardest case for a disguise, but Stachel glared into the man's face and told him there would be no Nightstick mission at all if he weren't permitted to go in under conditions agreed upon by Polly Loomis. "It's your funeral," the man had grumped upon his completion of the London call. "Kill yourself if you want. We'll win this crappy war anyhow."

Stachel, Randelmann, and Heidemann attended to their separate dressing needs, being carefully polite when meeting by chance in the hallways or parachute room. The Dijon OSS holding area was based on a large château about fifteen miles east of town, where a small stream wound through the estate's restricted acreage. For wartime, there was considerable luxury to be noted, since Wild Bill Donovan had decreed that agents awaiting paradrops should be given every comfort as an indication of how much value the U.S. of A. placed on their services. There were game rooms and a bar, and even sheets for the cots, and music came from phonographs brought in especially from New York. Plumbing was a problem, as it was everywhere in France, so the agents and their dressers and radio mechanics and case officers spent much of their time running bucket brigades between the château and the ice-clogged stream.

There was little time for all this for Nightstick, since they had arrived on the morning of the day whose night would mark the advent of their mission. Considerable attention was given to the papers they would be carrying—dates had to match the cover stories, and movement permissions had to be properly stamped and initialed—and there were two run-throughs of each of their cover stories. The chief dresser, primarily to restore face lost in his retreat on Stachel's disguise, made a fuss over Randelmann's Soldbuch. The man, red-faced and pompous, complained that the handwriting that recorded the various unit assignments "looked too god-damned English," and he wasn't satisfied until a forger from the Documents Section made out an entirely new Soldbuch and aged it with floor grime and tobacco stains.

Stachel's gear was simple: a black suit bearing a Frankfurt label; a cleric's black hat; a ministerial collar, which the dresser called "a celluloid turtleneck"; wallet with papers and ID; black, old-fashioned shoes; underwear from a Wiesbaden variety store; an overcoat of gray wool, very old and fabricated of material known to have been manufactured in Hoechst. He would carry only 150 Reichsmarks, since a preacher would be suspect were he any richer, and operating sums would be forwarded later through Bern and Whisper himself.

Elfi was issued a severe, skirted suit of serge, starkly nurselike and somber. With it went a medical kit, with a pitiful collection of rolled bandages, iodine, a few compresses, adhesive tape, aspirin, a thermometer, and a stethoscope —all of German origin. She was also permitted a small purse containing 100 Reichsmarks, her ID, medical worker's ration book, and items related to feminine maintenance, from comb to sanitary napkins. She herself had selected the inventory —subject to overruling by the chief dresser—since she would, essentially, be playing what she was and had been.

It was Randelmann who had given Elfi and Stachel the worst moment in the long series of adjustments they'd had to make since Wilmington. The two of them had been sipping coffee with Tarbell in the parachute harness room when Randelmann stepped through the door in his Gefreiter's uniform. The Feldgrau was worn and tacky; the Hoheitsab-zeichen—the silver Nazi eagle on the right breast—was pewter-dull and frayed; the jackboots seemed to have been to Mars and back; the service cap was sweat-rimmed. The whole was the sum of many melancholy parts, and Stachel was fairly certain of what Elfi Heidemann was thinking: The uniform was a material representation of what Germany itself had become. (God knows *he* felt that way.) The Wehrmacht uniforms at Camp Ritchie had been stage props—clean, creased, symbolic. The German equipment, from compasses to machine pistols, was the stuff of Hollywood. But this, this sad and battle-grimed set of rags, evoked simultaneously the once-proud hopes for the Fatherland and the amorphous, indefinable shame that had replaced them. All the rationaliza-tions over what his homeland had become were now reduced to a denominator of inescapable reality.

* * *

They returned to Germany by the light of a quarter-moon on Saturday, March 14, 1945.

The meteorologists at Dijon had forecasted generally stable conditions over Oberbayern between midnight and dawn.

The order-of-battle specialists at G-2 had pronounced the parachute pinpoint area to be devoid of any significant organized military activity.

Both had been wrong.

When the members of Nightstick went out the hatch of the C-47 at three-second intervals, they were spun about and entirely disoriented by severe gusting that dropped them —sprinkled was a better word—over a five-kilometer stretch of snow and forest being traversed by elements of the 108th SS Panzer Division, en route to the defense of the Rhine.

12

THERE WAS A RINGING.
Then a light—the diffused rippling that moves at the bottom of a mountain lake.

She considered the light for a time, then recognized it as dawn at the window. The ringing had to be the doorbell, since the phone sat in ebony silence on the night table no more than a foot from her head.

"For God's sake, Polly, what's all the noise?" Thompson's voice was muffled by the pillow he had pulled over his face.

"Someone's at the door," she said, husky with the afterpain of alcohol and prurience.

"Who in hell is it? Tell them to go away."

Collecting herself, struggling against the dryness of mouth and the guilt and remorse, she remembered two things, each in order of its importance to her. First, the ringing—two longs and two shorts—was Schroeder's signal, not only to identify himself but also to stress urgency. Second, she didn't really like Thompson, a large and beet-hued man with an inexpertly foul mouth (he said damn, when hell would sound better) and only a fifty-fifty chance of ever climbing beyond his rating in the State Department Foreign Service, which was not very high to begin with.

Somehow lucid again, she said, "I think it's your wife."

"My *wife?* Oh, God." The bedding heaved, and Thompson arose like a pink whale, clutching for his clothes and making small whimpering sounds. "How did she find me here? She doesn't even know you—"

Polly, suddenly malicious, said, "We were pretty high-profile last night, I'm afraid. You made quite a fuss over the bill at Klingl's. You left a broad wake."

"Oh, God. Oh, *God.* She's an absolute bloodhound."

"Here's your tie. You can go out the back way. Through the kitchen. No. That way. Through the arch."

When he had gone, clattering and cursing inexpertly, she pulled on her robe and went to the door, smiling to herself. She hadn't had the slightest notion whether or not Thompson had a wife. Lord, what *was* it about Switzerland that seemed guaranteed to loose the wantonness in her? Back home, she wouldn't give a clod like Thompson a second glance; here in Bern, she would probably hop in the sack with Bo-Jo the Dog-faced Boy and later go looking for King Kong. *Damn* it.

"Ah, Schroeder. Sorry to keep you waiting. Come in."

"I regret having to disturb you, Fräulein. But a message has been received via the Blue Network, and, since it carried a Z designation, I came at once."

"Of course. Want a drink?"

"No, thank you. I'm still on duty."

"So what's the message?"

Schroeder turned his hat in his hands, trying not to look at the underwear and stockings on the carpet before the fireplace, the empty bottle on the sofa. "It's from Whisper," he said politely, as if it were a rare privilege to carry such tidings.

"Well, what does he *say?*"

"Nightstick did not keep the rendezvous. The truck waited

at the intersection, as stipulated, until made to move along by
military police from a Panzer unit passing through. None of
the members of Nightstick showed up as planned."

She ran a hand through her hair, trying to absorb the
impact of this news. She vowed she would never drink again.
She might, when this was was over, become a nun. "The
safe-house near Gmünd—did—"

"No, Fräulein. No trace. Whisper fears Nightstick has been
lost to the enemy."

"Very well, Schroeder. You did well to advise me."

"Will there be a return message to Whisper, Fräulein
Loomis?"

"Signal at once. Keep a watch on the intersection and at the
safe-house. They may still show up. Sign my code name."

"I'll take care of it. Anything else?"

"No. I'll be at the office in an hour."

"Yes. Well, then. Wiederseh'n."

She closed the door behind him and stood for a time
listening to the ticking of the cuckoo clock and struggling to
subdue the anxiety that had compounded the sickness in her
belly.

Picking up the phone, she dialed Max on the special line.

"Max? Polly. I want you to get a message through to
Wiseguy. At once. Most urgent."

"It's about the mysterious disappearance of Nightstick?"

"Oh? You know?"

"I heard the traffic. I can tune in on your Blue Net, among
other Allied sendings."

"Don't you ever go to bed, Max?"

"The Fatherland has promised me two weeks of sleep
instead of an Iron Cross." He chuckled. "They will be
awarded me on my ninetieth birthday."

"Wiseguy must be informed."

"I've sent word already. It will take time to get to him, of
course. He's so super-cautious, so preoccupied with his

security cover. The tiniest leak would be disaster, I understand."

Curious, she asked, "You don't know who Wiseguy is?"

"Of course not. I'm only a message center, a letter drop. To
know could get me killed, my dear Fräulein Loomis."

13

THE WIND HAD DIED, almost with vexing magic,
soon after Stachel touched down in a rectangle of slushy
meadow. His landing was soft and soundless in the sogginess,
and he was able quickly to collapse his parachute and bury it
beside a line of trees marking the pasture's southern bounda-
ry. At first he thought he had landed precisely on pinpoint,
but standing in the dark of the trees, looking out at the rolling
country, which was pale blue in the fading moonlight, he saw
none of the features so carefully identified in the map sessions
at Dijon. There was no stream to the west; the twin hills to
the north were not there; and the map had shown no village
such as he now saw to the northeast, with its steep-pitched
roofs and onion-shaped church tower pointing to heaven. Nor
was there any sign of Randelmann and Elfi.

Since there was nothing to do but to make for the village
and whatever roads might pass through it, he made a final
check of how he might appear to curious eyes. All incriminat-
ing gear—parachute, knit cap, compass, knife, Colt .45 with
shoulder holster, first-aid kit, knee pads, coveralls, and
folding shovel—were now underground. Clergyman's
clothes, including hat and seedy topcoat and high-top snow

boots, wet but in place. Scarf and mittens, unaccountably missing. Papers intact.

He held to the woodland shadows and, stepping carefully so as to avoid unnecessary noises, made his way downhill. A lane, apparently heavily trampled by cattle since the last snowfall, met the tree line a hundred meters farther on, and he followed this in the direction of the village, thankful that his footprints were no longer evident. He had done what he could, brooming the dirty wet snow with a pine branch, to cover the traces of his landing, but he worried that some observant cowherd might want to register a bit of good will with the local Gestapo and report those that were left. The sky and its filmy clouds told him that rain would be falling in a day or two, but he needed it now if he was to clear the site and be on his way with impunity.

"Halt."

The voice was soft, undemanding, almost casual. But its very indifference intensified the surprise and shock.

"Oh. Good morning," Stachel said, struggling to match the soldier's tone. He blinked as a flashlight went across his face.

"You're up early, Herr Pastor," the man said. "May I see your papers, please?"

"You startled me. I didn't see you there in the shadows."

The soldier, a patch of darkness against the hedge at the village's rim, ran the light over Stachel's documents. "It's a Landser's duty not to be seen when on perimeter guard," he said. "Especially when the night produces spies on para-chutes."

"I'm not sure I follow you," Stachel said gently. "The military mystifies me. Spies, you say?"

The man slung his rifle and returned Stachel's papers. Out of some shade of loneliness or boredom, or even in response to Stachel's clerical guise, he became confidential. "They caught one a little while ago. Over by Oldendorf. Didn't you hear the plane? You must have, walking cross-country as you were."

"One hears so many planes these days," he laughed softly—"and I am an absentminded fellow."

The man grunted. "I am, too, unfortunately. I could have easily made sergeant long ago if I could only keep my mind on detail. But you, Herr Pastor Ritter, should be more careful. You can't wander through a bivouac of one of the Führer's SS Panzer divisions without courting trouble. These boys have all been rotated from the Eastern Front, where they have learned to shoot first, then ask for papers. Me, I've been reassigned from soft duty at Reichenhall. And that makes you lucky."

"Dear me," Stachel said. "I meant no wrong. As you have seen, I'm on my way to a new charge at Lauderbach, and I've learned to travel at night because the roads and towns have become so, well, feverish in the daytime."

"True. We are about to deny the enemy his entrance to the Reich." The trooper's voice was heavy with sarcasm.

"Odd that you should mention Oldendorf. A member of my flock in Vogelheim has asked me to look in on an ailing aunt who lives in Oldendorf. I was on my way there."

"Oh? If you were on your way to Oldendorf, why were you coming down that lane? Oldendorf lies in the opposite direction."

Stachel's mind sped. Smiling sheepishly, he said, "I was lost, actually. That's why I'm so glad to see you. Perhaps you'll be kind enough to point an absentminded old man of God in the right direction. Eh?"

"Well, the easiest route is from the crossroads in the village here. Turn right, follow the paved road for two kilometers, then bear left at the fork. Oldendorf is over the rise a way. But be careful—the whole area is packed with tanks and other armor, and the SS boys are mean and angry. They seem to take the Fatherland's misfortunes quite personally."

"I'm grateful for your advice," Stachel said, meaning it. He paused. Then: "By the way, who was the spy they caught tonight?"

"I haven't the foggiest. I simply heard the chatter coming from the captain's command radio while I was down for soup. A spy came down and was caught by the SS. Period."

Stachel knew it would be a mistake to press the matter. "Ah. I see. Well, then. I'll be off, if it's all right with you."

"Bon voyage, as the Frenchies say. Give my regards to God."

* * *

Stachel was stopped three times on his way to Oldendorf. The road was lined with trucks and tank-recovery vehicles, looming huge and silent in the darkness preceding dawn. They smelled of grease and gunpowder and raw earth, and the clusters of men sat about shielded fires, wrapped in tarpaulins and smoking and trading low-voiced, good-natured obscenities. Stachel himself joined a small group of hikers —three Saxon women and a pair of Ukrainian laborers en route to Munich for work with the railroad construction battalion—because to walk alone was to serve as a focal point for idle speculation at best, official suspicion at worst. The checkpoints proved to be no problem; the troopers on duty were tired and cold and no longer stimulated (if veterans of the Russian front could ever again be stimulated by anything) with the news of the captured spy. They waved the little group down the road with indolent swings of their hands, yawning and vacant-eyed. No officers above the rank of Sturmbannführer had been in evidence.

As he went along, Stachel felt a depression more terrible than any he had experienced, even in his drinking days. Part of it, he knew, was due to the return to Germany, the sense of doom and heartbreak and fear, all around, pressing in. But mostly it was the ambivalence of his side trip to Oldendorf —the absolute need to know who had been caught, Randelmann or Elfi, and the numbing fear that he would find out who. Randelmann was a good fellow, funny and brave and

88

guileless and loyal, and his loss would be a pain among pains; but Elfi's loss would be beyond pain, beyond his present ability to accommodate, even as a thought.

Trudging through the rutted slush, he wondered what had become of Bruno Stachel, the ruthless opportunist who once could lie, cheat, manipulate, even kill with surgeonlike self-mindedness. How much more comfortable—easy and undemanding—life had been in those long-gone days when he considered no one but himself. Why was the world so enamored of love when love obviously was such a gross inconvenience?

Was he in love with Elfi Heidemann? Really?

Who could say? After all these years, who could really say? Who could tell him why he was now so empty?

His thoughts careened, then fixed on the image of himself as a schoolboy, reading quotations beside the high classroom windows in the gray winter light. And out of the image came the barely remembered lament of St. Augustine: "Too late have I loved you, O Lord, too late have I loved you. Memory is indeed a sad privilege."

*   *   *

The security at Oldendorf was much tighter. Stachel and his silent little band joined a small crowd waiting at the stone bridge that led into the village. A huge Scharführer, lantern-jawed and malevolent under his steel helmet, was barking orders and waving his hands, all of which seemed aimed at clearing the area "of all you dirty-faced cow plops" so that "the Führer's armor can resume its march."

The day was already bright in the aftermath of dawn, and the sun would soon be up, and it occurred to Stachel that "the Führer's armor" would be making a serious mistake to try a move across open roads in broad daylight. Whoever was in command either was an idiot or had never understood how thoroughly the Americans controlled the sky over southern Germany.

"Bastards," a man said next to him. Then, after recognition: "Excuse me, Herr Pastor, I didn't see you here."

"No offense."

"I simply get so tired of all these potato-heads telling us to do this, don't do that. I can't even return to my own village now that all these big tin cans have refueled and want to go somewhere else to make their mess. When will it all end?"

Stachel gave the man a sidelong glance, his curiosity overcoming for the moment his inner pain. The fellow was dumpy, with a bulbous nose and bad teeth, and he was sacklike in his farmer's work clothes. A man in from the fields obviously. "I'd be careful if I were you," Stachel said in a low voice. "If that big fellow in the Stahlhelm hears you, you could be more than tired."

"Oh, I know, Pastor, I know. I saw what they did to that spy they caught. But I'm not afraid. I'm too tired for fear anymore."

"You saw the spy?"

"In the village square. Hanging upside down from a lamppost. With a sign reading, 'So die the Yankee vermin.'"

"Was it a man or a woman?"

It was something very much like a slow-motion film in the cinema, where a tree falls in an agonizing, inexorable arc, or where a horse leaps a hedge, a shower of turf following in lazy complexity. The flashes and eruptions came first, then the enveloping concussion and sound. The farmer, agape yet mute, disappeared in a rolling of smoke, and an oriel in the building beside the bridge caved outward in a slow cascade of timber, mortar, and glass. The air itself was crackling and laced with the livid, witless crisscrossing of tracer bullets. The planes came and went at rooftop height, bellowing and keening, and when they had gone for their far-off turning, the bridge, the town, the slope of hill beyond formed a panorama of Hades—burning junk, writhing bodies, cries and screams and drifting fumes.

The planes came back three times. They were American, of course, silver-gray and impersonal, the jaunty white stars on their wings easy to see even in the blur of their treetop passing.

The 108th SS Panzer Division would be late in reaching the Rhine.

The village of Oldendorf, among others, would be an eternity in forgetting that day.

* * *

Stachel made his way into the ruin, stepping around a burning tank, climbing over a fallen tree, and twice stopped to ask if the spy had been a man or a woman. The SS trooper, sitting in frozen disassociation on the doorstep of a house without walls or roof, gave no answer; the woman simply stared back at him with large blue eyes that didn't see. Eventually he found what had to have been the village square, but the rubble was so high and dense, the ruin so complete, he stood in motionless dismay and knew that his answer would not be found here.

In an alley at a corner of the square there were a dozen wounded and dying, aligned in a tidy row, like soldiers' packs awaiting inspection.

She was kneeling, closing the eyes of a chalk-white child.

"Elfi."

She looked up at him, her green eyes glazed. "I tried to help her," she said, "but she was too far gone."

He held out a hand. "Here. Let me see you."

She arose and stood before him, her face streaked, her black suit gray with dust. "Randelmann is dead. They caught him and beat him to death with rifle butts and crowbars. They hung him up by his heels."

"You saw him?"

"Yes. I came into town when I heard. I was afraid it might be you."

91

She began to cry then, soundless heavings of her shoulders. He held her close, tightly, rocking her gently.

Once, when his sight was clear for a time, he saw the farmer. The man stood in the alley's shadow, gazing at him with curious, piglike eyes.

14

THEY WALKED for most of the day. The road, a narrow and winding lane of slush that led from meadow to rise to glen to meadow, was lined at first with the remnants of the panzer unit, a thin trail of stalled vehicles, around which men scurried like the dazed survivors of a trampled anthill. But later, far beyond the attack zone, a quiet set in, a country stillness that seemed even more dreadful than the strafing itself.

Stachel helped her along, holding her arm when the ruts were deep, saying nothing when her sobbing resumed. The crying was intermittent, seemingly reflex, like a cough, and he understood that she was suffering a form of shock. Once or twice he tried to persuade her to sit beside the road, to rest, perhaps catnap. But she would only press on, one step after another, as if she were pursued by demons. He eventually lost his sense of time, and he went along, satisfied simply to be with her.

At a crossroads he induced a woman on a farm cart drawn by a swaybacked gray to take them on. They climbed atop a bundle of fagots and sat, huddled together for warmth, while the cart teetered over a branch road that, a sign said, led to Bad Tölz.

"Is there any public transportation at Tölz?" Stachel asked the woman.

"Who is to say? I know nothing of that area. Besides, everything is different these days. I could tell you yes or no, and either could be wrong, thanks to this rotten war." She glanced back at him, over her shawled shoulder. "How far are you going, Pastor?"

"Tegernsee."

"That's where your church is?"

"No. I'm being assigned to Lauderbach. But I must do some business at Tegernsee first."

"You have a long way to go. And your wife looks in bad shape."

He was about to correct her, but decided it was easier to let the matter pass. "She'll be all right. She had a bad time in the airplane attack at Oldendorf. She's tired and still in a bit of shock, I think."

"That was a terrible thing at Oldendorf. Hildegard Ottmann was there and saw the whole thing. I met Hildegard at the Konditorei in Weilheim, and she told me."

"There are terrible things everywhere these days."

They rode on for a time, the woman making clucking noises at the lethargic horse, Stachel sitting in silence, an arm around Elfi for mutual comfort. She was quiet now, gazing straight down the road unrolling slowly behind them, and he could sense that she was returning to a kind of equilibrium.

"It's getting toward evening," the woman said. "I have a room at the farmhouse. Perhaps you would like to pass the night there."

"That would be fine. I can pay."

"No need. It's the least I can do for a man of God."

*　*　*

It was an Einhaus, one of those large, old, plaster and timber places in which the cows lived below and the family lived above under the great slanted roof. Inside, it smelled of age

93

and woodsmoke and cooking and, from the stalls below, the faint sweet traces of cattle, and hay, and manure. The woman sat them on a corner bench, near the tile oven, and served them some potato soup and a heel of black bread, instructing them amiably to eat while she readied the room. But Elfi ate nothing, sagging in the corner, drifting into sleep.

"Look at her," the woman said on her return. "Out like a candle, poor dear. Your wife's a nurse, eh?"

"Yes. She's usually very hardy. Exhaustion has her now, though."

"Well, then, get her upstairs, Pastor. Nothing wrong with her that warm water and a good sleep won't fix."

"You're very kind, Frau—"

"Leopold. I am a widow. Herr Leopold died in a raid on Munich. He had gone there for a new plow blade. Two years ago, it was."

"I'm sorry. My name is Ritter. From Hesse."

"Good. Now—upstairs, Pastor Ritter. The two of you. Hand your clothes out and I'll clean them up a bit. I make my own soap, and it's not bad."

"You've already gone to a great deal of trouble for us."

"Nonsense. It's my pleasure. I get lonely here, with my man gone. Neighbors work my farm for me and let me share. My son and his wife lived here with me, along with my father, but father died three months ago and my son and his Gertrud went to Munich, where he works with the Winter-Help and she's with the Bund Deutscher Maedel, or some such. I don't understand any of these things. I don't understand anything anymore."

Not knowing what else to say, Stachel said, "God will see you through, Frau Leopold." He hoped his tone was like that of Pastor Ehrlich, who presided over his boyhood church in Bad Schwalbe.

"Ah, yes. I'm a Catholic, Pastor, but my elders taught me always to assist the clergy of all faiths. So you are welcome in my house."

94

He placed her on the bed and undressed her, sponging her with the warm water from the basin Frau Leopold had provided. For a woman in her forties, she was quite well formed, but in their new-found relationship he felt that it would be unseemly to dwell on such things, so he worked with as much clinical detachment as he could muster. Even so, he was aware of a contradiction in him, appreciation of the beauty she presented and regret that her mystery had been revealed to him at the wrongest of times.

There was a heavy chill in the room, so, after he had passed the bundles of their clothing to Frau Leopold outside the door, he quickly washed and climbed under the feather quilt beside Elfi, who, from the sound of her breathing, had fallen into a deep, absolute sleep. He held her close to him, feeling the warming, and luxuriating in the smoothness and the clean smells and the sunset colors on the ancient ceiling.

It occurred to him in the stillness that this was where he had always belonged; here, at this level of meaning and fulfillment, there was a confluence of all the twists and turns and subtleties of personality and experience that made up the enigma known as Bruno Stachel. From infancy to middle age, from tenderness to brutality to tenderness, the movement of his life had plunged him onward, like a ball in one of those crazy, blinking, raucous pinball machines in the Officers' Club at Ritchie—bouncing, spinning, careening, but inexorable in its progress to a conclusive rest in the gut of the thing. Unaccountably, for all the peacefulness in which he drifted, he felt a sudden, intense pang, a sense of being shot through with an arrow. This woman here beside him: she had, in truth, been beside him through all the wasted years, and now that he had at last acknowledged his fundamental need of her, she could be lost to him at any moment.

He slept.

*   *   *

The sunset had gone, and the dim light was coming now from the opposite window. She was resting on an elbow, her face close to his, her eyes dark and solemn.

"What is this place?"

"A farmhouse," he said. "A woman brought us here. You were exhausted." He wondered if he should say more, reassure her, guarantee that she had been succored, not savaged.

"I don't remember."

"There was a man in my squadron, in the old war. He would sleep like a log before a combat mission—even drowse in the cockpit of his airplane while warming the engine. Then he would fly and fight like a maniac. Afterward, he could barely make it to his cot, where he would sleep for hours. It was a kind of shutting-out, I guess."

She continued her staring into his eyes, seeming to think about this. After an interval she said, "I'm not a weakling, you know."

"I know."

"I'll be all right now."

"Of course."

"I was so afraid that I'd lost you. And when I saw you standing there, with your hand held toward me, I—I went to sleep."

He pulled her down to him, and her head filled the hollow of his shoulder, warm and sensual. "Why did you come into this madness, Elfi? I've heard your explanations, but never your reasons."

"I came into it when I learned that you had come into it. Miss Loomis told me that you'd probably never survive without my help. That this mission needed a woman you could trust."

He sighed. "Well, score another one for Polly Loomis. She told me you had come into it. And I knew you wouldn't survive without my help."

They fell silent again. Then, against his throat she mur-

96

mured, "I thank God for Polly Loomis."

"Yes. She's done us a wonderful service."

They made love then, slowly, lingeringly, with the intensity and preoccupation of the explorer and the scholar and the wine taster—an engrossment of the mind and senses that simultaneously shut out and gathered in all the sweet pain of a lifetime of waiting.

15

FRAU LEOPOLD GAVE them a breakfast of sausage, cheese, and tea. They ate in a corner of the big kitchen, exchanging superficial pleasantries with her and trying to handle the morning of their mating with insouciance. It didn't quite come off, however; Stachel had awakened to a vision of himself as the stereotypical gray little husband standing on a street corner in his gray little suit, consulting the watch on his vest pocket chain and waiting for the Mrs. The image had frightened him, so his portrayal of Pastor Ritter arising from a routine sleep with his routine wife had been, he suspected, considerably less than inspired.

More difficult, though, was the question of how to deal with Elfi Heidemann. He had wanted them to be lovers, but now that they were, warning flags were flying. First, in his natural state he was too capable of ruthlessness and selfish excess to expect a lasting relationship with her. She was fastidious and correct; he was earthy and blunt. She was sensitive and spiritual—even religious; he was none of these.

In her lovemaking, there had been the furious attention to detail that one who has been starving gives to a buffet. She had overlooked nothing. But how long would this honeymoon abandon persist? How long would it be, now that her sexual fast had been broken, before she began to consider him a candidate for reclamation, domestication, and conversion to her brand of piety?

More had happened in the steam of the night just past then mere reduction of a decades-long fever; he had developed a wariness that said he belonged to her—but not too much.

* * *

For Elfi, too, there remained some shadows.

The parachute landing had gone well for her. A soft collapse in a snow-patch already made irregular by winter stubble and a previous thaw. Some quick work with the folding shovel and a short walk through a forest to a paved road. In time, a lift by a friendly Wehrmacht truck driver who seemed genuinely concerned about "a nice lady nurse poking along these dark roads, alone."

It was in Oldendorf that the shock and sense of isolation had come. She had alighted from the truck in the town square, which was bustling with troops, to learn from a villager that the uproar was due to "an Ami spy who came down from a plane" to land in a tree outside an SS mess tent. The subsequent four hours had been a time of dreadful indecision and loneliness.

Randelmann could have been dead when they rolled him from a truck and strung him to the pole. It was impossible to tell, what with the battering and blood and nakedness, and she'd known it was the major only because they had not removed his army boots.

She must have wandered then; there were no clear images, only dim recollection of the fear that Stachel, too, had been caught somewhere out there in the darkness and that she was now alone, forever. Perception had become clearer with

Stachel's appearance in the alleyway, but not until she was lying on the bed, warming under Stachel's inexpert sponging, had she become fully aware.

She blushed now, remembering how she had continued to pretend to sleep so that he wouldn't stop, or go away. It was as if Randelmann, by dying, had quickened all of her life processes, from breath to sensuousness. From his death had come a brittle clarity, a keenness, a depth of appreciation of the juices in her, and Stachel's silent ministrations had been like a priest's at an altar. Still, the subsequent consummation of her long and ambivalent passion for Bruno Stachel had not left her free of doubts. Toward morning, after the initial explosions had subsided and they had drifted into indolent variations on the theme, she had made a secret evaluation of the new status. Stachel was not given to bedroom oratory, but she suspected from the deferential way he had taken her, that he was building a pedestal. She'd endured much of this kind of thing in Otto, her husband, bless his departed soul. His infuriating politeness, his cool determination never to appear gross or grotesque, more of that she did not want, and it bothered her to see even small traces of it in Stachel. She wanted to be ravished, not reverenced.

But sexual matters notwithstanding, she was simultaneously elevated and depressed by what seemed for her to be the transcendent lesson in Randelmann's death. During the period in which she'd feared Stachel, too, was dead, she had considered surrendering herself to the SS, discovering as she had that she'd rather not live without him—whatever he did, said, was, or was not. A wretched world would simply pass over into intolerable boredom if he weren't in it, somewhere.

So here she was now, nibbling cheese and pretending interest in a farm widow's small talk while trying to assimilate the irony of her condition: Only when death was literally at hand had she acknowledged what she had been living for.

* * *

They came in with a crash.

Stachel's first reaction was annoyance. Why was it that the German military always did things with crashing sounds? Clicking of heels. Goosestepping. Manual of arms. Opening of farm kitchen doors.

"You are under arrest!" The voice crashed around the low-ceilinged room. "Any unauthorized moves and you will be shot."

Frau Leopold squealed and dropped a dish. Elfi put down her fork, slowly. Stachel eased back in his chair, placing his hands on the table, palms down.

The kitchen seemed filled with them, although there were only three SS troopers, each large and square and helmeted. They stood with their rifles at the ready, their jaws set in heroic righteousness, their eyes darting about in the unwavering vigilance the Führer had prescribed in their training manuals. It was obvious they were waiting for something they deemed to be important, and, after a portentous interval, the something strode through the door in the form of the bulb-nosed, bad-toothed farmer Stachel had encountered at the village bridge. Only now he was in a Tyrolean suit, complete with Lederhosen and feathered hat, and he swaggered, with a cigarette held between thumb and forefinger in what suggested to Stachel an absurd caricature of Eric von Stroheim.

"So then," the man said, "I would like you to put your papers on the table there. Then I would like you to go to the wall and stand facing it. Over there, by the cupboard." He coughed dryly. "You, trooper, guard them. You other two, search the house for the radio. And weapons."

Frau Leopold, her voice filled with anguish, complained, "Why do you look for radios and weapons here? I am only a poor widow—"

"Silence, you old cow. One does not argue with the Gestapo, eh?"

"Gestapo? Oh, my God. I've done nothing. Nothing. These people are—"

"These people are spies. And your house is where they planned to do their dirty work." The man came to where they stood. He smelled of cigarettes, Schnapps, and old sweat. He ran his hands over Stachel's chest, hips, and legs. From the corner of his eye Stachel could see the hands move up and down Elfi's legs, then linger on her breasts and, finally on her buttocks. The man did not search Frau Leopold, but went directly to the table, where he sat and riffled through their documents.

"There is no trace of radios or guns," one of the troopers announced from the doorway.

"Did you look in the manger? The outbuildings?"

"Yes, Herr Kaspar."

"Well, look again, man. They're here somewhere."

Stachel, reviewing what he knew of the Gestapo (even its leaders knew precious little about the agency), decided that Kaspar was probably one of the lowest in the pecking order—a field agent assigned to a kind of precinct duty. Or he could actually not belong to the Gestapo at all, being instead a field security agent of one of the armed services on detached service with the secret police. Whatever he was, and despite his amateurish, loutish ways, he represented impending catastrophe, and Stachel used the silence to do some careful observation and heavy thinking.

His gaze wandered to the window and the terrain beyond. A lane led from the rear of the house to a frame shed, the lower half of which housed a woodpile, now considerably depleted by the winter just past. A fence line ran from the shed to a small copse atop a rise of land. The rest was pasture and cropland, a great gray wash of fields, unbroken except for an occasional tree and another clump of farm buildings about a half kilometer away.

As he evaluated potential escape routes, his eye was caught

by a pale glinting of sunlight on glass. It came from a corner of the distant barn, and, focusing on this, he was able to make out a man—large and wearing a military cap and what seemed to be a long, black SS coat—his arms bent in the attitude of one who examines the distance through binoculars.

Stachel thought about this.

Who would be watching Frau Leopold's house?

Von Lemmerhof? Or one of his aides?

No. Von Lemmerhof would not risk exposure. In fact, he was obliged not to in his deal with Polly Loomis. And it would hardly be one of his high-ranking SS assistants—for the same reason.

Herr Kaspar coughed again. "You Ami spies certainly have impressive documents. These look more authentic than the authentic ones. And that's bad news for you, Herr Pastor Ritter, or whatever your name is. These papers look too good. Real papers have a mistake here and there."

"My church forbids mistakes," Stachel said. "It's against our religion to make mistakes."

Kaspar laughed. "You're a comedian, too, eh?"

"It's the Eleventh Commandment—'Thou shalt have a chuckle now and then.'"

"I'll have to admit you're a droll fellow, all right. Plucky, too, considering the messy fate that awaits you."

"Perhaps. But you will be a long time having your own next chuckle, Herr Kaspar, when you find that I am indeed who I am. And when you find that I am personally acquainted with some very high-ranking party functionaries."

"You? A country preacher? Come, now."

"Must I remind you that the Führer himself had very modest origins? Some of our most elevated officials have known obscurity and poverty, Herr Kasper. There is nothing that says a few of them wouldn't have cherished their long-time friendship with an obscure man of God in an obscure Hessian village."

Kaspar arose from the table and came to the wall to

102

examine Stachel with curious eyes. "Yes," he said. "Plucky. And imaginative."

"You can avoid great embarrassment by releasing Fräulein Stolz, Frau Leopold, and me. I assure you, Herr Kaspar, we are indeed authentic. And Reichsführer SS Heinrich Himmler will be among those who are most annoyed at your high-handed treatment of old friends."

"There was a plane. Two separate reports—one from Ludwig Bechmann, the air warden at Klingdorf, the other from an SS sentry near the Weilheim highway—say three parachutes came down. One, a soldier, is accounted for. That leaves two. All soldiers in the area are identified after unit roll calls. That means the other parachutists were civilians. The only civilian strangers noted in the area, according to roadblock checks and cross-country sweeps, are a clergyman and a nurse, who were seen embracing each other." He added with an oily inflection, "An odd activity for a man of God, seeing that his bed partner is not his wife."

"You told me you were man and wife," Frau Leopold snapped indignantly.

"No, Frau Leopold, *you* said we were," Stachel corrected.

"My home is a proper home, I'll have you know."

"Shut up, all of you," Kaspar growled. "For people under arrest by the Gestapo, you certainly do a lot of gabbling. Good God, don't you have enough sense to be frightened?"

"We are not frightened," Stachel said piously, "because we have right on our side."

"What in hell is that supposed to mean?"

The trooper reappeared in the doorway. "Sorry, Herr Kaspar, but there is no trace of a radio. No guns, either."

"See?" Stachel put in.

Kaspar sighed with exasperation. He gathered up the papers on the table and, glancing at the trooper, said, "I'm taking this so-called man of God and his trollop to headquarters in Weilheim. You and your buddies can return to your unit in Oldendorf."

"Won't you need help guarding them?"

"No. I'm an old veteran at this kind of thing. Handcuffs, and such."

"How about this farm wife here? The fat one?"

"We won't hold her for now. I believe she's innocent. But she will not so much as mention this whole incident, even in her prayers to God, will she?"

"Oh, no, I promise, I promise," Frau Leopold whined.

"If she does, she'll be hung on a lamppost, won't she?"

"Oh, God. Please believe me—I'll say nothing. Ever."

"Pardon, Herr Kaspar," the trooper said. "How should we report to my commander? He'll expect a report, of course."

"Tell him you have helped me capture the suspects. He needs to know nothing more. But do give him my thanks for his help. My superiors at Weilheim will be grateful, too. Heil Hitler."

* * *

The morning mist had cleared, and the sun, brilliant and warm, brought an amiable yellow glow to the snowy Bavarian countryside. Stachel leaned back in the seat, his eyes closed, enjoying the warmth.

"Are you comfortable, Fräulein Stolz?" he said over the car's straining.

"These handcuffs are too tight. But otherwise I'm all right,"

"Herr Kaspar will remove our bonds after we've moved down the road a bit."

"Why would I do something like that?" Kaspar drawled, shifting gears for the rise ahead.

"Because you're General von Lemmerhof's contact. It's my guess that when we missed our rendezvous and you picked up the radio chatter about spies, you came to pull us out of the hole."

Kaspar smiled and said, "It's been touch-and-go. The general will be very glad to see you."

104

Elfi sat upright and glanced at Stachel, slumped beside her. "How did you know this?"

"Herr Kaspar was entirely too good-natured and addled for a Gestapo agent. I was even joking with him. Nothing amuses a Gestapo agent."

"Acting is not one of my talents," Kaspar agreed. "I am, in fact, a mere Gefreiter in the Wehrmacht. I have been General von Lemmerhof's chauffeur and orderly for two years. I would do anything for him." He added this last as if he expected it to be challenged. Which was no surprise, Stachel mused. He knew Kaspar's type: intelligent, mercurial, vicious, and amoral—a streetwise predator who would profess loyalty to a dandelion if it were to provide a moment's advantage. Kaspar might present himself as a chauffeur, an orderly—a mere noncom in the army—but one could be sure that behind Kaspar's pseudomodesty beat the heart of a Genghis Khan.

"Where did you get the three blind mice, Kaspar?" Stachel asked.

"The soldiers? I merely presented my bogus Gestapo credentials and requisitioned their services from the headquarters company of the Panzer battalion in Oldendorf. Amazing, the wonders a set of Gestapo credentials can work."

"You're going to have to work another wonder, Herr Kaspar."

"Oh? What's that?"

"There is a large black Mercedes following a kilometer or so behind us. Unless I miss my guess, there is a large blackcoated man in it. A man who has been watching us with great interest."

Kaspar laughed softly. "Now you have touched upon one of my real talents. I might be a rotten actor, but I am the Wehrmacht's absolute marvel at driving. Hold on, and I'll show you."

16

POLLY MET TARBELL at Dijon, per round-robin telex from the safe-house in Bern to Geneva, to London, to SHAEF, and then to Harrington, where he had been standing by for the radio work with Nightstick. He was not particularly glad to see her, inasmuch as he had been enjoying England in this waiting period, and now the thought of cranking up for some hairy flying over a very angry Deutschland was rather much for a man who, after days of easy drill and nights of good whiskey and a smooth-bodied WREN named Gladys, wasn't really sore at anyone.

There was a feeling of spring in the breeze, and the sun was warm as they strolled beside the stream, which here in France was called a river but at home would be called a creek. Tarbell prided himself on being enough of a gentleman to make small talk until she came down to the point of the meeting, and so there had been considerable chitchat about the thaw, the coming breach of the German Rhine defenses, their favorite movies, and who would win the pennant next season. But after they'd left the château and were ambling beside the gurgling water, her face lost its cocktail-party brightness and settled into what appeared to be real worry.

"We've lost Nightstick, Amos."

He gave her a quick glance. "Lost? You mean—"

"Randelmann was caught in the landing, killed by German troops. Stachel and Heidemann are apparently all right, but they're practically neutered, radiowise, now that Randelmann's gone."

"Was the radio lost with him?"

"I'm afraid so. At least, we must assume it was. He was carrying it when he went out the hatch."

Tarbell nodded thoughtfully, not so much because he was

considering the communications problem but more because it was now clear what she expected him to do about it. "So," he said, "you propose that I fly over and drop Stachel another set."

"No. Not exactly." She paused to consider a jonquil rising from a patch of soggy snow.

"What then, exactly?"

"I want you take the radio to him. And operate it for him."

He gave her a look. "You want me to parachute into Germany with another J-E set? Is that what you're saying?"

"We stand to lose the entire intelligence value of Nightstick and Whisper unless we can talk with Stachel and his team."

"Where is he—Nightstick—now?"

"I haven't the vaguest. We've had no word yet."

"How do you know they're alive—Stachel, Heidemann?"

"We don't, really. All we know is that our usual sources have not reported them dead."

"Usual sources? What sources are those?"

"Sorry. No need-to-know." She gave him a small smile of regret, which, he knew, was as sincere as a Parisian waiter's.

"Well, here's something you need to know, Polly Loomis —I can't speak German like a native."

"Germany is teeming with displaced persons these days. Russian defectors, Danish farmers, French industrial workers, Belgian store clerks—you name it. You hear more accented German in Germany today than you hear German. Besides, yours will be a controlled drop in controlled territory, so you won't have to wander around talking to anybody but friends."

"Oh, sure."

A cloud passed over the sun, and he felt the chill. Above the meadow, beyond the stream, a swarm of birds arced and circled and called out in thin, pitiful cries. He sensed their hunger, and, remembering his boyhood in Nebraska, experienced a stir of homesickness. So now the due bill was to be paid. Now, after all the years, his government was calling in

107

the marker for his free education, his warm clothes, his full belly, his escape from anonymous poverty. *Time's up, buddy. The freeloading is done. Get in there and die.*

"When do you want me to go?"

"As soon as I get word of Stachel's survival and location. I should be hearing at any moment now."

"What if only Heidemann survived?"

It seemed to Tarbell that a suggestion of sorrow showed in Polly's eyes. It was only a momentary thing, but it had been there, he was sure.

"Then you will not have to go," she said, shrugging.

"Why did you send her in the first place, Polly?"

"We've been through all that."

"Did it ever occur to you that Nightstick was overmanned? Stachel and Randelmann were all the team needed. Heidemann was always excess baggage."

She shook her head, her eyes angry now. "That's not true. And it's not up to you to decide such things anyway."

"Well," he said, his own anger rising, "I just want you to know that you aren't getting away with it."

"With what, Amos?" she snapped.

"You didn't expect Heidemann to last a minute, did you?"

"You're saying I sent her on a one-way ride?"

"Something like that."

Her face was red, and he thought for a moment that she might strike him. But then, as if a breaker had crashed and ebbed, the fury vanished, leaving a kind of detachment. "That's absurd," she said, shrugging.

"No matter to me. Your personal affairs, and all that." He hesitated; then, deciding that the need for sparring was long gone, he gave words to the rest of it. "You don't really need someone to take Stachel his radio, to work it for him. He's perfectly capable of catching a drop and setting up a station himself. Why me?"

"Are you afraid to go, Amos?"

"Of course I am. But I'll go. It's just that, once again, you're overdoing—putting butter on chocolate cake."

"All right, Amos—knock it off. You will stand by for a drop. You'll be given the go as soon as word comes in."

"Who'll be on the J-E in the plane?"

"An RAF specialist named Riggles. You will operate with the same recogs and alerting codes. If you're captured and the Germans turn you around, you will alert us to that fact by using precisely the language they give you to read, interrupted twice by a clearing of your throat. The combination of uncharacteristic speech pattern, word choice, and throat sounds will tip us off. All your transmissions will be recorded by the airborne J-E, of course."

Tarbell glanced at his watch. "It's almost noon. How about some lunch?"

She exchanged glances with him, and he could see that his peace overture had been accepted. "All right," she said, her eyes warming to the idea, "it'll help to pass the time."

"Vot means dot, Fräulein Boss?"

"I should be getting word from one of those sources you're so curious about. Sometime this afternoon."

"That soon?"

She nodded. "If the prognosis is positive, we'll give you a full briefing at once. After dressing, you should be on your way. Tonight."

"I can hardly wait."

17

KASPAR'S DRIVING WAS as good as he'd claimed it to be. Of course, the little Opel sedan was no match for the Mercedes in terms of horsepower or speed, but the roads were narrow and twisting, and Kaspar, working the gearshift furiously, managed to sharpen the turns and race down the hills so as to keep the following car always just out of sight. Near Wessobrunn, site of the ancient Benedictine monastery, he left the Weilheim road, cut across a farm lane to a dirt secondary road that doubled back to Haid and then northeast through the rolling woodlands to Diessen.

"How do you like that?" Kaspar said, pleased with himself. "The Mercedes is probably in Weilheim at this very moment, wandering about, its man-in-the-black-coat wondering whatever happened to our cute little Opel."

"Speaking of Weilheim," Stachel said, "won't the commander of those three soldiers you requisitioned at Oldendorf check with the Gestapo office at Weilheim to see what disposition was made of the spies you captured?"

"Who knows? My guess is that he'll let well enough alone. At least for a while. These days everybody hesitates to question the Gestapo about anything. The Gestapo is very quick to take offense when somebody pries into its affairs. At any rate, that's what I'm counting on."

"There's another problem," Stachel muttered. "We're supposed to be at the north end of the Tegernsee, but if we keep going in this direction we'll soon be in Munich. And if you don't slow down a bit, we'll overshoot Munich and end up in the North Sea."

Kaspar laughed, appreciating the exaggeration. "I promise to deliver you in Munich, as planned."

"Then what was all that business about the Tegernsee?" Elfi sounded tense, short of temper. "The truck with the flat tire, the inn called the Herzoghof—what about them?"

"Mere security precautions, my dear Fräulein Stolz. We had arranged to have you arrive in stages, so to speak, so that you would progress through various barriers of identification and confirmation. Your final destination has always been Munich. But your rather messy arrival has changed things."

There was no more conversation for a time. Kaspar

concentrated on his driving, taking them from Diessen straight north along the western shore of the Ammersee. The lake was cold and dull under the graying skies, and it seemed fitting, Stachel thought, that the once-beautiful morning had taken on such a doleful color. This road would take them directly past Sonnenstrahl, the country estate where he and his wife, Kaeti, had spent so many miserable years before her death at the hands of a Nazi assassin, and the graying skies were matching the uneasiness and melancholy that had taken him over. Those had been the unhappy times, with the drinking and the acrimony and the vengeful infidelities, the flat and fallow wilderness of his life. Sonnenstrahl was a monument to the fear and loneliness that tyrannizes those who are so filled with concern over yesterday and tomorrow that they have no ability to handle today. Kaeti and he had lived that way.

Elfi must have caught some of this, knowing as she did much of the mournful story. She sat in her corner, her lips compressed, staring out at the lake and seeming to be lost in some distant part of her own past. He thought about reaching over and taking her hand, but decided that it would only seem mawkish and uncharacteristic of him, and she would be embarrassed, not reassured.

To hell with it. To hell with Sonnenstrahl.

It was just a place.

*   *   *

At the road junction at the northern end of the lake they turned due east for Inning, but outside the town there was a checkpoint marked by a camouflaged sentry box and a string of wooden x's to which had been fastened an unruly coil of barbed wire. Behind this was a heavy machine gun attended by two SS men, who sat with their backs to a stone wall and shared a cigarette. Their officer, a lieutenant with sad eyes, sat at a small table beside the road and checked the papers of a line of civilians who waited in silent patience.

A Sturmmann stepped into the road and held up a hand, and Kaspar brought the car to a halt.

"Let me do the talking," Kaspar said over his shoulder.

They sat, mute and unmoving, as the soldier came to the car and, leaning, peered through Kaspar's half-open window. "Park over there," he said, pointing.

Kaspar held up his Gestapo credentials. "Let us through."

The Sturmmann squinted at the green folder. "Sorry, sir, but my orders are to have all persons pass by the Obersturmführer's desk. There's a spy alarm in effect." There was an uneasiness about the man, Stachel noticed.

"I'm on official Gestapo business. I must not be delayed."

"I'd appreciate your telling the Obersturmführer that. If it were up to me . . ." The Sturmmann's voice fell off, in the manner of one who would call off the war if only they'd let him.

"Sorry, soldier, but I haven't time to play your officer's little games. Give him our apologies, and tell him I'll call him from my office in Weilheim."

The Sturmmann straightened slowly, stepped back from the car, unslung his machine pistol, and leveled it at them, his eyes grim now, and very blue in the morning light. "Obersturmführer Weigand!" he called out. "Come, quickly!" To Kaspar, he grated, "Don't move an eyelash, understand?"

Stachel exchanged a quick glance with Elfi, and he saw fright. He wondered if she could see his own.

"What in hell are you trying to pull off here, young fellow?" Kaspar snapped. "Have you lost your senses?"

"Herr Obersturmführer! Quickly, please!"

The officer came at a quick step, reaching to unbuckle his pistol holster. "What is it, Hauser?"

"This man—he says he's a Gestapo official from Weilheim."

The Obersturmführer, a pudgy fellow with a Hitler mustache, had his pistol out now, and he held it in front of him as if it were a hot pan. "Oh, does he now. Well, then, we'll just

112

have to see that he is returned to Weilheim, nice and safe, eh?"

"What is wrong with you two?" Kaspar demanded. "I am on secret state business, and I demand that you get out of my way. Do you hear me?"

"Out of the car, all of you," the Obersturmführer ordered. "There is an all-points advisory. Emergency alert. An arrest-on-sight order. Any man claiming to be a Gestapo representative from Weilheim is an imposter."

"Where did you hear such nonsense?" Kaspar shouted.

"My commanding officer called," the officer blustered, a tiny uncertainty in his voice.

"You will answer for this personally, I assure you, Obersturmführer. You are in very serious trouble."

The officer glanced at the Sturmmann; then, seeming to realize that he must maintain an air of command, he stiffened. "Out of the car, I said."

Stachel decided that it was time to play the only card they had remaining to them. He leaned forward, so as to be clearly seen by the Obersturmführer. Evoking every shred of High Command arrogance he had witnessed and accumulated in twenty years in the hierarchy, he scowled. "You have two choices, Weigand. The first is to allow us to proceed on our way without delay and with no reports or alarms to impede us. In this way, you will have permitted me, a special aide to Reichsführer SS Himmler, to carry out undercover duties of enormous import to the Reich. Or, second, you can persist in this idiocy and make a fuss, and detain me and my associates here, and thereby reap the combined fury of the Gestapo, the OKW, and, no doubt, the Führer himself. Either way, we must get it over with quickly, since the success of my mission is in the balance. Which choice will it be? Eh?"

The young officer reddened, and his eyes became indirect. "I have my orders."

Stachel exploded. "You goddamned cretin! I'll not sit here

113

for one more instant and listen to your whining. Take me to your commanding officer. At once, do you hear?" To Kaspar, he roared, "Open the door! I want to get this over with so that I can get about the Reich's business!"

The Obersturmführer returned his pistol to its holster. "But what shall I tell my commander? I—"

"You will tell him nothing! Absolutely nothing! The slightest whisper of this to anyone, Weigand, will mean summary execution for you, for this trooper here, for your commander, and for anyone else who so much as mentions this to his own mother! *Do you understand?*"

"Yes. sir. I understand." To the Sturmmann, Weigand snapped, "You will say nothing of this incident to anyone, Hauser. It is an undercover Gestapo matter."

"As ordered, sir," the trooper said briskly.

"Now get this infernal automobile moving, man! I simply cannot bear to look at these idiots any longer."

The Obersturmführer clicked his heels and gave the Deutscher Gruss. "Heil Hitler."

"Drive! Drive, goddammit!"

* * *

They rode for some time in silence, each absorbed in his own measure of shock, relief, and savor of survival. The gloom that had taken over was not helped by the alterations in the passing landscape. As Kaspar drove them through Percha and then northeast toward Harlaching and Munich, the gentle Bavarian countryside—the meadows, the cathedral dark and the lights of the great Förstenrieder woodlands, the poor but tidy farm buildings—became, in gradually increasing shades of melancholy, a scene from Dante's *Hell*.

The sides of the road became littered with the junk of war, husks of cars and trucks—holed and rusted and burned to a red flaking, devoid of tires or headlights or any useful accessory. There were splintered trees, and bomb craters, sparse and scattered at first, then beginning to thicken and overlap in a kind of hideous smallpox. Troops seemed to be everywhere, hurrying on crisscrossing errands or slumped disconsolately along the muddy berms, staring vacantly at their officers, who stood in little gesticulating knots and debated some segment of the prevailing disaster.

Germany, Stachel saw, was beyond disaster. The Munich horizon ahead was a guarantee of at least fifty years of starvation, pestilence, and rot. There would be no Germany for a half century to come—only a gigantic trash heap, rat-infested, stinking of death and decay and hopelessness, and peopled by predatory savages. If it was now this awful, this shattered and ghastly while the war continued, there would be no words for what would follow the inevitable defeat.

Kaspar tried to break the spell. "That was clever of you back there, Pastor Ritter. Your facing the man down that way. He was ready to run us in."

Stachel shifted in his seat and took a deep breath, feeling a sickness in his belly. "It was not clever, Kaspar. It was mere recognition of the rotten truth—today's German does not fear the enemy. He fears his own people."

18

THEY REMAINED ON the east side of the Isar River, easing slowly through the choked streets of Haidhausen. Turning east on Preysingstrasse, Kaspar drove as far as Metzgerstrasse, where he made a left turn around an up-ended trolley, skirted a cluster of track laborers struggling fiercely to fill an enormous bomb crater with dirt, and headed north past the St. Johannis church to Ismaninger Strasse and, eventually, the Maximilians Anlagen.

There had been four more checkpoints, but Kaspar's credentials had carried them through without incident.

"So many questions," Elfi said once. "So many people mistrusting each other."

Kaspar nodded. "It gets worse every day. It's hardest on the common soldier, actually. The closer the Amis get, the tighter the restrictions on travel, and the ordinary man in uniform, moving from one station to another, has all kinds of fussbudgeting to endure. His travel papers have to be stamped daily at designated spots and times, and his Soldbuch has to be precisely right, or he'll be in real trouble with the eager SS boys who man the roadblocks and checkpoints. I don't know how the Wehrmacht can operate anymore. It's choking to death on its own paper work, its own suspicions of itself, as the Pastor says. As for the rest of us—well, you've seen. Identities, excuses for travel, movement permissions, ration-stamp checks, searches of food baskets—as if there were any food—drivers' licenses, credentials, credentials, credentials. My God, it will never end. On and on and on."

There was a large fire to the west, somewhere near the Hauptbahnhof. Sirens sounded far off, and a tower of oily black smoke rose above the moonscape of rubble and snag-tooth ruins profiled against the lowering sky.

"How often do they come? The bombers, I mean."

"Too often. Although Munich has not fared as badly as some cities. Only sixty-some raids since the war began, someone was saying the other day." Kaspar shook his head in resignation. "Even so, you can see what the Ami swine have done. Horrible. Just horrible."

Elfi said in a low voice, "It doesn't seem to be so bad on this side of the river."

"Of course not," Kaspar humphed. "It's Eisenhower again. He wants to save all these beautiful mansions and embassies

116

and town houses for the Ami troops. Have you seen the I.G. Farben building in Frankfurt? My God, the Ami bombers have flattened everything for blocks around. Then, sitting there as pretty as you please in the middle of a lovely park, directly across the street from rubble no higher than my knees, the Farben building sits untouched. The word is that Eisenhower plans to use it as his headquarters when he arrives in Germany, and he doesn't want any of the windows broken or the toilets not to flush. Isn't that a nerve?"

"One thing it is," Stachel muttered, "is precision bombing."

"One can't argue that."

"How much farther, Herr Kaspar?" Elfi said.

"A few more blocks. Up this street into Bogenhausen, then left a block toward the river. You'll like the house."

* * *

It was a formidable place, with steep-slanting tile roofs, gray stucco façade pierced by deep-set casements that frowned out at a walled garden, and heavy ornamental gates at the driveway entrance. There were clusters of yews, and several large shade trees, bare and black and menacing somehow. The war had left it unscarred, but the house would never be the better for that, Stachel judged; it was an unhappy place, and no doubt had been from the day its foundation had been laid.

Architecture was not his primary concern at this point, however. The black Mercedes had appeared again, fleetingly, passing ghostlike through an intersection a block to their right as they moved through the suburban quiet of Bogenhausen. He was about to ask Kaspar for guesses as to who might be riding such close escort, even anticipating their route, but he dropped the idea at once, reverting to his favorite adage —when in doubt, do and say nothing—because the fact remained: Kaspar could, or could not, be what he claimed for himself. If Kaspar had seen the Mercedes, he'd made no mention of it for reasons yet to be learned; if he had not, there was nothing to be gained by Stachel's bringing it up. The net of all this was a vague sense of danger unrecognized.

"You're wrong, Herr Kaspar," Elfi said.

"Wrong? About what?"

"I do not like this house."

"You will, my dear Fräulein Stolz. You will like it more each hour, since it's your only protection from a big, bad world all around. You'll see."

* * *

Inside, the house was even more oppressive. There was a baronial entrance hall, with heavy woodwork and mounted staghorns—dark against white plaster. A staircase was to one side, leading to a balcony that ran along the three inner walls and provided access to six upper rooms, whose doors were closed. A fire flickered sadly in a chimney corner, giving little warmth. Oriental carpets, dull with years, muffled their footsteps and deepened the stillness of the place.

Kaspar led them down a short hallway to the library, a square room with three walls of books, floor to ceiling, and a wall of french doors opening on the garden. "Wait here," he said.

Elfi sat in a leather chair beside the fireplace, where a log hissed and made soft snapping sounds. Stachel stood by the doors, gazing out at the melancholy trees.

"Are you all right, Bruno?"

"Yes. Why?"

"You look so—sad."

"A return to the Fatherland is hardly a hilarious experience these days."

"It's not just that. I've never seen you look like this."

He shrugged. "For all the time you've known me, you really haven't seen much of me."

"I know you better than you think."

"It keeps coming to me—a kind of overall view of what's

happened in the world, over and over. Just a handful of men, using whole populations in a big, deadly game to prove who's the smartest. From the beginning, just a few men in each century, each playing the game, each feeding his piece of population with the patriotism line, the God-is-with-us line, the national well-being line. And each sits in his palace, fat and smug and full of the sense of his smartness, and sends his population out to kill the other populations for no more reason than to feed his own ego, to prove to the other palace-sitters that he's the smartest. Only now it's out of hand. The killing gets too big, and you have a Munich like that across the river. A London. A Stalingrad. A Berlin. And the smug bastards simply shrug and say, well, so much for that game, let's get ready for the next—completely oblivious to how big the killing is, and will get. Sad, you say? I want to cry my eyes out."

She arose from the chair and came to where he stood. "You can't carry the sins of others," she murmured.

"Others? My God, lady—I was *one* of them."

"Hold me," she said, reaching out.

"Germany is gone. Everything I've done in my life has seen to that."

"No. A burned-over field always comes back." She shifted in his embrace and peered into his eyes. "So we were accomplices in arson. So now, with God's help, we'll make amends."

"God? Who is God?" he snapped. "I've been hearing about God all my life, and all I see is more insanity. You people who prate about God make me want to vomit. What do you—or anybody—know about God?"

"My mother used to say we are like children playing in a house, unaware the cellar is burning. When our parents rush into our room, pick us up, and throw us into the garden, we think they've lost their senses, and we're shocked, outraged. What we've seen as our parents' insanity is, in fact, their wider knowledge and love saving us from our ignorance.

God's always throwing us from windows."

"You mean all that out there is God's love at work? Now it's you who's insane."

She was about to say more, but there was a sound at the door and she broke away to stand by the desk, waiting.

* * *

Von Lemmerhof was, to Stachel's mild surprise, in full uniform. He entered the room at a slow, contemplative pace, a marvel of faultless Luftwaffe blue and glistening leather and braid. The Knight's Cross glinted at his throat, and his monocle, reflecting the light from the window, gave his square, meticulously barbered face a sinister cast—a glass eyepatch on a heavyset pirate.

"Good afternoon, Stachel. Welcome home."

"Herr General."

"And you, Frau Heidemann. Are you well?"

"Passably."

The general nodded toward the chairs grouped near the window. "Sit down, you two. We have some plans to make."

They sat, and Stachel noted that von Lemmerhof seemed ill at ease—a peculiar manifestation in one of General Staff rank. Officers of such lofty status simply never communicated anything but cool inscrutability, even in the presence of the bombastic Führer himself. But Lemmerhof half-sat on a corner of the desk, swinging a glistening, booted leg and trying too hard for nonchalance.

"Your landing was badly done," the general said. "You jeopardized the mission, even threatened my personal position."

Stachel stared at Lemmerhof in angry disbelief. The shock of seeing for the first time what the war had done to the once beautiful city around them persisted, and to have this box-headed Prussian whining about threats to his personal position was infuriating. "Isn't that too frigging bad," he snapped.

"Be careful, Stachel. I am in charge here."

"You are wrong, Herr General. I am in charge here. I am the American team captain, and nothing takes place unless I order it. You are now lower than any private in the American Army."

Lemmerhof, his face pale, grumped, "Nevertheless, without my approval, you'll go nowhere, are nowhere."

"And where will you go without me, Herr General? Back to Berlin, perhaps? To the Führerbunker, where you can announce your disapproval of how the war is turning out? How you've decided to throw in with the Americans?"

Elfi held up an impatient hand. "Please, gentlemen, we have no time for this kind of thing. You, Herr General, must understand that our bad landing was due to weather, time, circumstance. You, Herr Pastor, must understand that the Herr General has many problems which press him heavily." She paused. "And you both must understand that I haven't come all this way to listen to a couple of brats argue over who can pee-pee farther."

Stachel, his native appreciation of impudence asserting itself, felt a need to smile. His woman was changing before his eyes.

Lemmerhof's capacity for drollery was nonexistent, however. He gave Elfi a lingering appraisal, as if she were a specimen in a museum. Then he pushed himself erect and went to the window, where he stood in moody contemplation of the garden gloom. "You are right, of course, Frau Heidemann. Recriminations accomplish nothing."

Stachel's flicker of amusement died in a flood of contempt. It was an instantaneous resumption of his earlier disdain—a flash recognition of just how far this man had fallen. No German general would ever tolerate impertinence from anyone, let alone a woman. He might smile a bit, to be sure; but then he would, in the elegant Officers' Corps waspishness, reduce her to a whimpering lump. But with Lemmerhof there was the smell of fear and defeat; he was a man who had passed over the frontier of panic and was now quietly lost, demoralized, frozen. Here, Stachel thought, was still another contradiction, in the compounding of contradictions that the Nightstick mission had represented all along: Guerrilla warfare called for audacity, cunning, courage, tenacity, selflessness—character traits which (as the late Ludwig Stachel liked to say when scoffing at politicians) von Lemmerhof lacked in abundance. How could any High Command, even one so muddled as that which could abet an Adolf Hitler, be so offhand as to appoint a loser like this to the command of the Werewolf project? It simply didn't make sense.

Elfi seemed to feel this same thing. "There is something else I'd like to settle," she said crisply. "My name. As nurse Inge Stolz, I've left a trail at a dozen checkpoints and will probably be carried on next Tuesday's Gestapo blacklist. Obviously I can't continue under that name, and I can't very well introduce myself around as Elfrieda Heidemann. So just what am I to do about all this, Herr General?"

Von Lemmerhof sighed. "Feldwebel Hansen, who is in charge of our documents and wardrobe section in the cellar of this house, is taking care of that. New identities and their corresponding papers are being processed down there. However, while you are in my presence, I shall continue to call you by your real names, since I have no gift for dramatics or let's-pretend." He turned and went to the desk, where he sat in the leather chair and folded his hands on the glowing mahogany. "So then," he rasped, "what do you have in mind?"

"We were hoping you'd tell us what you have in mind," Stachel said, shifting in his chair. "All this is your idea, after all."

Lemmerhof's face registered no reaction to this heavy reminder of his treason. His hands unfolded, then folded again, and Stachel thought he saw a trembling in them. The general coughed dryly, then said with a subtle air of distraction, "Kaspar tells me that you lost your radio with your other associate. What was his name? Randelmann? This is most distressing, of course."

"Why? We can have another dropped in."

"It, ah, delays things. Alarmingly."

"We have plenty of time. Until the end of the war, as a matter of fact."

"No," Lemmerhof said quickly. "There is no time."

Stachel felt Elfi's puzzled glance. He said, "What do you mean, General?"

"Never mind. I'll explain later."

"Explain now, please. Tell us what we've dropped into here. What's going on."

Von Lemmerhof sighed again, a rising and falling of his shoulders. "We are assembling groups of Hitler Jugend and Bund Deutscher Maedel personnel in the mountains south of here, both in Germany and the adjoining Austrian Tyrol. These units are to be officered by Waffen SS people, with a support complement of Luftwaffe and Gestapo specialists. Logistics will be handled by army quartermaster units and whatever transport we can muster."

Stachel interrupted. "Are to be. Will be. All this sounds to be in the future. We understood that things were further along than this."

"Well, there have been many delays. The war has been going badly. Transportation is at a virtual standstill. Railroads destroyed, cargo vehicles without fuel, Autobahnen and secondary highways under the constant patrol of Ami planes. Good personnel are few—most of the best have died in the fighting or in the air raids. And now this latest, critical delay—the loss of your radio and its operator. We can't do a thing until that radio man is replaced."

"That's not true," Elfi put in irritably. "I'm a perfectly good courier. Messages might not get through as fast, but I can get them to the Swiss border in a day's time with the right papers and passes."

"We need the radioman," the general said doggedly.

"What do you suggest we do in the meantime, General? Play skat? Picnic in the garden?" Stachel's patience, never in long supply, was about gone.

"Your first duty, I should think," Lemmerhof said with faint sarcasm, "is to be properly documented and dressed. Feldwebel Hansen is drawing up papers that identify you, Stachel, as an SS Standartenführer attached to me for special duties. Frau Heidemann will carry the Kennkarte of an engineer specializing in fortifications. This will authenticate any errands you ostensibly run for me. You should be documented and dressed by late this evening. Meanwhile, the new radio operator is scheduled to parachute in early tomorrow morning."

Stachel and Elfi traded looks.

"Who is this new man?"

Lemmerhof shrugged. "A courier from Bern tells me it's a fellow posing as a Luftwaffe sergeant. Karl Folger is what they are calling him. Kaspar will meet him at a drop point near Königsberg at oh-four-fifteen hours tomorrow."

"Kaspar and I will meet him," Stachel said.

"Correction," Elfi said. "Kaspar, Stachel, and I will meet him."

There was a silence. Then Stachel, leaning forward in his chair, said, "Tell me, Herr General—how much of this Werewolf is known to whom?"

"You mean here, in Germany?"

"Of course."

The general thought a moment, his eyes distant, considering a mental organization chart. "Only the tactical units directly involved, and each works with a certain measure of autonomy. I am in overall command as Chief, Special Operations, Alpine Defenses. But my identity as such is known only to a handful of individuals. This was deemed necessary for security reasons at this early stage."

"Deemed by whom?"

"You mean, to whom do I report? Who is my superior?"

"Mm."

"I don't know."

"You *what*?" Stachel experienced a mixture of amusement and disbelief.

"For the same security reasons, I receive my orders by pouch, delivered by a courier named Otto Gautzsch. He is an SS Brigadeführer."

"That's a rather high-ranking courier, I'd say."

Von Lemmerhof straightened, his monocle glinting. "Of course. I am, after all, of rather elevated rank myself."

"Where does this Gautzsch come from?" Elfi asked.

"Berlin, I believe."

Stachel said, "That means your current assignment is known to all the important people then. Right?"

"Well, no, not really. There are some who disdain the Werewolf idea. It's defeatist, they say."

"Who, for instance?"

"The Führer himself, among others."

"The Führer himself is enough, I'd say. With Hitler against the idea, we're all in rather special peril, wouldn't you agree, Herr General?"

Von Lemmerhof fingered the large cross at his throat. "Thus the security precautions," he said dourly. "We have to watch out, not only for the Fatherland's enemies but mainly for those in the government who agree with the Führer that the German armies must remain intact, in the field, and beyond retreat or surrender."

"And who would those be?"

"I don't know."

"You don't know a hell of a lot, do you, Herr General."

"Only what I'm told through Brigadeführer Gautzsch."

"Don't you go out? Review developments in the field?"

"I am forbidden to."

Stachel shook his head in resignation. "Tell me, Herr

General von Lemmerhof—just what in pluperfect hell are you preparing to offer the Americans? What bill of goods have you sold the other side?"

The general looked away, a pinkness in his cheeks now. "Things won't always be this indefinite," he said. "As I learn, the Americans will learn."

"Dear God above," Elfi murmured. "We're not even at the beginning."

They sat in a long, deep silence.

19

"HEAR THAT?" she said in the twilight. "Rain against the window. Some hail, too."

"It always does that in Bavaria," Stachel said. "The sun can shine on one side of the street and it'll be raining on the other side."

"It's a good sound when you're in a warm bed."

"Speaking of which, don't you care if the others know you're in here with me, instead of in your own room?"

"Others? What others? That old nincompoop Lemmerhof? Kaspar? The orderly? What do I care about them? So we're lovers. Who cares?"

"Careful. Be gentle with Lemmerhof. He has the room bugged. He didn't suggest we take a nap because he likes us."

She laughed and, turning her face to the ceiling, said in a clear voice, "General von Lemmerhof is a fat old nincompoop. And whoever is listening is sure to agree with me."

Stachel humphed. "You're not as saucy as you make out to be. You saw me checking the room for devices."

"How did you know I saw you?"

"When I stood on the chair to put a towel over the microphone in the chandelier, I saw you in the mirror. You were peeking through the connecting door."

She laughed again. "You're impossible. I'll never be able to get away with anything with you. All my other lovers will simply have to go. You'll know every move they make."

"That's what worries me the most about you."

"What—all my lovers?"

"No. Your low aptitude for deceit. You're a pretty good person otherwise. But as a schemer and liar, you're a miserable flop."

"That's a rotten thing to say about the lady you've just made love to."

"You mean the lady I'm just about to make love to."

* * *

"Are you awake?"

"Mm."

"We'll have to get up soon. The new papers, the clothes, the car—they'll be ready by oh-one-hundred hours, the general said. It's twenty-three-thirty-one now. If we're to meet the paradrop, we'll have to leave the house by oh-two-fifteen."

"You sound like a wife."

"I am a wife. We might not be married, but I'm your wife. I always will be."

"I was joking."

"Well, I'm not."

"Tell me something, Elfi-Inge-Heidemann-Stolz—what do you really think of General von Lemmerhof?"

"He's no nincompoop, actually. But he very definitely is a fish out of water, I'd say. There is something about him that seems out of plumb. I can't imagine the High Command appointing him as chief of the Werewolf thing."

"Precisely. There's something very queer about all this. I

keep going over it. Why all the rigmarole over B-17s and belly landings, only to pop us down on parachutes? Why three people on this mission? It doesn't take three. I could investigate, supervise, and run the radio myself. Why such insistence on three? And, as you say, why such a lummox as Lemmerhof as the key man?"

"Unless he isn't really the key man."

"A-ha. You are with me."

"But who, then?"

"That, my dear lady, is the question. And that is what you and I must find out. Not for our beloved Ike Eisenhower, champion of all that's shining and holy, but for you and me. If we are to keep our lovely round buttocks intact, we must answer that question."

20

IT WAS A wretched night for a paradrop, one of those spells in April when winter and spring meet over the mountains and fight to the last drizzle. Elfi sat in the rear of the VW recon car (a vehicle the Equipment Identification man at Harrington called the Wehrmacht's answer to the jeep), stiff in her mannish woolen suit and faded overcoat, which had the pliability of a doormat. She had spent most of the ride watching Bruno, trying once again to digest the fact that she had become the mistress of this very peculiar, maddening man. As she huddled in the little square car, suffering its racket and feeling the thousand bumpings and tremblings, her mind unrolled a dreary panorama of the male vanity and attitudinizing she had endured in her life: from her father, military and towering and smelling of bay rum and leather, who would nod emperorlike after his day at work and waggle her chin between his thumb and forefinger and smile frostily with his lips and not at all with his eyes; from her husband, cool and detached one moment, mawkish and fawning the next; from the physicians, arrogant and distant, self-created gods, who would treat her like a draft horse in the hospital and like a ten-penny whore outside. And from Stachel, who contained some of them all and yet was like none of them, in any way, ever. And only with Stachel, the monster-angel, had she—for the first time in her miserable female life—felt close to what she was meant to be. Not what her father's, or Otto's, or the doctors' egos demanded she be, but what God had meant her to be. She looked at him now, square and haughty and masculine in his Waffen SS greatcoat and his visored cap with its glittering death's-head, and she felt a rush of adoration and gratitude—a silent explosion of thankfulness that, for all the years it had taken, her search had ended. Here was her man. He owned her. She hated being owned, but she exulted in being owned. She hated the way he treated her, but she worshiped him for the way he treated her. The dear, sweet, son of a bitch.

She laughed aloud and shook her head in private dismay.

Stachel, riding in the front seat beside the busily driving Kaspar, turned to glance at her. "What are you laughing at? There is absolutely nothing funny about this stinking road, this stinking night."

"That shows how much you know, Herr Standartenführer Franz von Kistner."

"You are a very peculiar woman, Fräulein Ingenieur Luisa Nagele."

"And you're in the position to know, yes?" She laughed again.

Kaspar sniffed. "There seems to be an awful lot of levity in a car that's off on a hazardous mission. Are all you Americans like this?"

Stachel joined her now. He actually laughed, a loud,

booming sound, and it occurred to her that never before had she seen him show more than a distant smile. It made her laugh all the more, this special moment.

"You're mad, both of you," Kaspar grumped.

*   *   *

They waited at the rim of the forest beside the great meadow, close to the tree whose branches held the hooded, upward-beaming flashlight. Kaspar, in his insider's way, confided that the light had been specified by the people in Bern who were collaborating with Herr General von Lemmerhof. (True to his Nazi nature, Kaspar could not admit to anyone, especially himself, that he and the general he served might be working for the people in Bern; it was collaboration, with the implication that it was the general who remained in charge.) American aerial navigation, he assured, was really quite inferior, and, while the airplane might find the area, there was no reason to expect that the incoming agent would be dropped accurately without a beacon lamp to help overcome the aircrew's ineptitude.

Kaspar could also see no reason for Elfi's presence at the landing site. He had told her, with the heavy tones of a displeased uncle, that the Herr General had ordered him alone to meet the paradrop. Elfi knew that it was prudent to risk only Kaspar in a paradrop meet, but it was clear that Stachel and she must be established as the command element, even if it meant increasing the risk.

She sat at the wheel of the VW, as Bruno had instructed her, ready to start the engine and make a dash if unfriendlies showed up while he and Kaspar waited in the field. The drizzle had turned to rain, and the pattering on the car's canvas roof had a lonely sound to it. Her earlier hilarity, which she recognized now as having verged on hysteria, had gone, leaving a kind of emptiness.

*   *   *

The plane arrived three minutes late.

At first there was a distant vibration, a feeling rather than a sound, and then it was a drumming beyond the rain. When it came low over the trees, rumbling and trailing a faint whistling, she had a momentary vision of the Americans in its gut—the close-cropped, smooth-cheeked youngsters with even teeth and with the smell of Vitalis and tobacco and with their puppylike obliviousness to the true wretchedness and savagery that existed beyond their Coca-Cola world. Three hundred meters distant they were, yet in their perception of the world down here it was three hundred light-years.

She felt a sudden uneasiness.

Her mind had been calm, despite her taut listening to the busy forest silence, her straining to catch sight of Bruno, Kaspar, and the new one. Then there was a sensation, almost a tingling in her spine, that told her there were others in the rain close by. Seeming to move independently of herself, she eased out of the driver's seat, feeling the soaking; as she went, her hand withdrew the machine pistol from its mounting clamp on the door and, fingers searching, released the gun's safety catch.

Sidling slowly through the darkness, she took up a position beside a dripping tree. Her breath seemed almost to have ceased, her heartbeat was a series of muted explosions in her rib cage, her eyes burned from their straining.

There was a time of suspension, in which the rain and the restless forest appeared to freeze, like a motion picture halted in mid-reel. Then out of the dimness of the great meadow came Stachel and Kaspar and a third man, who carried a case and whispered excitedly.

When they arrived at the VW, a light went on, brilliant, cruel in its instantaneous revelation of the car, the forest, and the men.

"You are under arrest!" a harsh voice announced from behind the light. "If you move, you'll be shot."

She could see Stachel's immediate anger, Kaspar's open-mouthed staring, and Tarbell's pale fright. They stood in a knot beside the VW, suspended like the world around them. The light, a hand-held searchlamp, moved forward, and in its reflected glow she saw four men in civilian clothes, each holding a pistol at the ready.

She had no way of knowing if there were others, but this was the only time given to her.

Aiming carefully, pressing the trigger in the slow, deliberate way they had taught her at Harrington, she opened fire.

The gun stuttered, rapidly, a staccato so swift it sounded like a tearing bed sheet—a rasping snarl that threw its own hideous glow before it. The four men went down as if sledgehammered, hats spinning, guns flying, arms flopping like ragdolls'.

"In the car, Bruno! In the car!" She heard her own voice as if it were coming from some great tube beside her. "Hurry! I'll cover you!"

"Where are you?"

"Get in the car, damn you! Drive! I'll get there! Go! Go damn it!" She fired another burst into the shadows, then began to run for the VW.

There were flashes in the darkness, and she heard the cracking of dry boards in the air about her.

The VW barked into life and its wheels spun in the wet forest loam. She caught the roof support and slung aboard. Bullets snapped, there were clangings and the tinkling of glass.

"There must be a thousand of them out there," Kaspar moaned.

"Only two guns," Tarbell said. "I see only two guns."

"But they've got a car. They'll be after us."

"Right you are, dear lady," Stachel said, gunning the car over an embankment and onto the highway. "Keep us covered to the rear with that pop gun you're so handy with, eh?"

"I dropped the gun somewhere. I don't have it."

132

"Oh, that's capital, that is," Kaspar whined. "Let me out. I'll chance it on foot."

"Here they come," Tarbell yelled. "They're about a quarter of a mile behind us and coming fast."

"Here's my service pistol," Stachel said. "It's better than nothing."

"They're gaining," Kaspar cried. "Oh, God. This is awful—"

Stachel steered the VW around a curve, and the tires chirped. He drove with blackout lights, whose diminished beams provided illumination that was next to valueless.

"Now there are two of them," Elfi announced. "Two cars. One after the other."

"Oh, dear Jesus," Kaspar whimpered.

"Is this the best this crate will do?" Tarbell asked Stachel.

"This crate is now doing better than it was designed to do. If you hold out your arms we might even fly."

"We'll never make it," Kaspar said, anguished. "They have a big Horch. One of the fastest cars—"

"Maybe," Elfi said, "but the other car seems to be gaining on them. It's passing. See? The lights are side by side."

There was a flickering to the rear, and the sound of stuttering coming through the strident motor noises.

"My God," Elfi piped, "they're shooting. The second car is shooting into the first."

"You're sure?" Stachel said.

"Of course I'm sure. The first car is skidding, or something. It's—it's crashing. It's turning over; over and over. Oh, dear Lord—"

Tarbell yelled, "Stachel! Why are you slowing down?"

"I'm not slowing down. I'm stopping."

"Why? For God's sake—"

"That second car's going too fast to stop. It'll have to pass us. I want to see who's in it, if I can. Whoever it is, he's on our side."

It was the black Mercedes. Big, slick. Powerful. Going at

full speed in a sizzling of rubber and a whine of well-oiled engine.

It was still too dark to see who was inside.

21

THE EARLY MORNING was gun-metal gray, with a rawness that defied clothes and sent little tremblings through the spine. As he drove, Stachel thought about people, from Elfi Heidemann to Hermann Göring and back again. (From the sublime to the ridiculous; he smiled inwardly.) He had learned early that the control of men rested in an understanding of them, not merely as individual specimens isolated on some glassy slide of the Now but as contexts, alive and in the round, who did thus and so today because they had done such and such yesterday, or ten years ago, perhaps. Long ago, in the First War, he had watched Otto Heidemann and learned of Heidemann's fatal preoccupation with his beloved wife, Elfi, and, in the learning, had played Heidemann like a marionette. Subsequently, he had recognized in a back-street Munich political fanatic named Hitler the route to power and influence; playing to the man's ego, exploiting his inordinate capacity to hear only what he wanted to hear, Stachel had used Hitler and could have (if he hadn't succumbed to personal flaws, such as candor, racial tolerance, loyalty to friends, and love of family and country), risen to the top of the Nazi ant pile. Göring, Himmler, Goebbels, Bormann—watching them had taught him that brain counterbalances brawn only when the brain comprehends the brawn's whole and sees beyond the strutting—the flexing of muscle—to the resident weakness it conceals. Thanks to the lessons of his life in the Third Reich, Bruno Stachel had fine-tuned his intuition for the elemental frailty in others and had developed an unwavering respect for his own.

The man called Kaspar had offered little challenge.

Kaspar, in the Opel ahead, had the smell of a man with a lust for money—the easiest of all flaws to discern and exploit.

Trailing in the VW, dressed in his new Standartenführer's uniform, impeccably credentialed, Stachel cleared the checkpoints quickly—but sufficiently far to the rear to escape any idle glance Kaspar might have sent to the Opel's rearview mirror.

From Bogenhausen Kaspar had driven to the shored-up Prinzregentenbrücke, which von Lemmerhof's situation map had shown to be open to civilian traffic, and, after crossing the Isar, beyond the Englischer Garten and into the center city. It was a numbing thing to move through the smoking mountains and valleys of broken bricks and shattered timbers and twisted steel; tautness behind his breast bone became, when he analyzed it, an unresolved sigh. The walls, sheared downward by collapse—with pictures still hanging, draperies still neatly folded at window holes, doors still firmly locked against empty sky, washbowls and toilets and bathtubs still dangling from pipe connections—were the most pitiful of all, a lugubrious exhibition of once-cherished intimacies. Overall was the stench of violated sewers and undiscovered dead.

Kaspar drove on, persisting through fire-control barricades, police cordons, and the haphazard roadblocks formed by rubble and craters and fallen trolley wires. Stachel kept with him, a dogged ghost in the haze of yesterday's fires: through the Hofgarten to the Ludwigstrasse at the Odeonsplatz, then right for a slow trip north to the Schwabing section, and, finally, a turn west through labyrinthine valleys in the mountains of ruin. At the corner of two nameless ruts that had been residential streets, Kaspar pulled the Opel into a cul-de-sac, where he turned off the motor and sat, waiting.

Stachel parked the VW behind a tilted kiosk a block away and, walking carefully, made his way to the Opel. He opened the passenger door and sank into the seat beside Kaspar.

"Good morning."

"Stachel. What are you doing here?" Kaspar's eyes were wide with surprise, and there was sudden pallor in his cheeks.

"Von Kistner. You have me mistaken for someone else."

"Oh, yes. Standartenführer von Kistner. What's up?"

"I want to talk to you about the Gestapo. You are waiting for your Gestapo contact, aren't you?"

Kaspar registered undisguised alarm now. He glanced about, his little eyes sweeping the piles of rubble as if looking for help. "I—I don't know what you mean. I'm just—" His voice faltered.

"Don't be frightened, Kaspar. I want to throw in with you." Stachel kept his voice cool, even, amiable.

Kaspar blinked and shifted uneasily in his seat. "You're moving a bit fast for me. What is it you want? Why do you think I'm involved with the Gestapo?"

"At the paradrop, in a dark night full of rain and only blackout headlights showing, there was no way to tell what kind of car the reception party was using to chase us with. Yet you said they were driving a Horch. That means you had prior knowledge. You knew they would be there."

Kaspar shrugged, trying for nonchalance. "But why do you assume it was the Gestapo? There are—"

"If it had been the Wehrmacht, or the SS, they would have been in uniform and would have driven military vehicles. Big civilian automobiles are in very short supply in the Reich. They're assigned—and very sparingly, at that—only to the Gestapo and its companion security forces, and a few big shots granted War-Important Work papers. So anybody driving a big Horch and packing automatic weapons simply has to be Gestapo. Right?"

"So you've got it all figured out. So what do you want of me?"

"In. I want in. I want to turncoat on the Amis and pick up some of that Gestapo money you must be raking in. I'm sick of risking my ass for a bunch of Yankee clods, getting nothing but do this, do that, and keep your fingers clean or we'll chop them off. Hell, Kaspar, you know what I'm talking about."

Kaspar eased back in the seat, visibly relieved. Money was something he understood, and it was apparent that he was pleased to see things returning to greed's familiar ground. "Yes," he said carefully, "I think I do."

"What kind of a deal can you work for me?"

"I don't know. I'll have to talk to somebody."

"Somebody? How about your controller?"

Kaspar raised an eyebrow. "Herr Dunkel? Hell, he was wiped out with the rest of the reception party—probably when the people in that Mercedes opened up on the Horch."

"Who was in that Mercedes, anyway? It's been following us around ever since I arrived."

"I haven't the least notion," Kaspar said resignedly. "I wish I knew. Herr Dunkel was worried about it. He was going to put a team on nothing but that."

Stachel nodded. "I see. Well, if Dunkel's dead, who are you waiting for now?"

"I don't know. It was my custom to meet Dunkel here every Thursday. Instructions. Pay. That kind of thing. I don't know who they'll send now. Or even if they'll send anybody at all."

"Surely they'll send somebody."

Kaspar showed doubt. "Well, I don't know. Dunkel was an ambitious fellow, always trying to look good as an innovator, a self-starter type. He made only routine reports to his superior, then would close out his cases with a burst of self-promoting surprises. In my case, he probably told them I worked for him, but little else."

137

"What have you done for him?"

"Some pretty good tricks. A couple of agents the Amis tried to drop in. I tipped Dunkel and he got the credit for capturing two OSS teams, practically single-handed. Then there were some black-market types, a couple of runaway Soviet prisoners. That kind of thing."

Stachel made the question casual. "How come you didn't turn in Lemmerhof? The general is a traitor. He'd be a big feather in Dunkel's cap and a big piece of change in your pocket."

Kaspar grinned knowingly. "I'm saving him. I'm not turning him in for any paper money. I want some of that gold all the big shots are stashing away these days. I've been with the general for a long time, and I rather like the old bastard, but the war's almost over, and one must be realistic, practical. If I don't watch out for me, who will? Right?"

"My feelings, exactly. But gold? What gold?"

Kaspar drew a long breath. "Oh, I can't say for sure. But there are rumors. Lots of gold and U.S. currency being shipped out of the Reich's treasury in Berlin for hiding in caves and lakes. That kind of thing. You can't tell me that some of the big shots aren't lining their own pockets. And I think Lemmerhof is enough to get me into that kind of game."

Stachel decided he should add a pinch of conviction to his own role. "Us. Not just you. I want a piece of Lemmerhof, too."

"Well, we might be able to work something out."

"You're sure no one in the Gestapo other than Dunkel knew about me, the general's treason, all that?"

Kaspar snickered. "Of course I'm sure. If Dunkel had shared that info with any of his bosses, the house in Bogenhausen would have been raided hours ago. And you and Lemmerhof and that snooty bitch you've been laying would be wearing piano-wire neckties right now."

"I guess you're right." After a pause, Stachel asked, "Who is this Gautzsch von Lemmerhof reports to?"

"I'm working on that. I want to find out who he really is, who he works for in Berlin, so that when I'm ready to sell I have the whole package, from the top to poor old Lemmerhof."

The overcast had lowered, to cover the sky with a monochromatic blear. There was the strong smell of impending rain. Kaspar sighed again, his eyes fixed on the agonized horizon. "God," he said bleakly, "but I'm sick of this filthy war. I want to go where I can sit in the sun and not keep pushing and worrying and looking for a Pfennig to hold things together."

"There's no place like that except paradise."

"I guess so."

"Well," Stachel suggested, "why guess? Why not go and take a look around?"

He shot Kaspar twice. Then he opened the door and dragged the body over a hill of shattered masonry and rolled it into a water-filled bomb crater.

To protect the Opel until he could send someone for it, he removed the distributor cap and the lugs from the right front wheel.

Returning to his VW, he drove back to the house.

22

STACHEL WENT UPSTAIRS and tapped at Tarbell's door.

"Come in."

From the doorway, Stachel said, "Are you all right?"

Tarbell was lying on the bed, in his Unteroffizier's uniform.

His eyes were heavy with sleep. "Good day, Herr Standarten-führer. Forgive me if I don't get up."

"Just lie at attention, please." He looked around the room. "It's cold in here. Do you need blankets or anything?"

"No, thanks. I'll be getting up in a moment. How long have I slept?"

"About four hours. I regret it couldn't be longer, but the war is waiting."

Tarbell swung his feet to the floor and yawned. "Do you always greet new visitors with such pyrotechnics? I mean, I've heard there's a war on and all that, but, my God—all that fuss over one silly little spy? A man could get hurt."

They both smiled, and there was an awkward pause. To break it, Stachel said, "How long have you been in the army?"

"About ten years. I was a Depression soldier. My old man was a scratch farmer, and I couldn't wait to get out of that miserable stretch of dirt. When I was old enough, I enlisted, and I worked hard, and eventually I was appointed to a flying cadet class. I was commissioned at the Army Advanced Flying School at Kelly Field in San Antonio."

"Where did you pick up your German?"

"My mother. She was born and reared in Frankfurt. Came to the States as a young woman. Worked as a maid in Milwaukee. You know."

Glimpsing another man's youth, Stachel felt his age, his own decay. Bruno Stachel: a compound of physical, mental, and emotional systems that had declined beyond reclamation and, in some special sense he would never fathom, had missed some kind of opportunity, somewhere, somehow. Why would this Stachel, whose dials had been set for sunny skies and adventures and accomplishment, be making talk with a bleary stranger in a bleak and dying city? What kind of secret rot permits a man to tune out the signal he has heard calling from Somewhere Else? What peculiar inertia keeps a man in this Here, when he suspects—knows—that he has always belonged in some There?

"You look rather tired yourself, Stachel."

"I've been more twinkle-toed in my day, to be sure."

"So where do we start, now that I'm here?"

"We'll have something to eat, then a conference with the general."

"From what I saw of him this morning he looks to be a rather formidable type."

Stachel humphed. "He's what our crew chief in Wilmington would have called"—he switched to English—"'nervous in the service.' A frightened, uninformed old man."

Tarbell held to German. "Did you hear, by the way. what happened to Finnegan?"

"No. What happened to our beloved crew chief?"

"It seems he had always had a yen to fly. Remember how we'd see him sitting in the pilot's seat, fondling the controls? Well, it was this yen he had, apparently. But three days after we shipped out for Europe, he cranked up Oh-Four-Niner and, all by himself, flew her to Norfolk."

"He'd never flown before?"

"He knew more about that airplane than any living soul. Except he'd never actually flown it. So it became too much for him, I guess, because off he went, without training, without clearance, without anything. Beautiful takeoff, solid cruise from Wilmington to Norfolk, with two P-47s chasing him and raising hell on the radio."

"Where is he now? In jail?"

"Who knows? He could fly Oh-Four-Niner, but he couldn't land her. He stalled out and spun in three miles short of the Norfolk runway. He was dead when they got to him."

"It takes a lot of skill to fly a B-17 single-handed."

"Well, no one ever accused Finnegan of being brilliant."

There was another pause. Then Tarbell staggered erect and went to the dresser and poured water into the basin. Splashing and sputtering, he said, "Speaking of skill, Elfi Heidemann is an absolute dazzler with a submachine gun. God, how she did mow those buggers down. What's hap-

141

pened to her, anyway? In Wilmington she was a self-effacing schoolmistress. In Munich she is Bonnie to your Clyde. How so?"

"I don't know. Maybe it's something in the water."

Tarbell dabbed his face with a towel, glancing at Stachel in the mirror. "Are you sleeping with her?"

"That's none of your business."

"Then you are. My congratulations. You must be blue hell between the sheets if you can work a transformation like that in her." He laughed softly.

"Let's change the subject."

"Very well. We'll talk about you. You've changed, too. When I first saw you at Ritchie, you were a snarling, acid, bastard-on-tank-treads. Now you are as composed as Grandfather Christmas. Which means that Elfi must be blue hell between the sheets, too."

"All right, Tarbell. Enough's enough."

Tarbell's eyes glinted with amusement. "Sure. Seriously, though, Elfi is a first-class woman. You're lucky. Now—how about a cigarette? Do you have any?"

"There's a pack of Zephyrs in the library. Cigarettes are hard to come by over here. Tobacco in any form buys more than money does."

"Ah, yes. Before we go to breakfast, then, I bring a message from Miss Loomis. She says that if you are dead, as we have feared, I am to replace you as team leader. But, since you are here, all pink and pert, I will revert to the status of what is obviously a fifth wheel on a very creaky cart. You need my radio, but you don't need me."

Stachel shrugged. "Sorry to disappoint you."

"That's all right. Better luck next time."

"But you are an embarrassment of riches, Tarbell. We've got three cooks in a one-cook kitchen."

"Four, if you count Herr General von Lemmerhof."

"As Finnegan would have put it, Herr General von

Lemmerhof couldn't find his own dingus if he didn't have a string tied to it. The general, like the rest of us, has changed. Only in his case, for the worse. He was, when I worked for him in Berlin, rather a formidable type, as you say. But he's now a frightened old fussbudget. With him in charge, General Eisenhower has nothing to fear from the Werewolf, I assure you."

Tarbell sniffed. "Then what in hell are we doing here? What's all the shouting about?"

"I don't know. I have a feeling something deeper is going on."

"Deeper?"

"I have a feeling we're serving as a bandage on the nose when the snakebite is on the ass."

Tarbell thought about that. Then: "Those people who tried to gather us in at the drop—who were they?"

"The Gestapo."

"Oh? How do you know that?"

"I asked Kaspar."

"Well, how would he know? He was with us. And, as I recall, a bit too anxious to be very observant."

Stachel nodded reasonably. "That's true."

Tarbell stared at Stachel, his eyes thoughtful, and Stachel could feel the searching and discovery that was in the other mind.

"Who was in that Mercedes? Who put the blast on our pursuers?"

"I haven't the least notion," Stachel said, using Kaspar's words.

"Doesn't Kaspar know?"

"Probably not."

"How do you know that for sure?"

"Because he told me."

"You believe him?"

"Yes."

"He's a Gestapo informant. He had those people waiting for me when I came down. Why would you believe anything he's told you? He's a very real threat to us, man."

"Not anymore."

Tarbell's gaze wavered, then dropped to the carpet. He was obviously beyond further comment.

"You see?" Stachel murmured. "I'm really not Grandfather Christmas, after all."

23

DRESSED IN THE tweed suit Hansen had provided from the cellar wardrobe, Stachel sat at a desk under a portrait of a glaring Hitler and for the fourth time riffled through Kaspar's papers. As he read, he thought about the Nazis and their wondrous society, of how they had created and destroyed this man whose wallet contained dirty pictures and matchbook covers and laundry tickets and a newspaper clipping that described Tahiti. There were the usual, too—ID papers, driver's license, ration cards, money—but they told him nothing beyond the fact that there had once been a fellow named Oswald Leon Kaspar; they had no suggestions as to why it had required Bruno Stachel—singly, specifically, personally—to cross so many years and miles to reduce Oswald Leon Kaspar to a pasty, barely visible lump under a meter of muddy water.

He reshuffled the lot, studying each item in turn and trying to penetrate the turbulent mystery behind them. One of the photos fell to the floor to lie facedown at his feet, and, reaching for it, he saw a lightly penciled notation on its matte backing: Gerda, 5/III/45; Rieglstr. 14; BFKZ 3317; AL 22; 005; MTG; Z; Ausg; D. Pondering this, he assumed that the woman in the picture, leering out from between chalky, elevated knees, was named Gerda and that her most intimate secret had been photographed on the fifth of March this year, at Riegelstrasse 14, perhaps. The rest, despite his imaginative efforts, remained indecipherable. The other pictures carried equally enigmatic captions, each including a woman's name, an address, and, after a series of numbers and letters, the initial D. Dunkel, maybe? Could these women be informants on the late Oswald Leon Kaspar's daisy chain? Could their information have been of significance to the late Herr Dunkel, erstwhile rising star of the Munich Gestapo? Or could it all be code, meaning altogether something else —something entirely unrelated to women or to addresses and dates? The only departure from the puzzling norm established by the notations was on the photo of Lisa, a sulking self-fondler: After the D a question mark had been added.

There was something else, too. He knew from personal observation that Tobart Strasse, Olsen Allee, and Findlgasse —streets noted on three of the photos—were obliterated, mere gullies in a weed-grown prairie of rubble in which no distinguishable structure remained. It was therefore unlikely that any of those three pictures could have been made at those sites on the dates designated, which were too recent to conform to the age of the ruins there. It was possible, then, that the streets represented a code, or part of one. Except maybe Lisa's—Baum Strasse, with a question mark. Baum Strasse, unlike the other streets, was in a section of the city he knew to have escaped heavy damage. Maybe Lisa's photo and its Baum-Strasse-with-a-question-mark was an inconsistency worth examining. He sat for a time, evaluating the hunch that told him so.

After reassembling Kaspar's wallet and placing it in the pocket of the raincoat Kaspar had hung in the hall closet, he went to the kitchen, where Elfi was clearing the luncheon clutter. She glanced up at him from her stack of dishes, giving him a friendly but not presumptuous smile. He liked her for this. They might be lovers, but she would be careful not to advertise the fact.

"Well, then," she said. "You're looking busy and official. Brown suit, fedora . . . Who are you now—a schoolteacher?"

"A tax accountant. Get your coat. You're due for a sally mission."

"Ah. Time to play soldier again."

"And hand me a piece of that black bread. With a little of the jam."

"You didn't get enough lunch?"

"Of course. But I'm a growing boy."

He watched her spread the dark-red preserves with lavish sweeps of a knife, and he wondered at the difference between this woman, with her clear eyes and faint-smile lips and creamy brow and silken hair, and the women of Kaspar's abominable photographs. He knew for a fact that she was capable of impulsive sensuality and that her enthusiasm for experimentation seemed limitless; so what then made her so different from the Lisas and Monikas, those suety wretches who flaunted themselves for a world of smirking voyeurs? Morality aside, what was the difference between the appreciative eyes of a thousand men or one? When did lust cease to be immoral? When did lasciviousness become uninhibited lovingness? Why should he give a damn?

"You're very thoughtful," Elfi said, placing the bread on a dish and passing it to him across the service counter.

"I'm writing a sermon."

"Watch out. That jam is dripping."

"So it is," he said, catching it with his tongue.

"Where am I going on this sally mission?"

"We. We are going. I'll tell you after we're in the car."

He stood by the window, eating his bread and jam and watching as she took off her apron and folded it carefully away in a drawer. She was looking very domestic, and he had

146

another small vision of life as it might have been for them had there been no wars or flying or drinking or willfulness and self-centeredness. Would she have bustled about some kitchen in some small house somewhere, humming tunes and baking bread and getting freckle-faced, knobby-kneed Brunos off to school? The thought was depressing. He wasn't at all certain he could have endured all that. One Bruno was too goddamned many.

"Where are the others?" she asked, pulling on her coat.

"Unteroffizier Folger is tinkering with the radio in his room. The general is making entries in his diary. Adolf Hitler is in Berlin, chewing carpets."

She gave him a look. "My, you are in a mood today, aren't you?"

"Just don't get pregnant, you hear?"

"What in the world are you talking about?"

"Anything I can't stand is pregnant women humming in the kitchen."

"Who's pregnant?"

"You'd better not be. And I mean it."

"Are you mad? I'm too old for that sort of thing."

"Well, I'm not."

She took up a cloth and dabbed at his chin. "Anything I can't stand is a mad tax accountant with jam on his face."

"You were very, ah, competent out there at the paradrop last night."

"So were you."

"I admire your way with guns. Except the way you lose them."

"I was frightened."

"You look cool enough this afternoon."

"I'm working on it. Very hard."

"The best antidote for the shakes is more action. Come on. Get in the car. I want you to drive."

"Why?"

"I'll be bailing out. You'll continue on as a decoy."

"Few women drive cars these days. What if I'm stopped at a checkpoint?"

He tapped her purse with his forefinger. "You'll be carrying your engineering credentials and War-Important Work pass. You are en route to Fürstenfeldbruck to study the airfield's drainage."

"And few women are engineers these days, by the way."

"But you're one of them, my friend. The general has planted documents at City Hall that prove you received your degree in 1932."

"What if the checkpoint holds me so the Gestapo can ask me engineering questions?"

"Then, dear Fräulein Nagele, you will once again have to prove your proficiency with firearms. It's a cruel world, as the saying has it."

*　*　*

As they rode, Stachel wondered why he was going to all this trouble. Their mission was clear and, give or take a few zigs and zags, rather uncomplicated: collaborate with von Lemmerhof. There was nothing in their charter to require trips down side roads. Still, Kaspar had been a part of the mission, one of the contributors to the Werewolf postulation, and whatever he might have known could have significance. This was a flimsy rationale for a sally, to be sure, but Stachel admitted grumpily to himself that he had never been renowned for his adherence to methodical, carefully planned procedure. Of all the crosses he bore, a restless curiosity was among the heaviest, and, coupled with his abiding expectation of the worst of motives in all men, he simply could not permit Kaspar's inscrutable little memorandums to go unscrutinized.

"Follow this street along the river to Hirschau," he said.

"We're not going into center city?"

"Not directly. The general's maps show a pontoon bridge above Hirschau. Cut west over that and along the secondary road to Moosach. From there we'll head southwest through Nymphenburg, where, I hope, I'll manage to leave you. You will continue south to Laim and then east through the city—by whichever route looks best—to Bogenhausen. I'll join you there, probably after dark tonight."

"What will you be doing?"

"Watching the comings and goings at Baum Strasse Seventy-three."

"What's there?"

"I don't know. That's why I'm taking a look."

"This is why you're wearing civilian clothes?"

"It wouldn't do for a uniformed SS Standartenführer to stand around some neighborhood all day. The residents would expect more for their tax money than to have a highly paid officer loafing on the corner."

Elfi became silent, concentrating on her driving. The day was raw and overcast, and the landscape was a study in grays. After inching through a clog of bundle-laden wanderers at the Oberfohring detour, she cleared her throat and asked, "Why are we going soch a roundabout way? And why are you leaving me in Nymphenburg?"

"For one thing, I don't want to wait in line for all the city checkpoints. A man could die of old age in one of those lines. For another thing, I want to lose that fellow in the black Mercedes. I don't want him to see where I'm going."

He saw her glance at the rearview mirror, a quick, nervous flicking of her green eyes. "He's with us again, then," she said tautly.

"He's with us always. Usually I don't mind. But today I want some privacy."

"What if he catches up with me and demands to know where you've gone?"

"He won't. He prefers his own anonymity where we're concerned. If things go right for us, he'll merely tag along behind your car, wondering why he ended up back in Bogenhausen."

"How will you get back to the safe-house?"

"Kaspar has left his Opel for me at a spot I know."

"Do you really trust Kaspar?"

"I didn't at first. I do now."

"What changed your mind?"

"We've had a very candid talk."

She considered this, and he could see she didn't know what to make of it. Just as well. He would break the news of Kaspar's pacification at a less demanding time.

* * *

When they had entered the Nymphenburgerlandstrasse at its outer reaches, Stachel told Elfi to turn east toward the city's heart. Out here the war's erosion was indirect, with only occasional bomb damage and a general disrepair to show for the passing of the Amis' dreaded Liberators and B-25s, which had worked such horrors elsewhere. The street was wide, brick-paved, and melancholy in the the gray light, and there was a strange lack of life along its hem. Now and then an old woman, picking her way on some dreary, market-basket errand; here and there some children, kicking a soccer ball in a kind of terrible, intense silence, or trudging glumly, school books slung on unhappy shoulders.

"See that overpass ahead? Where the street makes a sharp turn under the railroad?"

"I see it," she said.

"Speed up now. Make the turn as fast as you can. Just beyond the overpass, slow down enough to let me out. But keep moving."

"All right. But be careful."

"You be careful, Fräulein Nagele. After all, you're the bait."

"Won't he see there's only one of us left in the car?"

"Not if you keep far enough ahead. He's a very careful tail. He always hangs far back, in the hopes we won't notice him. He follows our car, not us."

"He's very tiresome."

"I'll see you at the house, Fräulein. Ta-ta."

She made the turn with a soft warbling of the tires and he was out of the car and snugly behind a concrete pillar under the bridge by the time the Mercedes swished through. Since it was more important to remain hidden than it was to identify the driver, Stachel made no effort to risk a peek. When all was silent again, he brushed the wrinkles from his tweed jacket, adjusted his Tyrolean hat, and stepped out to the sidewalk.

"Hiding from the Gestapo?" a voice asked from above.

He glanced up to see a girl sitting on the retaining wall, legs swinging. Her eyes were bright blue and amused under her red knit cap. He guessed she was about ten years old.

"Everybody's hiding from the Gestapo these days," he said.

"Don't worry about me. I won't talk."

"Who are you?"

"Trudi Eberhardt. I live in that house over there."

"Tell me, Trudi—if you had to get to a street near the old Hirschgarten, which way would you go?"

She sniffed. "Me, I'd follow the railroad tracks. Up that way is Dachau, but down that way is the main station. I'd walk along the tracks toward the station, then by the bombed-out Kaserne I'd leave the tracks and go across the road to the Garten section. It takes longer, but it's safer."

"You wouldn't go directly along this avenue here?"

"Not me. Too many checkpoints. If you stay on the railroad you look just like all the other people who walk up and down, looking for pieces of coal that have fallen out of the trains. The SS doesn't check the coal snappers much. These days, anyhow."

"You're very nice to tell me all this."

"That's all right. I don't like cops."

"Why?"

"They took away Herr Gittl one night. He's the man who

151

lived next door. He used to give me candy. His wife used to teach me how to bake things. They took him away and she died."

"I wish I had some candy to give you."

"I haven't had candy in a long time. But nobody has, Mutti says."

"Where's your Vati?"

"He fell at Stalingrad."

"I see. That's your house, you say?"

"Mm. The one with the missing shutter."

"Do you believe in fortune-telling, Trudi?"

"I guess so. Sometimes. Why?"

"I'll tell your fortune. Right now. I predict that you will get a box of candy one day soon."

"Ha."

"You'll see."

24

THE BUILDING AT Baum Strasse 73 was a yellow stucco drabness that dominated the block, both by size and by virtue of its sign—a line of Gothic letters across the façade that read Fuglein Kompanie, Möbelspeicher und Transportgeschäft. Beside the building and to the rear of an alley was a large garage where, presumably, as operator of a furniture warehouse and moving-van firm, Fuglein housed and maintained its trucks. Stachel walked past the place twice, once on the far side of the street, once on the near side in the hope that he might see through the casement windows, all of which had been crisscrossed with tape to prevent shattering in the event of a nearby bomb blast. From any aspect, there was no clue as to why Kaspar had noted the address in his pornographic filing system.

Happily there was a small Bierstube and hotel at the corner, and he was able to acquire a table whose window gave a direct view of Fuglein. He ordered eine Halbe to justify his possession of what the barman obviously considered the choicest table and pretended to read the newspaper brought to him with the watery beer. Only two other patrons were in evidence—one an old man who slept in a far corner over a copy of *Illustrierte Zeitung* and the other a gaunt and rheumy fellow whose left leg was missing and who stared at the wall and sipped from a stein. The barman, barrel-bellied and suspendered and mustached, sat on a stool and studied his fingernails. No one spoke, each seeming to be preoccupied with deep and private pain.

A woodburning truck grumbled out of the Fuglein driveway shortly before 1400 hours, and a woman left the front door to walk up the street and out of sight about five minutes later. No other events disturbed the moving van company's dreary afternoon.

There was a thumping, and Stachel turned to see the one-legged man approaching with practiced swings of his crutch.

"Are you finished with the newspaper?" the man asked in a soft hoarseness.

"Yes. There's nothing in it anyhow."

"I like to read about the Wehrmacht's glorious vic‌ːᵤⅈes over the Ami swine. Of how we magically seem to hold the line despite the Amis' advance of fifty kilometers a day. Of how we'll win in the end when our V-2 bombs wipe out everything between the Rhine and New York City."

Stachel gave the man a lingering, evaluating stare. "You seem to enjoy danger, my friend. That's pretty seditious sarcasm. How do you know I'm not a cop?"

"So arrest me. Execute me. I'm not afraid of dying. I'm

afraid of living. I'd do the job myself if it weren't against my religion." The man smiled dourly and winked. "Besides, you don't smell like a cop. You going to drink your beer? You haven't touched it."

The barman, not so sure of Stachel's un-policemanlike aroma, decided to declare his fidelity. "Is he bothering you, sir? If so, I'll throw him out. He's one of our local characters, the neighborhood malcontent."

Annoyed with the barman's obsequiousness, Stachel nodded at a chair and told the one-legged fellow to sit. "Help yourself to the beer, as you call it. Actually, I think it's cow piss, and if you drink it you'll invite the death you seem so anxious to acquire."

The man sat down, sighing and hooking his crutch on the table's rim. "Ah. That's better. Ludwig Auer is my name. Afrika Korps retired, if you can accept the term. I live in the house next door with my daughter and her seven hundred illegitimate children, all brats with running noses and dirty pants." He took a long pull at Stachel's Halbe.

"She runs an orphanage?"

"No. She runs a baby factory. Every fellow she meets make her pregnant. She simply can't say no to a pat on her ass."

"Well, you'll have to admit she's creative."

Auer glanced at Stachel, his drinker's eyes revealing an acid amusement. "Yes, I suppose that's so. How come you're not in the army? You're an oldish potato, but not too old for the Volkssturm."

"I have flat feet, asthma, and tertiary syphilis."

"They've excused you for such skimpy reasons? I'd heard the Wehrmacht was getting lax, but, my God—"

"When did you, ah, retire, Herr Auer?"

"When an Englishman stitched me with his machine gun near Tobruk. I lay in the sand for three days. Then some accommodating Landser came along, threw me into his VW, and drove me to an aid station. Although they eventually relieved me of my leg, the High Command wanted me to become commanding general of the Wehrmacht whore battalions, but I declined the honor, choosing instead to return here and drink myself into dignified oblivion. My most pressing problem is finding enough alcohol to do the job."

Stachel signaled the barman. "Another Halbe for the neighborhood malcontent, please, so that he might be helped along his road to oblivion."

"He's been there all his life, if you ask me," the barman humphed.

Auer regarded Stachel with what could have passed for interest. "Speaking of jobs, what's yours, Herr—"

"Knabe. Alfred Knabe. I'm a tax specialist for the Reich. I'm here to begin an audit of that moving van company across the street. But I can't work up any enthusiasm for it today. I'm simply bored stiff, and I can't face another ledger."

Auer nodded sympathetically. "I know the feeling. But your task shouldn't be too difficult over there. They've been open only a couple of months. How much money could they have made in a couple of months?" He licked his lips. "Especially when nothing seems to happen day in and day out."

"They aren't very busy?"

"Ha. Busy? My daughter says they have a platoon of big shots who do nothing but sit behind closed doors and burn their own trash. A truck goes out now and then, but only for an hour or two. Some busy business, eh?"

Stachel put money on the barman's tray, and the man returned to the shadows behind the taps. "What does your daughter have to do with Fuglein?" Stachel asked Auer.

"She's a scrubwoman there. Between fornications, that is."

"Oh." Stachel tried not to appear too interested.

"Peculiar place, apparently. Lots of phones. But they hardly ever ring. Lots of people. But they all have clean desks, empty wastebaskets, and sit around as if they're waiting for something. The biggest stir, she says, was one day last month when a customer showed up. A Luftwaffe fellow with a Tin Cravat. They made a big fuss over him. But he didn't stay long."

"Tin Cravat? I don't understand military terms—"

Auer smirked. "The Knight's Cross. That big Iron Cross all the headquarters heroes wear at their throats. It used to mean something, the Knight's Cross. But now they hand it out for efficient ordering of paper clips and toilet paper. The foxhole Landsers now call it the Tin Cravat, I'm told. In whispers, mostly, since it doesn't do to have the headquarters heroes hearing such sacrilege."

"I see."

Auer drank heavily from the second beer, his eyes turned to the ceiling in bleary concentration, and Stachel thought about all this. Fuglein Kompanie was a front for something, obviously, and Kaspar no doubt had seen it to be an activity worth noting down. Which suggested that Fuglein might be illegal or treasonous, since Oswald Leon Kaspar had not dealt in wares that could not be peddled to Herr Dunkel and the Gestapo. But a brass hat from the Luftwaffe? A Tin Cravat wearer? How did this figure in?

"Well," Stachel said, smiling resignedly, "I can't put it off any longer. I must be off on my thrilling mission among the credits and debits. Nice meeting you, Herr Auer. Give my regards to your energetic daughter."

"Where's your briefcase?"

"I never carry it on the initial call. It's disarming."

"Makes sense."

"Want another beer on me?"

"Do birds want to fly?"

Stachel went to the bar niche under the archway to the rear. Handing the barman a couple of small bills, he said, "This is for the oblivion account. And treat yourself while you're at it."

"Thank you, sir." The portly man nodded amiably and dropped his voice. "I truly hope Ludwig didn't bother you.

He's a grumpy sort, and he drinks too much, but he's not really a bad fellow. He's had a hard life."

"I'd be grumpy, too, if I had left a leg in Africa."

"I worry about him and his open dislike of the Regime. He'll get in trouble someday if he doesn't watch his mouth."

"Are there any rooms at the hotel? I'll be returning in a day or two to start real work across the street."

"We've got a nice room for you. Second-floor front."

"Here's a binder. Hold it for me. If I can't make it a friend of mine will. I'll tell him to give you my name—Knabe, Alfred Knabe. And, incidentally, our tax visit to Fuglein is confidential."

"Very well, sir. Not a word."

*　*　*

Stachel crossed the street in the waning afternoon light, feeling the chill of the die-hard winter. Some of the trees were showing buds, but the wind retained a dampness that cut through his tweeds and set his eyes to watering. As at all times of danger, he seemed to acquire a special awareness of detail, feeling the wind, seeing the cracks in the pavement and the tints of mold forming on the stucco beside the main entrance.

The reception room was dimly lit and as silent as a cathedral. A woman of about fifty sat at a typewriter behind a reception desk and smiled at him with fake cordiality as he approached.

"Good day, sir," she intoned. "May I help you?"

"My name is Braunek. I'm from the municipal buildings inspector's office. I'm here to check out the electrical wiring."

"Oh?" the woman's carefully constructed smile fell into lower gear. "We've had no notice. I mean, your inspection is most inconvenient. There's a staff meeting under way, and I'm afraid there's no one to show you around."

"No matter. I know where to look."

She would have made a good guard sergeant. "Well, Herr Braunek, I'm afraid unescorted visitors are not permitted."

Stachel feigned annoyance. "Please, dear lady, let's not quibble. I'm a public official, doing his duty. I'm not a visitor, or a customer, or anything else."

"May I see your credentials, please? An inspection order, perhaps?"

Stachel's mind raced about for means to parry this nasty little development when a door opened in the hallway behind him and a man's voice said, "Frau Benner, will you bring in the Odenwald correspondence, please? And the bill of lading for the Brinckhoff piano removal."

The door clicked shut again, and the woman pushed back her chair, stood up, and turned to a metal file cabinet behind her desk. "I'm sorry, Herr Braunek, but as you can see, we're very busy today. If you'd be so good as to return tomorrow with an inspection order we'll make the entire plant available to you."

"Very well. I'll be here at oh-nine-hundred, sharp," he said darkly.

*   *   *

He didn't mind leaving now. Frau Benner had placed a mirror above her file cabinet, presumably to practice her welcome smile, and he had caught a full view of the man who had needed the Odenwald whatever.

Hans Berger, SS Sturmbannführer and saber-scarred Prussian who, as a personal friend of Reichsmarschall Hermann Göring, was a ranking official of the Forschungsamt and chief of communications intelligence there.

With Berger involved, Fuglein Kompanie, Möbelspeicher und Transportgeschäft, was very definitely of interest to Ami intelligence.

Home Plate most certainly would want to put an agent on it.

25

THE CARRIAGE HOUSE of the Bogenhausen place
had a modified mansard roof, with a flat sloping area cover-
ing its tool and storage ell. This section was surrounded by lofty
evergreens grown thick and opaque in years of inattention.
The whole formed a kind of small, treetop amphitheater in
which Tarbell could operate his radio unseen from ground
level—and even from the house itself. The RAF Mosquito
made its first appearance on schedule, which was at 1355
hours of Tarbell's second day in Munich. It circled so high in
the pale sunlight it was beyond vision, a fact established by
Stachel and Elfi, who lay on the roof beside Tarbell and stared
into the distant blue haze while he chattered away, giving
recognition signals and countersigns. The radio was, Tarbell
had assured them in his superior way, an improved J-E, the
absolute latest in espionage technology, enabling direct
discourse at conversational level, free of static or garble.

"How about German planes?" Elfi asked. "Won't they see
the Englishman and shoot him down?"

"Of course," Stachel said, enjoying the sun's faint warmth,
"except for one thing. There are no German planes."

"I can't believe that. There must be some."

"Sure. But some means none, in air power. The Luftwaffe
is nearly out of planes, out of skilled crews, out of gas and oil.
When it flies at all, it might as well not."

"Be quiet, you two, I'm sending now, and I can't concentrate on these notes with you two buzzing in the background."

"Tell our friend hello from me," Elfi said.

"I said shut up, damn it." Tarbell switched to English.
"Airboy, this is Nightstick. We are established and operating
as per plan. But there's disappointment among the team. The

Werewolf thing simply hasn't jelled yet, and there seems to be no hard plan. Whisper is next to nothing as a leader. Some HJ people are trying to organize in the Tyrol, and Nightstick leader will attempt a recon of this activity this P.M. and tomorrow A.M. Suggest another Airboy contact at, say, fifteen-thirty hours tomorrow's date. Your transmission. Over."

Tarbell had been right. The new radio was a living dream of a thing; the faint, clipped British voice came through Stachel's auxiliary earphones clearly, like a distant ghost's.

"Right-o, Nightstick. Have recorded you. Message from Home Plate to you. Please note as follows. Most urgent to Whisper—'Der Schmetterling kommt jetzt an die Reihe.' Repeat—'Der Schmetterling kommt jetzt an die Reihe.' Your transmission for acknowledge. Over."

"We are to tell Whisper, quote, 'Now it's the butterfly's turn.' Anything else? Your transmission. Over."

"No further comment or instructions, Nightstick, old boy. Toodle-oodle, and out."

Tarbell shut off the set, then sank back from his deep-knee bend to rest on his elbows and squint at the sky. "Toodle-oodle. Sheee. They all sound like David Niven in *The Dawn Patrol*."

"The English are among the world's best, for my money," Stachel said in German so as to include Elfi in the conversation. "I've fought them. I've been friends with them. A few of them, that is. Tough, splendid, cool people."

"Then why are we Germans fighting them?" she chided.

"Because the Führer wants to show them we're tougher, more splendid, cooler people than they are. It's important that they know that."

"Why?"

"Because we're tired of being admired for our diesel engines and sauerkraut. We want to be loved. And we've kicked the crap out of everybody to prove how lovable we are."

"The Führer is a very wise man indeed. Who could ever

160

have devised a more noble philosophy than that?"

"The radio works well, eh?" Stachel said.

Tarbell nodded, openly pleased. "Better by far than the original Joan-Eleanor, I'd say. It was like we were having a three-way chat in the neighborhood saloon. And, even if the Nazis were listening, they couldn't have gotten a fix on us. Neat as hell, I'd say."

"Maybe next time," Stachel said, "the Englishman will play us some Benny Goodman records. Or send us the Fred Allen and Jack Benny show."

"Benny Goodman," Elfi said. "I know that name. He played music in the American barracks at Hastings. He seemed to be very popular. Do you like American jazz music, Bruno?"

Tarbell stood up, a dark tower against the sun, and slung his radio pack over a shoulder. "Come on. My God, are you going to lie there and gabble for the rest of the war?"

"What about it, Fräulein Nagele? Should we lie here and gabble?"

"I'd like to, Standartenführer von Kistner, but we must go to Oberbayern and the Tyrol. There are some people we've missed kicking into lovability."

*   *   *

Von Lemmerhof was at the desk in the library, writing indifferently on a pad of yellow lined paper. His face, pink with a recent shave, was creased and gloomy and seemingly forever lost even to the hope of a smile. He looked up, and the monocle dropped on its string.

"What is it, Stachel?"

"Frau Heidemann and I are off to inspect the troops. We should be back sometime in the next day or so."

"You have all your papers, maps?"

"Yes. Your document man in the basement has taken care of all of it. He's a good man, all right."

"The best."

"Unteroffizier Folger will remain here with the radio. You are responsible to him in my absence. Meanwhile, you have something I want."

"What's that?"

"Your Tin Cravat. I want to wear it on my trip."

Von Lemmerhof lifted the monocle and screwed it into his eye. A redness had come into his talcumed cheeks, and his gaze was full of outrage. "My Knight's Cross? You want to confiscate my Knight's Cross?"

"Not confiscate. Borrow. It will give my already considerable weight as an SS Standartenführer even more dimension. It will be, ah, a door opener. Right?"

"I despise that term—The Tin Cravat."

"Don't blame it on me. It's what irreverent old campaigners call it behind the backs of new headquarters heroes. It's foxhole slang, Herr General. Usually whispered, I understand."

"Such a demeaning term for such a noble decoration."

"Well, as we Yankees like to say, 'Don't you know there's a war on?' Things will simply never be the same again. The old values topple, and all that."

"You've become a thoroughly detestable man, Stachel."

"Thank you, Herr General."

Von Lemmerhof slowly removed the medal from his throat and handed it across the desk. "That decoration was given me personally by the Führer," he said in a barely audible voice.

"Cheer up, Herr General. Your expectation of a German surrender should soon be realized. Then you will be able to spend the rest of your treasonous life in recollections of all the fun you once had among the world's most hated men. You should be laughing and singing, Herr General."

"Detestable."

Stachel turned to make for the door. "By the way, Herr General, there's been a message from Home Plate. It's directed to you, personally."

"Well, what is it?"

"Der Schmetterling kommt jetzt an die Reihe."

Von Lemmerhof pushed back his chair and slowly rose to his feet, a subtle something replacing the frozen sourness there. "My God, Stachel," he said throatily, "you simply cannot go off to the Tyrol now."

"Why not?"

"That message—it has enormous and immediate implications. Something very important is to take place."

"Tell me about it."

"I—I can't. It's not for you to know. Not yet."

"Well, then, as an Englishman of my acquaintance likes to say, 'Toodle-oodle.' "

* * *

Stachel checked the VW for fuel, flashlight, terrain charts, road maps, trip ticket. He placed an extra magazine of ammunition for the machine pistol under the driver's seat and blankets and tent-rolls in the back in case they were unable to find lodgings. As he worked, he reviewed the situation: someone in Berlin relaying orders through Brigadeführer Gautzsch to Puppet Lemmerhof, who is kept on a severely limited information diet. Yet the puppet convinces the Amis that they should send three trained agents to the Reich to spy on, and regulate if possible, an intrigue the Puppet still knows little or nothing about. Peculiar. Very peculiar.

26

POLLY'S OFFICE WAS in a side street overhung by medieval half-timber façades and bottle-glass windows in oriels. It was somber-Swiss, dark with time, and it was not to her liking, since she was a fastidious woman. But she had, in this case, subdued her taste for elegance, because the sleaziness supported her cover, which was the sale of watches and jewelry, for her real business, which was trying to keep the Wiseguy Affair moving and in balance and headed for a successful conclusion.

She stood at the window, staring into the night beyond the rooftops and chimney pots, and sought to ignore the smell of restaurant kitchens and disinfectant and manure and auto exhaust that drifted from below. She was thinking of the past—a dreary idling for one so preoccupied with today and tomorrow. The uneasiness and discontent were especially heavy, perhaps because she had become increasingly awed by the enormous implications of the Wiseguy affair, but more probably because she was sick of herself and her duplicitous life and her constant involvement with sordidness and the second-rate. How, she wondered, do you tear loose? How do you stop? Can you really, at forty-two, make a U-turn? Why should you want to? And, clinically, how could you simply walk away from the schemes, the plots, the connivings, the angles—all of them teeming with people whose survival hung on your decisions and words? How do you dismiss a network of spies? How do you disengage? Call a meeting? Send out letters?

She supposed all this morbidness was due to her embarrassment at dinner last night. There had been a little scene when Olive Detweiler, wife of the legation's communications officer, had drunk too much and delivered a heated denunciation of "those cold-eyed government broads who snatch government husbands with their snatches and if the shoe fits, Polly Loomis, shove it up your valise." There had been some very important people in the party, and although Jim Detweiler had managed to get Olive out of the club and into a cab, an awkward superpoliteness had come over everybody and she'd gone home early—too early, since it was a sign of retreat in face of accusation, or some such rot. Few were likely to have known of her occasional dalliance with Jim, a nice guy virtually starved for tenderness, and so Olive's vitriol was probably dismissed by most as the rantings of a drunk. But *she* knew. Polly Loomis knew. Polly Loomis *was* a whore. And Polly Loomis was suddenly very tired of it.

She turned from the window and sat in the swivel chair, which emitted an irritable squeak that went around the room as a lonely echo. She shut her eyes for a time, hoping that, by switching off sight, she could switch off thoughts of Bruno. He always came to her mind when she was down. If she were ever to find peace it would never be with him on the same earth. Because when she was down and hurting, the thought of him out there somewhere, reachable but beyond her reach, would press her down further and hurt her all the more.

Downstairs someone turned up a radio, and an oily man's voice relayed the news as if he had personally caused all these things to happen and aren't all you sons of bitches out there lucky that I'm in charge of the world? The Allied armies continue their exploitation of the breaches in Germany's Rhine River defense line; Remagen, first, and now, at the beginning of April, crossings as far north as Wesel and as far south as Mainz, Worms, and Karlsruhe; the German news agency reports the bridgeheads are all under control and, in most cases, being turned back with tens of thousands of Allied casualties; the BBC reports that the German reports are false; the Germans report that the BBC report on the German report is a report without foundation. News of push, pull, fight, claw, snarl, hate, and greed. Greed. Greed disguised as altruism, patriotism, fraternalism, and paternalism; greed masked as smiling friendship, as the smirk of righteousness. The world turned on greed, and she hated the world and its greed. She knew all about greed; she'd built a life on it, and, as a consequence, she hated herself above all things.

The phone rang—a clamor that announced yet another manifestation of greed. *The phone*, she thought. *The ringing of a phone is my theme song. It rings, and I answer, and I listen to the greed, and then I make a judgment and speak. For more than fifteen thousand days I've lived, and in most of them I have heard the phone and uttered my judgments. When they bury me there should be no softly humming organ; there should be an a cappella choir of ringing phones.*

"Hello?"

"Max here."

"Where the hell have you been? I've been waiting to hear from you since noon."

"It's not a simple matter to get through to you at times. Your phone is busy more often than not. Besides, I've only just now heard from Wiseguy."

"Is he in Berlin?"

"Of course."

"When is he coming south?"

Max was silent for a moment, and the radio downstairs had abandoned chatter for an accordion band and a yodeler. She heard him rustling some papers at his end of the line, and the contrast between the saccharine-innocent mountain music here and the enormity of what lay behind Max's notes there was patently mad.

"Why are you laughing, Fräulein Loomis?"

"Was I laughing?"

"You're a cool one, all right."

"Answer my question, Max."

"He's coming south within the next two days."

"My God. That means Nightstick has to be in position by tomorrow at least."

"At least."

"Any indication when Wiseguy will contact me directly?"

"Not as yet."

"How about you, Max? With things going the way they are, will you be going back to Germany? Or will you be staying here? Claiming asylum? What?"

Max sighed. "I really can't say, Fräulein Loomis. Things are rather in a turmoil now."

"Well, if you stay, let me know. I can always find a job for a good man like you."

"Thank you." He paused, then said unctuously, "It would be a privilege to serve you."

She hung up and sat in the silence. For the first time in years she had an unaccountable need to cry.

She began to work on the incoming mail instead.

27

IT TOOK THEM most of the day to drive the sixty-some miles from Munich to Kufstein. American planes were especially active, thanks to the sparkling sky and the spring-like temperatures. It was as if, Stachel thought, the P-51s and Thunderbolts and Lightnings were bugs over a meadow, brought out and caused to dance in the air by a pleasant sun. But their comings and goings worked hell below; the roads were jammed with burning wrecks and hardly a bridge was left intact, anywhere, and the checkpoints seemed to be at every curve of road.

He kept to the back roads as much as possible, pushing the VW to the limit and twice fording streams when the highway ended abruptly at water's edge. Even so, it was better by far than what they would have found on the major highways. A trooper, pouring gas at a back-country station converted to SS depot use, told them of a nasty Ami attack near Rosenheim that had destroyed a convoy and wiped out a Volksgrenadier battalion. Stachel was wary of such extravagant talk, but there was little doubt that life was most difficult on the Autobahnen these days, and he planned to stay as far as possible from them.

Elfi was very quiet, and he suspected that she was still dealing with the hangover of her shooting binge. Killing was something best left to experts; impassioned or frightened first-and-only-timers often suffered more than those they packed away. He kept a sidelong watch on her, and tried making little jokes now and then to get her mind off melancholy reconstructions.

"The Tegernsee is beautiful today, isn't it?" he said. "The water's bluer than I've ever seen it, and those white puff clouds are really something special, eh?"

"It's lovely."

"Seeing the lake reminds me of Gunter Seidl. He was a pilot in the Luft post service after the first war, before the Luftwaffe came out of wraps. One day he heard his girl friend was sailing the Tegernsee with her father on his fine big sailboat. He flew down here, saw the boat riding at anchor with a party under way. He swooped low to wave hello, but he flew too close. The lower wing of his old AEG clipped the mast and turned the boat upside down, throwing everybody into the water in a shower of beer steins and potato salad. His crate wobbled into a crash landing in a backyard in Wiessee. And when it was all over he learned it had been somebody else's sailboat and that his girl friend was at home in Munich all the time."

"Was anybody hurt?"

"Well, no. Only their feelings, as the saying goes."

"Seems a silly thing for a man to do."

He nodded slowly. "I suppose so."

After a time of driving he said, "You seem rather down today."

"Sorry. I'd like to be better company, but something's been on my mind, and it worries me."

"Something I've said or done?" He felt vaguely like a husband.

"Of course not. It's just a personal thing."

"It helps sometimes to talk things over."

"I don't even know how to give this words. How do you talk about something when there aren't any words for it?"

"Well, what's it about?"

"That gun fight the other night. When I shot those men."

"Ah. I thought that was it. You had the look I've seen on people's faces after they've been in combat. Well, let me reassure you—the first time's the worst. After a while it wears off, the feeling of guilt and remorse. It may take time—I've seen men anguishing over having taken a life for days, even weeks—but it goes away. So don't feel bad. They were the enemy."

He concentrated on his driving, but he could feel her silent inspection.

"You've got it wrong," she said eventually. "I don't feel bad about having killed those Gestapo people. On the contrary. It was almost as if I were intoxicated. After all those years of crawling for them, of fearing them, it was so good to be standing up to them at last. Guilt? There is no guilt. I enjoyed it. And that's what frightens me."

In his astonishment he found he had nothing more to say.

*　　*　　*

The command post was in a farmhouse on a sweep of high meadow between Kufstein and Worgl. They had found it by driving southwest on the highway through the Inn valley and turning off on a dirt lane that showed heavy use. Von Lemmerhof's directions had been sketchy, since he himself had never made the trip and had only Kaspar's offhand reports to base them on, so their arrival had been due in considerable measure to Stachel's intuition. Follow a churned-up country lane and you're almost certain to find soldiers at the end, had been his guess.

If the black Mercedes had tailed them, it had been very successful at remaining out of sight.

Stachel parked the VW in the farmhouse shadows and, making for the doorway, returned the stiff-armed Deutscher Gruss given him by a heel-clicking SS trooper on guard there. Elfi, solemn in her tailored tweeds and snap-brim hat, followed suit.

"May I help you, Standartenführer?" the trooper asked briskly.

"Your commanding officer—where do we find him?"

"Up the stairs and along the corridor to the rear room. Major Weiss is there. May I escort you?"

"Remain at your post."

Inside, the house was a paradox. The walls were hung with contour maps, mimeographed general-order sheets, memorandums; the rooms were bristling with desks and file cabinets and plotting tables and typewriters; the shelves were choked with field manuals, reference books, binoculars, steel helmets, ammunition boxes, canteens, gas masks—the orderly clutter of the military. Yet, contrary to its readiness for business, there was no business. Nothing moved, not a phone rang, not a voice spoke.

When they entered the commander's office—a large room with a low, beamed ceiling and a row of casements that displayed a sensational Alpine view—a squat, sandy-haired major turned from the window to give them a cool inspection. Bringing himself to a casual semblance of attention, he grated, "Afternoon, Standartenführer. Madam. What can I do for you?"

"I'm Standartenführer von Kistner. This is Fräulein Nagele, who is a construction engineer and specialist in fortifications design. General von Lemmerhof has asked us to look in on you and your operation here."

The major's thin lips showed a trace of scorn. "Well, operation is hardly the word I'd give it. You can see for yourselves that this is hardly a beehive of activity."

"I would like to know why," Stachel said, keeping his tone cool, in the manner of top brass. "After all, Major Weiss, you are supposed to be setting up a major resistance facility."

"Ha. Supposed to be is the key phrase, Standartenführer." Weiss made a sweep with his arms. "As is quite evident, I'm all dressed up with no dance to attend. I have an office, I have maps, I have orders from a general I've never seen, I have one stinking VW recon car, and two weapon trucks, one gas pump, and a squad of SS screw-ups to run errands and stand guard over a facility that nobody would want to take anyway. What's worse, I'm supposed to use my few men and trucks to make tire tracks and footprints across meadows. I'm supposed to build barracks on hilltops, fake gun positions beside roads, trenches, pillboxes—all of them out in the open where the Ami planes can photograph them, strafe them. I ask you —what kind of secret operation does its operating out in the open?"

"How come there were no guards at the highway? We weren't challenged once on our way in here." Stachel helped Elfi to a chair.

The major snorted. "Except for the man at the door downstairs, they're all in St. Johann, helping to unload trucks."

"What trucks, Major?" Stachel said, sitting on a camp stool.

"Who in hell knows?" Weiss stomped to the windows again, where he stood, regarding the view with vast disgust. "I get a phone call this morning—the only time the phone has rung in two days—and this voice in Munich tells me to send my men to St. Johann. There is a supply shipment to be placed in a warehouse. Well, frankly, I was glad to get the bastards—pardon, Fräulein—out of my sight for a while.

God, what dunderheads. No wonder we're losing the frigging war. Pardon, Fräulein."

Elfi sniffed and nodded frostily, and Stachel felt an urge to smile. He did not, however, since it was important that he match her play-acting and convey High Command disapproval of all things made of men and God.

"Watch your language, Weiss. One must not let one's impatience obscure the amenities." He wondered if he looked as foolish as he sounded.

"Apologies. But I get so double-damned frustrated. How is a fellow supposed to carry out his orders when he doesn't get clear orders from people he doesn't know in a headquarters he can't visit on an operation he isn't allowed to talk about to anybody who cares anyhow? Jesus to Jesus!"

"Language, Major."

"Oh, to hell with the language. Why don't you bring charges against me for public indecency or something? Have me dragged out of this stimulating command and shipped off to a deadly dull post at Remagen or some place where I'll be bored to death by Yankee paratroopers?"

"I'll have you bored to death by a firing squad if you continue this insubordination."

Major Weiss ran a hand through his sandy hair and gave Stachel a narrow-eyed study. "Say," he said sardonically, "that's an idea. I might form my own firing squad if I could only find the sons of bitches, who, when they aren't unloading trucks, are sneaking off to the village to spread-eagle the local barmaids."

Elfi began to laugh, a soft sibilance that quickly advanced to an outburst. Despite himself, Stachel smiled, and Major Weiss stared at them both in open surprise.

"I'm sorry," Elfi managed, "but I know just how you feel, Major. I've felt the same way about things for months now."

Stachel said, "You're lucky Fräulein Nagele and I have a sense of humor, Weiss. Otherwise you'd be in deep trouble by now."

The major gave Elfi a glance full of new interest. "I'm sorry, too," he said disarmingly. "And I really do beg your pardon, Fräulein. And yours also, Standartenführer. I've simply had a vile time. I want to serve the Fatherland but nobody will let me."

Stachel nodded and changed the subject. "Tell me, Weiss, this voice from Munich, as you call it. Did the voice have a name?"

"Gautzsch. He said he was SS Brigadeführer Gautzsch. He said he was assistant to Reichsjugendführer Axmann and was concerned that a shipment of small arms and ammo consigned to Hitler Jugend personnel might go astray before it got to its warehouse in St. Johann. He said that he wanted me to send a party over there to supervise the unloading."

"Have any HJ people shown up for duty with you yet?"

Weiss shrugged. "There have been a few visitors from Berlin whose names I don't remember. A few snotty old men and some Bund Deutscher Maedel hens, all satisfied with themselves and full of bean breeze. But no troops. No teen-agers with hair on their chest and fight in their eyes. Promises. Just promises."

"How about weapons? Supplies?"

"Ha. A few cases of rifles, a Vierling or two. A box of Panzerfausts. Nothing you could give the Amis a headache with. I swear, Standartenführer, if Berlin wants to set up an honest-to-god Werewolf operation, something's got to happen fast. The Yankees will bring their grandchildren sight-seeing in the Alps before we can fire a shot down here."

Stachel nodded, permitting himself to show a trace of sympathy. "Well, that's why Fräulein Nagele and I are here. To look things over and make a report to the general."

"This General von Lemmerhof—who is he, and why don't I ever see him?"

"He has been placed in command of the Werewolf thing by the chief of staff himself. And, frankly, I don't know why you haven't seen him. It mystifies me, as well."

"Perhaps," Elfi put in, "he's off in the village with your SS squad, eh, Major?"

Weiss gave her a direct, fond stare, then grinned, obviously taken with this unusual woman. "It might do him some good at that." After a pause, he asked, "How come a lady like you is involved in engineering, fortifications? My God, the only engineers I've ever known are lardy old men with all the charm of dyspeptic alligators."

"If men can dance ballet, why can't women build forts?"

"Mm. I've never thought of it in that way."

"Perhaps we'd better take a look at that warehouse, Fräulein Nagele," Stachel suggested. "How do we find it, Weiss?"

"There's no direct, easy way. Take the main road to Worgl, then head east on the paved highway. Number One, it is. Ordinarily it's about thirty kilometers, but the road's been cut here and there, and the detours call for mountain goats. West of St. Johann, you'll see a sawmill and a cluster of houses. There's an inn, too; called Der Schwan. Turn left at the inn, on the side road there, and head north about a kilometer. You'll see a large barn on the right, next to the brook. That's it."

"Any troops there?"

"Whenever I've been there, I've seen a platoon of Waffen SS, half on guard here and there, half on housekeeping, rest period, so on. Up the road is a Flak outfit with a few Vierlings. Nothing sensational."

Stachel nodded and made a note or two on his pad, as he'd seen headquarters types do. "Very well. We'll find it." Giving Major Weiss a level, sincere stare, he added, "I'll look into things, Weiss. It's a waste, having an energetic type like you on duty in this wilderness. I'll see what I can do."

"May your days be blessed and filled with chocolate-covered diamonds, Herr Standartenführer. Come. I'll walk you to your car."

They went downstairs and out to the VW, with Weiss as

solicitous as a headwaiter. As they climbed into the car and settled in for the drive, the major peered under the canvas roof, his eyes showing curiosity.

"Excuse me, Standartenführer, but I simply must ask you before you leave—have we met somewhere before?"

Stachel shook his head. "I don't believe so, Weiss. I'd have remembered."

"Well, of course, and I should have, too. But I have this deplorable memory for names and faces and all that social Quatsch, and I thought maybe you and I had had a nip or two together somewhere, All I know is that, from the moment you walked in this afternoon, I've had this absolute conviction I should know you. Your face is somehow familiar to me."

Elfi laughed and said, "I think he looks like Konrad Kramer, the film star. Many people think he does. Don't you, Major Weiss?"

"Well, perhaps a bit around the eyes," Weiss said politely, "but it's more than that. It's—well, it's not important. But I had to ask you. I'd have stayed awake all night wondering, otherwise. I'm always losing sleep over irrelevant things. So, then—have a nice trip."

28

A CALM HAD settled over the mountains, and they drove through them, amiably taciturn, in the manner of old friends who had come a long way together. The sky had turned a royal blue, and the long, golden slants of sunlight trimmed the peaks with the delicate traceries of evening.

At one point Elfi glanced at him and said, "So what do you think about all that back there?"

Stachel hunched a shoulder. "It looks to me as if the Werewolf is a paper tiger. Somebody is setting up a nothing to do nothing."

"Somebody?"

"Well, it certainly isn't our esteemed friend General von Lemmerhof. It's apparent he hasn't the slightest idea of what's going on or the slightest intention of finding out."

Elfi rubbed her eyes and stifled a yawn. "Our mysterious SS Brigadeführer Gautzsch, then. He gives orders to the general, he gives orders to Major Weiss. I can only wonder two things. Who else does he give orders to, and from whom does he get his own orders?"

Elfi added, "I have the distinct impression that both Lemmerhof and Gautzsch, whoever he is, would have much preferred that we hadn't had our little chat with Major Weiss. I don't think they want us to know that the Werewolf thing is so flimsy. But if that's so, why didn't they use force or something? Why didn't they physically interfere?"

Stachel gave her a wry glance. "Because our health and well-being must be very important to them. You have your distinct impressions. Well, I have mine, too, and the main one is that Lemmerhof and whoever is behind him would do just about anything to keep us in good humor. We are the key to something. I'm sure of that."

"Then why did someone try to wipe us out when Tarbell parachuted in?"

"That was nothing more than Kaspar's trying to make some money. He was on the Gestapo payroll."

"Is he still?" The question implied that she'd already guessed the answer.

"No. I retired him from service."

She thought about that for a time. "Which means," she said finally, "that if Kaspar had been any more than a paid Gestapo

176

informant and the attempt to arrest us at the paradrop was part of a large scheme to destroy us, we—"

"We'd have been destroyed by now." He took a deep breath. "No, the official goblins don't know about us. But we are being set up for something, and I suspect there are some unofficial goblins we do have to fear."

"How about Major Weiss? Do you think he recognized you as Bruno Stachel, famous aviator?"

"I don't know. I rather doubt it."

"One thing for certain—he couldn't keep his eyes off your Tin Cravat."

"The general's Tin Cravat."

"Whatever. But the major is an ambitious man. I think he would do most anything to acquire his own Tin Cravat."

Stachel fell silent, his thoughts wandering.

* * *

She was instantly sorry she had mentioned the medal because she, perhaps more than he himself, knew how sensitive he was to these things. He made no secret of the fact that his Blue Max, the top award for meritorious military service in the first war, had been granted him by the Kaiser for an action he'd been too drunk to remember; and he swore that Hitler had given him the Blood Order—a medal awarded primarily to those who had been with the Führer in the fateful November 1923 Putsch—for his heroic participation in a march he'd in fact stumbled into, hung over and bleary after a night on the town. Bruno pretended dry amusement over all this history, and he'd been cynically indifferent to borrowing Lemmerhof's Tin Cravat, but she knew, with the certainty of a woman, that the pain of shame and unworthiness weighed heavily on him. It was difficult for one who despised hypocrisy in others to confront the fact of his own.

And I ought to know, she thought sourly.

In the beginning, familial propaganda had served as the

base for girlish mysticism, which saw God as a gigantic, unseen Tinkerer who fussed with the world like a wise and kindly general deliberating sand-table strategies. With adolescence, this Spartan concept had broadened and mellowed. Christ ceased to be mere Captain of the Good Guys and became the Tinkerer himself, slumming in masquerade. And at the turn of womanhood she'd become quite bookish about it and settled into a gentle emotionalism in which Christ, as the spring source of the civilizing forces of honesty, tolerance, justice, and decency, deserved her loyal and conscientious support. A Vote for Christ is a Vote for Gracious Living . . . . See Elfrieda Heidemann for details.

Until the calamity represented by Adolf Hitler, which revealed her for what she was: a cartoon Christian, a play-acting nurse, a sanctimonious reformed drunkard, and, all in all, a pompous phony.

Compassion for the fallen? Discernment of the evil? Support for the persecuted? Where had they been? Certainly not in her actions. But worse, where had her individual salvation been? Certainly not in her heart, because she had never, from the beginning, believed that a busy, decent fellow like God would have anything to do with a wretch like Elfi.

And now these new things in her—this serene capacity for fornication, to practice uninhibited, enthusiastic, and probably perverted sex with a man not her husband; this appalling readiness to kill, to enjoy the destruction of life, above and beyond any considerations of self-preservation. These were the culminating hypocrisies.

She had completed the transformation: She had at last become the kind of person she had always claimed to dislike the most.

And it would only get worse. The sex was too much fun, the killing was too satisfying, and her faith—whatever it had or had not been—was not up to the times and the needs.

God, if you're truly there somewhere, forgive me—I despise the Nazis, but I am like them.

*   *   *

The inn called Der Schwan had become a service club for transient soldiers, and its foyer and main lounge were filled with troops and their Klamotten—knapsacks and helmets and rifles. The low ceilings were almost obscured by smoke from ersatz tobacco, and the clamor was intense. Everyone seemed to be talking at once and at the top of his voice, and a radio in the corner by the stairway blared the eternal, omnipresent "Lili Marlene." Stachel went no farther than the entrance, since a full colonel in the Waffen SS, a wearer of the Knight's Cross, would be the center of much attention in that crowd. Turning away, he went down the steps and across the road to the VW.

"It's what the sign says it is," he told Elfi. "A Soldatenheim. A rest center for soldiers on leave, or being transferred from here to there and back. It's no place for us."

"Well, it's too dark to take a look at the barn. We'll have to spend the night some place."

Stachel peered through the twilight at the crossroads, and its scattering of houses, all dark behind shutters and blackout curtains. There was a sentry box beside a roadside crucifix, whose carved Jesus suffered in wooden solitude for those wayfarers who might stop for a prayer or two, and Stachel decided that the man on duty might have some ideas.

"Are there lodgings in the area?" he asked, slapping his gloves against the palm of his left hand in the slightly menacing manner of the Officers' Corps.

The man came to a brittle attention, jaw thrust out from the shadows of his Stahlhelm. "I believe the Standartenführer might inquire at that large Hof across the way. The one with the red shutters."

"I need fuel, too. Is there an SS Tankstelle nearby?"

"Not that I know of, sir. I've heard that fuel can be obtained at the airstrip near Nebelburg, on the plateau there. But I can't say for certain, sir. Most vehicles that come through here are woodburners."

"Airstrip? What kind of airstrip?"

The soldier's voice was thick from a head cold. "Regret to say, sir, I don't know, sir. It's just something I heard at the canteen. I was talking to a Luftwaffe mechanic last night and he said he was on duty out there and that this—last night—was the first he'd had any time off from a special project he was on."

"How do I get to Nebelburg?"

"Take this road here, up the hill beyond the big barn that's being used as a warehouse and motor pool, take the next left, and stay on that road until you get to the village of Going. Turn west there. Nebelburg is on the plateau at the foot of the Wildem Kaiser Range."

"Is there fuel at the motor pool?"

"Beg the Standartenführer's pardon, but those fellows up there wouldn't give a starving dog a kick in the ass. They are on some kind of special duty, and they keep to themselves."

"I see. Well, then, Nebelburg it is."

"It's a bad ride at night, sir. Perhaps you would benefit from a rest at the Hof and go in the morning."

"Good thinking, soldier. I might just do that. Good evening."

"Evening, Standartenführer. Heil Hitler."

Stachel returned the man's salute and sauntered back to the VW. When he got there he found Elfi sitting pale in the chalky light of hand torches held by two burly SS troopers. Standing in the reflected glow, looking smugly triumphant, was Major Weiss.

"Ah," Weiss said, "there you are. We've been waiting for you."

"What's going on here?"

"I finally remembered," Weiss said happily. "I thought and thought, and I finally remembered. You're Bruno Stachel. The great Bruno Stachel, flier of planes, idols of the ladies, and traitor first-class. And you are my prisoner."

29

"TELL ME, STACHEL —how in hell did you get all the way over here from America? My God, but you have a nerve. Whee."

Stachel stood quietly in the lowering night and blinked into the light with tired eyes. So. The inevitable had occurred. There was bound to be one, and here he was.

"What do you propose to do, Major Weiss?"

"Do? Why, I'm taking you two back to my headquarters, where I will hold you for the proper authorities. Then, once I've received proper credit for having captured one of the Reich's most-wanted criminals, I might just get that transfer out of that godforsaken hole I've been loathing for these past million years." Weiss was so elated Stachel would have not been surprised to see him dance.

Elfi said, "Perhaps we'd better let Major Weiss in on what we're doing here, Herr Stachel."

"I think not. He is after all, a mere army major."

Weiss snorted. "I know what you're doing here. You're spying for the Amis, that's what."

"Major Weiss," Elfi said coolly, "we are engaged in Geheimekommandosache—a most secret and sensitive mission in behalf of the High Command itself. We—"

Weiss broke in, "Come now, lady, don't try to sell me *that* Quatsch." To the two SS men, he snapped, "All right, we'll split them up. Stachel will go in our VW, with you driving, Thoma, and me in the back seat. We'll manacle the lady to the grip bar in their car and you will drive ahead of us, Vierecke, so I can keep my eye on both cars and both prisoners."

"As ordered, Herr Major."

The beams from the flashlight flickered as the troopers turned to the job. The man called Thoma slung his rifle and headed off for the other car, and Vierecke leaned his weapon against a tree, groping in his belt for the manacles dangling there.

Three soft snaps sounded in the gloom.

Weiss bent over slowly, as if peering at a bug at his feet, then folded in sections, like a carpenter's rule, to lie in a shapeless lump in the dark. Vierecke sat down, legs out-thrust, arms folded across his middle, slowly tilting sideways to die. Thoma said, "Ouch," almost annoyed, like a man pricked by a thorn. Then he fell, his helmet bouncing on the gravel.

"My God," Stachel grumped, "I thought you'd never get that peashooter uncorked."

"The silencer snagged on something in my handbag."

"It's good that those three were so busy admiring me, one of the Reich's most-wanted criminals. Otherwise they would have seen you struggling with the damned thing."

"What do we do now?"

"Help me lift them into their car. Then follow me in this one to that bridge to the southwest of here."

"The one that's fallen into the gorge?"

"That's the one. We'll roll them and their car off the end. After we empty their fuel tanks, of course."

"How about that sentry over there by the Soldatenheim?"

"I don't think he heard anything or he'd have come running."

"Surely he saw those rotten flashlights," she muttered.

"If he had, he'd have made a fuss about the breach of black-out regulations. He's probably dozing."

"Thank God for little favors."

* * *

They drove their tiny convoy through the now-completed darkness to the long hill, where the highway descended from a plateau to the chasm cut by a million years of snow runoff roaring down from the crags to the south. At the beginning of the downhill course, Stachel steered Weiss' VW off the road and waited until Elfi had pulled to a halt behind him.

"What's wrong?" she called.

He climbed out of the car and walked back to her. "I see hooded lights down by the bridge. I think it's a party of engineers working under camouflage nets. They must be trying to improvise a crossing over the broken span."

"What's your plan?"

"Do you have any lip rouge?"

"What?"

"A lipstick. For God's sake, woman, don't you carry a lipstick in that handbag of yours?"

"The Führer frowns on makeup."

"And I frown on Standartenführers, but I'm wearing one of their play suits. Come on—the lipstick, please."

"I can't see in this darkness."

"Use the hooded flashlight clamped to the dashboard."

With the help of the same light, he pulled a terrain chart from the VW's map pocket and, turning its blank side up, flattened it on the car hood. He scrawled a message with the lipstick.

"What does it say, Bruno?"

" 'Death to the Nazi Occupier!' Signed—'Women for a Free Austria.' "

"So we leave the bodies here with their car, and from the

message found with them, the authorities will think that partisans killed these people."

"God, but you're clever, Fräulein Nagele."

* * *

Traffic was fairly heavy on the highway approach to Nebelburg, which, Stachel thought, could be an advantage, since the more troop activity the less likelihood of undue fuss over the presence of a Standartenführer. He was too old, of course, for most of the lower ranks, the fact that had prescribed his cover after his clergyman's guise had been blown. It would have induced even more curiosity and questions if he had chosen to go civilian, since a civilian calling on military commanders and making military inquiries could, in the edgy lay mind, mean one of two extremes: Gestapo or enemy agent. The equivalent of colonel was high enough to put lower-ranked personnel on the polite, deferential side, and not so high as to raise the suspicions of general-grade officers. While an SS Standartenführer was a formidable figure in any milieu, his chances of blending in increased in direct proportion to the numbers of troops knocking about.

He shifted the car to low gear behind a woodburning bus whose rear-mounted cylindrical gas generator emitted a foul-smelling smoke. Ahead of the bus were three horse-drawn artillery pieces waiting to make a left turn on the west-bound highway for Kufstein and the Bavarian plain. On their way to hold the line at the Rhine, Stachel mused, drawn from some obscure post in some backwater of the war. Everything was headed north and west these days; everything but the schemers and their postwar machinations, their little Werewolf games for the benefit of a gullible Eisenhower.

Beyond the crossroads, where the highway entered the village, there was a road barrier flanked by a sentry box and a small wooden provost shack. A line of horse wagons, two Wehrmacht trucks, a treaded personnel carrier, and a knot of civilians waited for a lieutenant to check trip tickets and ID cards. After considering the situation for a moment, Stachel gunned the VW out of the line and drove briskly to the checkpoint.

"What are you doing?" Elfi said in a low voice.

"I have too much rank to wait humbly in line. A Standartenführer who waits in line is no Standartenführer, my dear Fräulein Nagele."

The lieutenant pushed back from his desk, then stamped officiously for their car. "Just what in hell do you think you're doing? By God, I—Oh. Excuse me, Standartenführer. I didn't see you in this rotten light."

"Who are you?" Stachel snapped.

"Leutnant Oswold Vestner, sir. Of the Geheime Feld Polizei, Kufstein detachment."

"Where do I find the airstrip here, Vestner?"

The lieutenant looked flustered. "Well, sir, that's a most confidential facility. I'm under the strictest orders to permit no traffic whatsoever to pass that way. Unless, of course, the Standartenführer has Marschbefehle that take him there on official business."

"Who gave such an asinine order?"

"All respect, sir, I know only that I'm to keep all personnel"—he inserted apologetically—"of whatever rank, from the area unless specifically authorized by my headquarters or if the individual seeking admission carries travel orders issued by OKL, Berlin, and endorsed by the airfield commandant. If you can produce such Marschbefehle, and the, ah, lady's Kennkarte shows she's not entered on the blacklist, I'll be happy to escort you to the airfield myself."

Stachel let his annoyance show. "Vestner, I did not request a lecture on your little protocols. I wanted simply to know where the airfield lies. Fräulein Nagele here is a construction engineer specializing in airfield drainage systems. It is her mission to study possible sites for auxiliary runways. We were on assignment elsewhere when this mission was assigned by radio."

"Sorry, sir. I'd like very much to be helpful, but I must obey my orders. Perhaps if you were to take a room at the Gasthof over there tonight, your situation could be clarified in the morning."

"I must obey my orders, too, Vestner. Out of my way."

"Before you pass, Standartenführer, may I see your papers?"

Stachel handed him the Marschbefehle signed by Lemmerhof and authorizing "an inspection tour of Tyrolean facilities." Elfi passed out her little gray Kennkarte, the ID card carried by all civilians over fourteen years of age, which in this case informed the world that here was Luisa Nagele, doctor of engineering, OKW, Berlin. Vestner took the credentials to the provost shack, where they could see him check the green-covered blacklist under a desk lamp.

Bringing the papers back, Vestner was especially obsequious. "I sincerely hope the Standartenführer and Fräulein Nagele will understand my inability to speed them on their way. But I do recommend the Gasthof"—he nodded at the blue-shuttered, white stucco building on the square—"where there are special accommodations for officers. The food is quite passable, too, and if—"

"Out of my way, Vestner."

Stachel slammed the car into gear and drove with a spattering of gravel to the Gasthof, where he pulled into a parking place, turned off the motor, and drew the padlock chain through the steering wheel. In the silence he sighed, and, giving Elfi a wide-eyed stare, imitated Leutnant Vestner's oily fawning. "Perhaps the Fräulein Ingenieur would like to dismount from the car and permit the Standartenführer to escort her to the dinner."

* * *

The old man at the desk had assigned them a room under the eaves—"the only one we have left, I'm afraid, but it has a nice view of the Kaiser Range in the morning light"—and, after a meal of rabbit ragout, brown bread, and a rather decent cup of tea, they went upstairs. They washed in a porcelain basin and, in the silence that had fallen between them, he saw evidence of a new mood in her. Where before she had been brittle and alert, there was now a certain aloofness—a sense of her withdrawal from the present. He wanted to ask her about it, but decided that it would amount to some vague sort of imposition, or intrusion. So he kept to himself, going carefully, even when, while brushing her hair, she said, "I feel awful."

"Oh? How so?"

"Depressed. All of a sudden. Very down."

"You've had a bad day, all in all."

"I killed three men this evening."

"And if you hadn't, we'd be dead tomorrow."

"I hate myself."

"You're a good soldier. You're brave. Smart. I consider it a privilege to soldier with you."

"I don't *want* to be a soldier. I—" Her voice fell off, and she sat on the bed, pale and unhappy in the candlelight.

He stood before her and took her chin in his hand, lifting her face to him. "Easy."

"Oh, God, Bruno. I'm a terrible person. I'm a rotten, two-faced, murdering hypocrite." Her mouth began to quiver, and there were tears. He sat beside her, taking her gently into his arms, saying nothing and letting her weep.

* * *

Her lovemaking was incandescent, feverish, grasping, demanding. She cried out once: a cursing in the darkness.

* * *

Toward dawn, he sat upright—rigid, listening.

"What is it?" she asked, instantly alert beside him.

"Hear that?"

"The roaring? The motor sound across the valley?"

"Yes. Do you recognize it?"

"It sounds like an airplane. We've been hearing them off and on, ever since we got here."

"But this is not just an airplane. Not just any airplane."

She listened, tensely, a smooth warmth against him. "You're right. I know that sound."

"You should. You've heard it enough, God knows. Wherever that airfield is, whoever is assigned there, one thing is certain—they're working with a B-17."

30

FOR SOME REASON, Tarbell found Stachel on his mind—a continuing presence in the mishmash of thought that had come and gone since he'd awakened. He sat at the radio on the garage roof, setting the dials precisely and listening to the restless trees, and, unprefaced by the slightest suggestion, he remembered the story (Who had written it? O. Henry?) of the country boy who goes to the city, falls in with a gang, and, abandoning the principles he'd been brought up to honor, becomes a pickpocket. On the street one day he sees a girl he had known back home. In her face he sees the long-forgotten purity and freshness of youth, and he collapses against a lamppost, red with shame and remorse and moaning, "I wish I could die." There was no purity and freshness of youth in Stachel, that was certain, and so why his mind had made this connection was unclear. Unless, of course, the anger and fear and resentment that obviously had twisted the German's life was, in fact, what O. Henry had been writing about.

His wristwatch said it was time, so he went on the air, and after the usual introductory exchange, Airboy's cheery British cadences came across the void.

"Hullo, Nightstick. Hope everything's tutti-frutti for you down there. Over."

"Hi, Airboy. Nightstick leader is on recon, as reported earlier. No word as yet, and all's quiet otherwise. Over."

"Good show. I have a word for you from Home Plate. Please copy. Message follows. 'Home Plate to Nightstick leader. Most urgent that you Peter-Pan Whisper to Home Plate tomorrow. Whisper will give you details on course to be traveled in Peter-Panning. Looking forward to reunion.' End message. Did you copy, Nightstick? Over."

"Message received, Airboy. Anything else? Over."

"Not a syllable, old shoe. Home Plate indicates transmitted message will give you altogether enough to handle. Over."

"Home Plate is right. Peter-Panning is difficult indeed when you haven't got anything to Peter-Pan in. Over."

"How dreadfully true. But I'm sure you'll manage. As Cornwallis said at Yorktown, 'You damned Colonials always come up with something.' Memorable words. Uplifting. Over."

"Trouble is, us damned Colonials is all a bunch of Germans. Over."

"Then maybe you can ride back on one of those V-2s, eh? Over."

Tarbell sounded a gentle raspberry: "To you, Airboy. Over."

"Toodle-oodle, Nightstick. Great gobs of luck. Out."

*   *   *

Securing the radio, folding the card table and camp chair, Tarbell stowed the gear under the tarpaulin beneath the mansard's eave and then went through the window and down the loft ladder to the garage floor. He felt old and tired and dispirited, as he always did after contact with Airboy. The wonderfully friendly voice was the voice of the world that was lost to him now, and when the set clicked off, he was impossibly alone and vulnerable in a world of great malevolence. The feeling intensified when he heard, far off, the whistle and blattering of a low-flying P-51, one of the seemingly innumerable American fighters that ranged so arrogantly over Bavaria. He thought of its pilot, and what he might say if he knew that the sound of his airplane's engine had brought almost intolerable homesickness to Amos E. Tarbell, Colonel, U.S. Army Air Corps, serial number 0-545169, grubbing about a backyard in Munich-goddamn-Germany.

He went through the kitchen door and up the service stairway to his room at the side of the house, where he sprawled faceup on the bed and listened to the morning. He wondered what it would be like to live in a house like this, with a woman, say. A pretty wife. He had never been much with women, having disdained the bordello and the easy liaisons of army towns; the first represented no challenge and the second was suspect, since he recognized his basic unattractiveness to the woman of taste. Should a female show interest in Amos Tarbell, one could only assume that she was nymphomaniacal or goofy-bored and thus a danger to be avoided at all costs.

Below, a car pulled into the driveway, and, curious, he arose and went to the window. It was a large black Mercedes, and, as he watched, a very tall man in a black leather field coat and SS officer's cap climbed from behind the steering wheel, slammed the door, and hurried up the walk and into the house. There were muffled voices, and the sound of movement in the lower hallway. He went to his door and stood there, listening.

"Morning, Gautzsch," von Lemmerhof's voice said.

"Are we alone?"

"Stachel and the woman are in the Tyrol today, much against my wishes. The American is on the carriage-house roof for a dawn radio contact. He's usually out there for some time, so I think we can forget about him. Stachel's my worry. I just hope he returns by tomorrow night, as promised."

The big man's basso rumbled in the stairwell. "No matter. Stachel will be back. He's very adept, and by the day after tomorrow it won't matter who knows what. Do you have anything to report?"

"No. Come into the library, and sit down, won't you?"

Gautzsch said, "No time. I just dropped by to see how things are going."

"All right, I guess. Stachel has been his usual insufferable self. God, what an unpredictable smart aleck. I'd forgotten how bad he is."

"Did you know that he shot your chauffeur?"

"Kaspar?" Von Lemmerhof sounded incredulous, shocked.

"Mm. It seems he learned that Kaspar was a Gestapo informant."

"I can hardly believe that. Kaspar's been with me too long for that kind of treachery."

"Sorry, but it's so."

"God. Are we still secure?"

"Yes. Kaspar had no real connections. He was a petty leech." Then, after a pause: "You should be getting the signal to fly out very soon now. The 'Schmetterling' alert precedes your action code by only two days."

"Perhaps that's what the Ami is on the roof for."

"I hope so. Wiseguy is very restless, anxious for things to culminate."

The general said, "Well, even gods have to wait, they tell me. Things are going well at Fuglein Kompanie?"

"So-so. General Linck is having trouble keeping Berger reined in. Berger is an activist, and that runs counter to the long-range plan, which calls for quiet waiting."

"Berger's an ass. I'll never understand why they chose him to head up Fuglein."

"He has a head for business, it seems. And with the kind of money we're dealing with, we need all the talent we can dig up."

"Mm."

"Well, I'd better be going. Send me a note if there's anything urgent. The phones never work these days. Like the gas and electricity. One bomb, it seems, and all services stop. God, whatever happened to good, old-fashioned German ingenuity?"

"These are bad times, Gautzsch."

"See you later, then, eh?"

There was an interval, then the sound of the car door's slamming. The motor whirred into life and the Mercedes crunched around the oval to hum off to the north and the boulevard.

Tarbell eased along the hallway to the back stairs, then, descending softly to the ground floor, opened and then shut the kitchen door with a slam. He went to the library and, peering through the archway, asked the general, "Who was here just now? I heard a car."

Von Lemmerhof glanced up from his breakfast tray. "Provisions delivery."

"Oh." After a slight hesitation, Tarbell said, "Are you interested in what Airboy had to say?"

"Why should I be interested? Stachel has all the say around here. No matter what I might think, Stachel will ultimately decide as to whether Airboy's message was interesting or not."

Tarbell clucked his tongue. "Such resignation. Such indifference. Such Weltschmerz. No wonder you Germans are losing the war."

"Don't laugh too soon, Unteroffizier Folger." Lemmerhof

gave the title a disdainful emphasis. "You might defeat an army, but you can never kill an idea."

* * *

Tarbell went to the cellar, where Feldwebel Hansen worked with his papers and stamps and printing presses. Hansen was set up at one end of the room, while the large pantry area at the other end was given over to wardrobe and equipment supplies supervised by a thin-faced old actor named Grinsel, who always whistled tunelessly and was said by Hansen to have once been associated with the UFA film studios.

"Where's Grinsel, Hansen?"

"He is visiting a friend at what's left of the Wehrmacht supply depot in Riem. Something about uniforms, as I recall."

Tarbell nodded. "I see. What are you up to?"

"I am forging American army vehicle trip tickets."

"Trip tickets? What for?"

"This, I understand, is to cover certain big shots against the day when you Amis occupy our fair land and the certain big shots need to run around in nonexistent cars on fruitless errands. It is hoped that these trip tickets will ease their passage."

Tarbell smiled. "Do I hear a tone of doubt in your voice, Feldwebel?"

Hansen snorted. "Doubt? You don't hear doubt. You hear scorn. What man in his right mind would expect Ami occupying forces to grant standard military vehicle trip tickets to German nationals who want to grunt around in their old woodburners? The Amis are sure to issue specially printed, probably serial-numbered, permissions to drive vehicles. Everything will be special. What's the sense in wasting this scarce paper? I ask you."

Tarbell decided to gamble. "These trip tickets are for Linck and Berger at Fuglein Kompanie?"

"Oh," Hansen said, shooting him a glance through his thick

193

spectacles, "You know about Fuglein, then. The general said you would not be made privy to that phase."

"Believe me, Hansen, I know a great deal more than either you or the general can imagine," Tarbell said smoothly. "As a matter of fact, it would behoove you to hold back nothing from me. Or Stachel. Or Frau Heidemann. In these matters we are your superiors, and you would suffer unpleasantly if you were to anger us. Especially our dear, gentle Stachel."

Hansen shrugged. "It's no great matter to me. I'm just waiting out the war."

"So then—what are you doing for Fuglein Kompanie?"

"Trip tickets, as I say. War-Important Work passes. Kennkarte. Drivers' licenses. Truck registrations. Business licenses. Tax stamps. Letterheads, billing forms. All that kind of manure."

"What do they need all those for?"

Hansen showed impatience with such a stupid question. "After all, if they're going into the moving-van and delivery business, they're going to have to have documents that make them look authentic. Why else, for God's sake?"

Tarbell recognized thin ice, so he backed off. "Sure. It was a silly question." He paused, then, to create a little good will, asked, "Is there anything you need? Anything I can arrange to make life a little easier for you?"

It worked. Hansen, obviously, was one who went through life feeling unappreciated. He gave Tarbell a lingering, softening glance, and then smiled sheepishly. "I could sure use a little female company. It gets lonesome down here in the cellar."

Tarbell returned the smile. "I'll see what I can do."

31

STACHEL AND ELFI were in the alley beside the Gasthof, putting their bags in the VW, when there was a rumbling, then a rising roar and clatter that intensified as the vehicles entered Nebelburg's medieval streets. The column was led by the inevitable motorcycle, with a pompous lieutenant filling its sidecar, followed by a tractor-trailer combination and three heavy cargo trucks, all battened down and enigmatic, and it ground to a halt in the town square beside a kiosk whose posters reminded the world that the Enemy Is Listening, Winter-Help Needs Your Gift, the Führer Will Lead Us to Victory, the Women of Greater Germany Strive Tirelessly for Adolf Hitler and His Goals.

"What are you doing?" Elfi said, struggling with the tent-rolls. "Give me a hand here."

Stachel, staring at the column reflectively, said, "In a moment. I'm thinking."

The lieutenant swung stiffly from the sidecar and strode to the canteen, where he disappeared through a door marked FOR OFFICERS ONLY. All motors had stopped, Stachel noted, which meant that the trucks would not be moving on for a time, and two of the drivers had dropped to the cobblestones to walk about, stretching their legs.

"Did you notice that there's a peculiar atmosphere here?" Stachel muttered.

"From the first. From last night, with all that business with Vestner at the checkpoint outside the village, with the airplane sounds. There's a tension. A feeling that something is, or will be, going on."

"The license plates on those trucks begin with WL, for Wehrmacht-Luftwaffe. They're not standard ground-force transports, they're air force. Which means they must be heading for the airstrip."

195

"Unless," Elfi said dryly, "they're returning from the airstrip."

"No. They would not be buttoned down so tightly if they'd been there, unloaded, then left. See how those tarpaulins are pulled? Like drumheads, they're so tight. That means there's a load inside."

"Which is more than I can say for this VW." Elfi humphed, lashing a tie rope to the rear passenger grip bar. "Are you ever going to help me, or am I now completely your wife?"

He gave her an amused glance. "You have yet to shine my boots."

"You know what you can do with your boots," she said, smiling and making a face.

It pleased him to see her relative cheeriness. Her gloom and self-accusation of the night before had left no trace in the morning, and this was good, because the day promised to be a risky one. Since dawn he had studied his terrain map, analyzing contours for likely airstrip locations. His plan had been to go scouting, and, if the field were to turn up, do what he could to examine it through binoculars from higher ground. But now, with the arrival of the convoy, another idea began to form.

"Come on," he said. "Get in the car."

"We're not finished here."

"We'll get it later. Right now we're going to run down to the provost office."

"Whatever for?"

"When I pull up outside, you stay in the car and start a conversation with whoever's on duty at the checkpoint table. I'll be going into the shack, and, if I'm lucky, I shouldn't be more than five minutes."

She climbed into the passenger seat, saying, "What should I talk about?"

"The weather. Soccer. How in hell should I know?"

They drove through the brilliant morning to the road junction west of the village gate, and, to Stachel's relief, saw that Leutnant Vestner had been replaced as duty officer by a pudgy Oberleutnant who sat in the sunlight and regarded the world with slightly baffled eyes. He forced himself erect and came over to the car, squinting.

"Help you, Standartenführer?" he said, glancing at Elfi.

"Do you have a road map in that office there?" Stachel demanded in the SS manner. "For this area, I mean."

"Yes sir. But it's fairly old and in bad shape."

"We're somewhat lost, you see," Elfi put in helpfully.

"I am not lost, Fräulein Nagele," Stachel bristled. "I'm simply looking for a shorter route."

"As you wish," Elfi drawled, winking at the Oberleutnant.

Stachel went into the shack, where a Gefreiter sat at a typewriter and pecked unhappily at a supply form. The man was not overwhelmed with the arrival of a glowering Standartenführer, choosing to rise slowly from his chair and strike a position halfway between attention and slouch. "Morning, sir."

"Where is your road map?"

"In the drawer here somewhere, sir."

"Well, let me see it. Why are you waiting?"

While the man began a dispirited rummaging, Stachel's gaze raced around the small room. In the corner, by the window, there was a desk, obviously the duty officer's, and, on the wall above it, a sheaf of mimeographed general orders. He crossed the room to pretend an interest in the orders, but as he stood there, peering, his hand went to the desk top, where he had seen an ink pad and stamp. Quickly, silently, he slid these into his left tunic sleeve and turned to face the Gefreiter just as the man arose from his search of a drawer to announce, "Somebody must have borrowed the map, Standartenführer. I can't seem to find it in all this clutter."

"I'm not surprised, given the condition of this pigsty. God, when was the last it was swept? And look at that window. Disgraceful. A sad commentary on what the German Army has become."

197

"Yes, sir, Standartenführer."

"What do you mean, 'Yes, sir'?"

"I don't know, sir. It seemed like the right thing to say."

"God."

Stachel returned to the sunlight to find the Oberleutnant leaning on the VW, assuring Elfi that it would be a distinct pleasure for him to show her the view from Weissgipfel if she could join him after his duty tour this day.

"That's very dear of you, Oberleutnant Elke. It excites me even to think of it, but that awful Standartenführer I must travel with plans an immediate return to Munich." She sighed.

"Can't you arrange to stay over, or something?" Oberleutnant Elke purred, unaware of Stachel's arrival.

"Certainly she can," Stachel rasped. "I'd be delighted to have her remain here. Women engineers are a mockery of the profession, and I'd be well rid of her."

The man spun about, crimson and flustered. "I'm sorry, Standartenführer, I—"

"Out of my way, you sex maniac."

*   *   *

Back at the Gasthof, Stachel borrowed the innkeeper's portable typewriter and took it to their room. He placed the machine on the small table by the open casement, then rolled in their Marschbefehle and began punching the keys with a finger.

"What are you doing?"

"Amending our letter of authority from Lemmerhof."

She read aloud over his shoulder. "'Endorsed and approved this office by undersigned this date. Please grant bearers access to all privileged information and stations.'"

He removed the letter from the typewriter and placed it flat on the wooden table. Loading his stolen stamp on the ink pad, he pounded it across the newly typed endorsement.

"'GFP—Kufstein,'' Elfi read. "What's that?"

198

"Secret Field Police, Kufstein office. Now, take that pen and scratch some initials in the lined space there. And put yesterday's date after it."

"Why don't you do it?"

"Because your handwriting is much worse than mine. This should be hard to read."

"I have a very nice handwriting," she said, scribbling.

"You have a way with Oberleutnants, too."

"Do you know that man put his pudgy little hand on my knee?"

"What do you expect? I've put my hand there myself now and then. It's a natural thing for a fellow to do."

She pulled a pillow from the bed and hit him with it.

* * *

The convoy rumbled along at a fairly good rate over the macadam highway from Nebelburg to Going. Then turning east toward St. Johann, it maintained its speed along the valley road below the Wildem Kaiser Range, a great gray wall of snow-spotted mountains that formed the vestibule to the towering Alpine crags farther east, west, and south. Between the Kaiser and the valley bed, where a sparkling river coursed, there was a broad, elevated shelf of open country dotted by farms and woodland patches. It was this plateau that had impressed Stachel as the most likely location of an airfield, and, indeed, it was this plateau for which the convoy seemed to be headed. He kept the VW at a proper distance to the rear of the truck column—far enough to suggest to the casual observer that he and Elfi were part of the parade, but not so close as to become an irritant for the convoy commander.

"Hold on," Stachel said eventually, "there's a gate and a guard station ahead. This is where we see how good our forged endorsement is."

"If there's trouble, do you want me to shoot?"

"Only when all else fails. We'll try to bluff our way as far as we can. Shooting should be a last resort."

She touched his hand with hers. "If we don't make it, I want you to know that I wouldn't have changed any of this."

"We'll make it."

"I didn't want to be a blubbering fool last night."

He patted her hand. "I'm glad you were. You did the blubbering for both of us."

* * *

The road, a secondary made of packed gravel, curved down a gentle hill. The guard station's twin houses, camouflaged with daubs of gray and green, flanked the road where the curve ended and the road resumed a straightaway rise to a fenced-off sweep of pasture. As the trucks thundered down the slope, the black and white barrier pole across the road lifted and a pair of guards, rifles slung, stood stiffly to either side, making the traffic policeman's arm-sweeping signal to pass through.

"They're not even slowing down," Elfi said.

"Then we won't either."

The motorcycle, the tractor-trailer, then the three trucks roared through the gateway, the turbulence of their passing sending up swirls of dust and causing the guard shacks to shudder perceptibly. Stachel gunned the VW ahead to where it clung almost to the shadow of the rearmost truck, and as they raced past the barricade he could see the soldiers standing stiffly, arms outthrust in the Deutscher Gruss.

"What are they doing now?" Elfi asked tautly, not wanting to look back.

Stachel sent a glance to the rearview mirror. "They are lighting cigarettes. At least that's what it looks like. There's a lot of dust back there."

"My God."

"Yes."

"They thought we were part of the convoy."

"Yes."

"Now all we have to do is get out again."

"Yes."

32

ATOP THE RISE and beyond a stand of evergreens, the plateau stretched for a mile or more, flat and treeless. In the mid-distance was a cluster of low buildings, heavily camouflaged with great nets and twists of green, purple, and gray cloth. The largest structure, obviously an aircraft hangar, was ingeniously draped so as to appear from the air to be a small hillock, and sitting on its crest, serene in the Alpine sunlight, was a full-scale chalet, complete with smoke from the chimney and geranium boxes under the windows—all but the smoke fashioned of papier-mâché. The airstrip itself was dotted with dummy cows in the attitude of grazing, and here and there were cardboard shepherds' huts, green with fake moss and gray with painted age.

The Convoy slowed to a crawl so as not to disturb this intricate make-believe, eventually pulling under the nets to halt, rumbling and chattering, in the dappled shadows in front of the hangar. Stachel steered the VW into a sharp right turn and drove behind the hangar, where he parked at the end of a tidy row of four identical vehicles.

"Now what do we do?" Elfi whispered.

"We make like engineers," Stachel said, turning off the motor. "Come on. Bring your clipboard and slide rule."

"Aren't you going to padlock the car?"

"No. We might have to leave in a hurry."

They went to what appeared to be a rear service entrance to the hangar, where Stachel tried the door and found it to be unlocked. He opened it, then peered through, carefully.

"What is it, Bruno?"

"It looks like a small office and parts department. Shelves with boxes, tools, that kind of thing."

"Are we going in?"

"Let's look around outside first."

"Where is everybody? It's so—deserted."

"Up front, I think. At least that's where the noises are coming from."

They sauntered along the hangar's length, pausing occasionally as if to make notes. As they went, Stachel's mind was busy with questions, one of which Elfi asked.

"I wonder why those guards didn't stop the convoy at the gate? It's absolutely un-German not to check Marschbefehle and Kennkarten and Soldbücher and bills of lading and birth certificates and golf scores and Strudel recipes whenever there's a gate and a guard. How come the guards here waved everybody through?"

Stachel said, "And why the Deutscher Gruss? I mean, how many trucks carrying potatoes and piston rings and paper clips rate a formal salute?"

"Weren't they saluting you?"

"They didn't even see me until the last second. They were saluting the convoy. And that's odd, Fräulein Ingenieur Nagele."

They fell silent, thinking about these things. A breeze, full of spring, stirred suddenly, bringing the suggestion of clover and distant flowers, and in a whimsy of mind, Stachel recognized the metaphor in a fresh, renewing world beyond a dying war's obscuring nets. It was a fleeting thing, a splinter of thought, but it stabbed him and hurt in some unspecific way. As always, he used action as an antidote.

"Let's try in here, shall we?" He opened a door in the side of the great building and helped her through.

The hangar was a vast cavern of gloom and drafts. The chill was so pervasive, so darkly insistent, it was nearly tangible, like ice water, and the thin light from the gently swinging bulbs far overhead seemed to cling to the high girders as if it feared the shadows below. Stachel's sense of oppression deepened as he closed the door behind them and surveyed the scene.

Standing central in the dusk, brooding in chilled silence as if mourning summer skies, was a Focke-Wulf 200, an enormous four-engine transport whose black-green surfaces glistened in the patina of countless polishings and whose nose lifted high and aloof above the knot of men gathered before it.

Stachel reflexively held out a hand to caution Elfi as his gaze focused on the scene. From the darkness in which he stood, he counted five mechanics standing respectfully under the airplane's wing, a dozen SS troopers at ceremonial attention across the partly opened hangar door, and, beyond them in the dappled sunlight, he could see the tractor-trailer, whose open rear doors revealed a plush interior furnished with easy chairs, coffee table, a desk, and assorted lamps.

"Look," Elfi hissed, her German sibilants sounding awe. "Those men. Those two men in front of the plane."

"I see them," he muttered.

They were standing in the hands-behind-the-back posture that had become the cliché stance of German military masters. Their uniforms were creased and spangled perfection; their conversation was muted and correct, in the fashion of academicians and morticians. They spoke little, however, preferring to listen to the obsequious monologue of an Oberst who, while pointing out various features of the airplane, managed to sound like a ten-Pfennig cicerone for sightseers on the Reeperbahn.

"Are they really—" Elfi was unable to complete the question.

"They are. Göring and Himmler."

"You are sure?"

"I've lived with the bastards long enough, God knows."

"What are they doing here? I mean, aren't they in Berlin with the Führer—I mean, that's what everybody thinks—"

Stachel held up a silencing finger. "Maybe we can hear what they're saying."

They listened intently, but because of the distance the echoes were heavy and garbled. The Oberst seemed to be making much of the auxiliary fuel tanks attached to the airplane's wing tips, and at one point Stachel could hear an assurance that "the ship has an unprecedented range for an aircraft of this type," and "plenty of room for passengers and cargo," but the preponderance was gibberish, all hollow and rebounding in the huge vault.

He gave in finally to the pressure of old memories, the weird nostalgia that came from the grotesque Hitler years. To see Hermann the Fat—broad, balloonlike in a pale-blue uniform—was to see his own past. He had known Göring since the final days of the first war, when Göring had been a slim, piercing-eyed combat pilot of wide renown; and he knew at this moment, watching the man, how close he had come to being what Göring was now—a mountain of self-indulgence, deceit, and drug-induced delusion. Himmler, the taciturn and reticent tyrant who had come from farm-country obscurity to preside as Hitler's policeman, had never been more to Stachel than someone with whom to make small talk at a reception; old friends they were not, but each of them knew—and was wary of—the other's capacity for duplicity.

Reassured by the atrocious accoustics, Stachel nevertheless kept his voice low. "It would seem that somebody important is getting ready to take a long journey."

"Could this be the airplane we heard this morning?"

"No. It was a B-17, sure enough. German engines have a characteristic sound, a kind of thrum-thrum sound, because they're unsynchronized. I've never paid much attention to what an FW-200 sounds like, but I guarantee you, I recognize four Wright engines working in synchronization, and that's what we heard. And what we heard was much closer than this hangar is to Nebelburg."

"What does all that mean?"

"It means that there's a B-17 around someplace. But it's out there on the meadow somewhere—west of here, toward Nebelburg. It has to be. I heard it. And so did you."

"Is that important?"

"I don't know. It could simply be one of the black outriders the Luftwaffe uses to keep track of American raiders en route to target areas in the Reich. Or it could be part of all this hocus-pocus. I'd like to find out which."

"Why? What does that have to do with our mission? Lemmerhof is our concern, not these people and their airplane. Not B-17s and your curiosity." Her tone was confused and filled with sudden irritation.

He glanced at her quickly. Their eyes met for only a moment, but he had caught sight of the very real fear behind hers. It struck him again, the remarkable good fortune she represented; she was not only a very handsome woman and a splendid lover, she was also a courageous, audacious, inventive comrade in difficult going; and yet, for all this, he had pushed her to her limit over the past two days. It was time to take her out of the line, as they used to say in his old wartime squadron days when a fellow pilot showed symptoms of shredding.

"We've seen enough for today," he said softly. "Come, we'll go back to the car."

"How are we going to get out?" Her voice was taut now, her nervousness on the surface.

"The same way we came in. We'll go down the road, wait for the convoy to take the big shots back to wherever it is they're going, and then trail them out the gate."

He took her arm and turned her toward the doorway behind them in the gloom. And as he did, another door marked TOILETTE opened and a man emerged, adjusting his visored cap, to walk straight for them.

Stachel, stunned, instinctively did the only thing available to him. He halted, crashed his heels together, threw back his shoulders, and stood motionless, eyes straight ahead, thumbs on trouser seams, and toes at a forty five-degree angle.

Bormann hesitated for only the tiniest splinter of time, his

205

small eyes staring directly into Stachel's, then he brushed on, making for the group beside the airplane, his heels clicking hollowly on the concrete.

33

THE RETURN TO Munich had been as uneventful as war allows. They used the Autobahn at first, primarily to determine how much of it was passable, but on a stretch near Miesbach, Ami fighters had caused a huge traffic jam by catching a motorized infantry battalion during its dash from somewhere to somewhere and reducing it to a mile-long junk pile. So they had turned north on a detour to Bad Aibling, then drove northwest through Peiss to another disruption that sent them to Haar, southeast of the city, and west into Bogenhausen.

Near Perlach she'd said, "You're so very quiet. You still think he recognized us, don't you?"

"There was simply no chance for him not to. He looked directly at me. He saw both of us. I've known him for years. He wants me for treason. He shot our friends before our very eyes one fine day in 1938. And on this fine day in 1945 he did not do a single frigging thing about it. Why? Why would that be?"

"I can't tell you, Bruno. I've lost all track of reality. Nothing makes sense anymore."

"Well, I think I know why."

"Then tell me, please," she sighed, elaborately long-suffering, "why did Martin Bormann, Adolf Hitler's deputy, refuse to acknowledge the presence of two traitors at a most-secret airfield hidden in the Tyrolean Alps?"

"I said I think I know why. But I'm still thinking."

She made no further comment, sitting beside him, hunched against the incoming evening's chill and watching the passing ruins with indifference.

He fell into moody reminiscence, evoking vignettes of his toadying cultivation of Bormann in the old Haidhausen beer-hall days; of his playing Bormann's greed and ambition against Göring's, and God help him, even Hitler's; of his lamentable inability to kill Bormann when the opportunity had come; of his helplessness when watching the Baroness von Klingelhof-und-Reimer—lusty, tender, silly-but-intelligent Lotte—go down in Bormann's gunfire. From these gloomy ramblings his mind went on a search for the elusive strand of fact that would have tied the whole thing together. That there was such a strand he was positive; a nagging certainty in his belly, or spleen, or kidney, or whatever makes a man certain, told him that in all the confusion and chicanery there was a Something—a single piece of revelation lurking just beyond recognition. It was in plain sight, he was sure of that, like Polly Loomis's artifact hidden in plain sight on the mantel, or her Bing Crosby's selling peanuts at a ball game. There was something obvious and hidden within reach, with a decoy directly in front of his nose.

According to his mother all those years ago, God works in wondrous ways his miracles to perform. Her claim won considerable support as he drove through the twilight along the Isar, because he experienced at that moment a kind of miracle of perception. His thoughts had been roaming from Bormann's evil to Elfi's good, then to life, to death, to airplanes, to Polly Loomis, to Amos Tarbell, to Wright engines, to hunger, to cars, to Göring, to Otto Heidemann, to his father, to Camp Ritchie, to sex, to the coming summer and his chances of living to see it. And then, in a passing from not-knowing to knowing, he could see—in framework, at least—what he had been missing. What was really going on.

"Damn."

"What is it, Bruno?"

"I'll tell you later," he said, steering the VW into the driveway circle.

* * *

Tarbell was waiting for them at the door, his faint, superior air in place, his Unteroffizier's uniform open at the collar. "You were out the whole night together," he said. "What will Mother say? What will our friends say? The whole town will be gossiping."

"Where's the general?" Stachel said, pulling off his gloves.

"In the study, writing notes. He's always in the study writing notes."

"Tell him to stay there. After we've freshened up a bit, I want to talk with him. With you and Elfi, too."

"What do you want to eat?" she said, making for the kitchen.

"Anything. We'll have it in the study while we talk."

"I've got a few things to tell you, too," Tarbell drawled.

"All right. I'll be there in a moment."

* * *

Evening softened the view from the kitchen window, and the rear garden, a bleak still-life of fences and brown lawn and dormant shrubs, was almost pretty in the lemon light. But, as always, it was a time of day that would stir nameless yearnings, and so she concentrated on the sausage and cheese and brown bread and made up a platter of them, feeling a loneliness.

But as she worked her mind served up a memory of that time in Köln, when she had been preparing supper for Otto, who had come home from the airfield and his duties as flight instructor to find her bleary from an afternoon with the wine closet. He had given her one of his little lectures, and, in the fog and rage, she had thrown a platter of sausage and cheese across the kitchen and run to her room.

In her subsequent remorse, she had written Otto a rambling, sentimental letter of apology, leaving it on his bureau for him to find when he came home the following day. And, presumably to prove he carried no hard feelings, Otto had sent her a new coat from one of those fancy shops on the boulevard. She had never worn it, saying it didn't fit right, and it had finally gone to Maria Loden, the widow on Zulpicher Strasse who was her friend from the Winter-Help, or whatever they called it in those days.

In those early times, she could look on personal unfulfillment as simply another aspect of life, like breathing or blinking or the weather, and over the years she had resigned herself—to the point of total acceptance—to the tiresome assertion that the Lord gives and the Lord takes away. But now, after a blink of time with Bruno Stachel, she was feeling intense resentment of the whimsicality God could bring to his supervision of mankind. How could any God capable of fashioning seasons and tides and heartbeats permit a filthy war that would take away the one man—the only human being—who had ever truly touched her? So who was the greater fraud: distruster Elfi Heidemann-Stachel, who could claim a trust in God's loving kindness, or God himself, who could, while taking a love away from her, claim a loving kindness?

For one thing was sure. Things were coming to an end, and, in the ending, her Bruno would be gone.

The Lord had given, and the war was going to take away. She knew it. She could feel it.

*   *   *

Stachel put down his coffee cup and glanced at Tarbell. "You said you have something to tell me?"

Tarbell, deep in one of the library's leather chairs, said

indolently, "Airboy's contact came in as scheduled this morning. Home Plate has ordered us to fly General von Lemmerhof to the base at Harrington. Tomorrow morning. Without fail."

Elfi gave him a quick glance. "Whatever for?"

"Ours is not to reason why, Fräulein Ingenieur." Stachel, seated behind the desk, gave the general a direct, challenging look. "I have a better question: What are we to fly?"

Von Lemmerhof clipped the end of a cigar with a silver cutter and studied the result with lowered, disapproving eyes. "I have arranged to hide an American bomber, a B-17, in a meadow in the Tyrol. Near a village called Nebelburg. It has been fully maintained by a most trustworthy crew. It is ready, at any time, to fly. Yesterday, Airboy gave me the alert; today Airboy has ordered the flight."

"So that explains all that training we had on the B-17, only to use parachutes instead." Elfi said laconically.

"A B-17 will permit us to fly out of Germany and into England without fear of being shot down by Ami fighters," the general said, studying the cigar as if it were a gem from a Pharaoh's tomb. "Hansen will drive us to the airstrip in my Mercedes. I am taking only one bag, one uniform. I suggest you three travel in an equally spartan manner."

Stachel shook his head. "No. We're not going. We are not flying the general to Harrington."

The others gave him uncomprehending stares. In the sudden silence the ticking of the clock on the mantel seemed thunderous.

"We've been *ordered* to fly the general to Harrington," Tarbell said, evoking the cardinal tenet of Military Religion.

"By whom? Polly Loomis? I don't owe Polly Loomis a thing."

There was another silence, even deeper, even more electric, unbroken until Stachel himself went on. "General von Lemmerhof is a fraud. He has promised the Amis the complete details of the Third Reich's plan to set up armed resistance in Oberbayern and the Tyrol. Yet he is, as we've all seen, so entirely in the dark, so truly unaware of conditions, so thoroughly inept and indifferent, and so altogether misleading in his claims of Hitler Jugend groups, SS Troops, Wehrmacht and Luftwaffe forces already on hand and digging in, it would be a fraud—a travesty—to foist him on the Americans. I not only refuse to fly him to Harrington, I am going to message Home Plate at the next radio contact that Nightstick will remain in Germany—going underground as a mole team and reporting incidental intelligence and targets of opportunity until such time as the American Army overruns us and we can surface."

They sat, listening to the clock and trying to absorb this rebellion and what it meant in personal terms. Stachel could see Tarbell's jaw working, Elfi's eyes studying the carpet, Lemmerhof's fingers toying with the unlighted cigar. If it were to come at all, Stachel decided, it would come now.

The general cleared his throat and said in a faintly strangled voice, "It's imperative that you fly me to Harrington. I shall tell you why. You have forced me to tell you why."

34

"VERY WELL, GENERAL," Stachel said, "let's hear it."

Von Lemmerhof at last placed the cigar between his pursed lips, and with a deliberate motion, lifted the benzine lighter from the table beside his chair and clacked it aflame. Puffing industriously, he sent up a cloud.

"I must meet with your people at Home Plate," he said

through the smoke, "to give them a report, complete with documents, on the real Nazi party resistance movement. Werewolf?" He waved the cigar disdainfully. "The Werewolf thing has been a pipe dream from the outset. It was conceived by a junior officer on the West Front, was considered by the Führer's advisers, and then placed on a shelf—half the consensus deeming it to be a crackpot idea, the other half seeing it to be militarily unfeasible and defeatist to boot.

"However, after the unsuccessful attempt to assassinate Hitler with a bomb last July, and after the Führer announced that Germany would never surrender—it would leave only scorched earth and the last German dead—Martin Bormann finally admitted to himself, apparently, that the war was lost and something would have to be done immediately to keep the Nazi party alive after the defeat. Despite all his public fanaticism in support of Hitler, Bormann has always put Bormann first. So Hitler's intention to fight to absolute destruction was, he felt, grotesque and unnecessary; it would be much better to salvage whatever possible of the National Socialist structure. So—"

Stachel broke in. "You mean Bormann planned treason?"

The general examined the ash on his cigar and shook his head. "Not treason per se. Bormann is truly too much of a fanatic for that. But treason, of course, if you consider it treason to give raging public support to the Führer's orders, while privately amending them. But Bormann has always manipulated Hitler in one way or another and this scheme is really not inconsistent in Bormann's total context. Bormann simply sees a need to continue the Führer-principle and himself as the logical one to meet the need on a long-term basis."

"Go on."

"Well," von Lemmerhof continued in his grating voice, "Bormann went secretly to Marschall Göring and Reichsleiter Himmler and suggested that the best way to keep the party organized and viable on a clandestine basis would be to establish a network of underground Nazi political cells *before* the German military collapse, which is expected no later than this coming summer. He proposed to take enormous sums in gold bullion and U.S. and English currency from the Reichs Treasury and bury it in salt mines at Merkers and several other places in the Bavarian arc. He would send reliable, yet obscure and generally unknown Nazis to Frankfurt, Mannheim, Stuttgart, Munich, and Bad Reichenhall to set up actual business enterprises—trucking companies, produce distributors, accountant firms, banks, construction contractors, and so on—which, financed by Nazi funds until self-supporting, could serve as covers and administrative headquarters for the political cells hiding in those cities and their surrounding population areas. When the Allies move in to occupy German national territory, these firms and their networks of Nazi reliables would be existing enterprises, all reputable and registered, that could be readily accepted into the Allies' postwar governance of the Reich. The aim is to work a long-range influence on whatever German national government eventuates, years ahead."

The general coughed, made a face, and placed the cigar in an ashtray. "Bormann further suggested," he continued, "that Göring and Himmler and he leave Germany prior to the military capitulation and live reclusive lives abroad, directing the overall clandestine party via intermediaries, until such time as they could return to Germany and resume open leadership." He paused, obviously awaiting the inevitable question.

Tarbell asked it. "Don't those three monsters understand? They're finished. The world would never accept them as German leaders, nor would the Germans themselves. Everybody has had enough of that bunch."

"Everybody but the diehards," Lemmerhof amended. "And since Göring, Himmler, and Bormann are practicing egomaniacs, they don't believe they're finished, either. In any event, that's the plan, and that's why I must take comprehensive reports to the Americans. I do not want

Göring, Himmler, and Bormann to succeed. Nor do I want them to survive. And to keep myself clear of war crimes charges, I am offering this intrigue in return for amnesty."

Stachel asked coolly, "How will Göring, Himmler, and Bormann leave the country?"

"By air," the general said, folding and unfolding his hands in his lap. "Bormann arranged secretly, with help of the millions he has diverted from the Treasury, to expand an airstrip near the village of Nebelburg, below Kufstein. He has placed a large transport plane there, an FW-200, the only German plane with the proper range, and a service force of some twelve to fifteen fanatical technicians. The plane will fly the three men and their families to Spain, where they will refuel for a trans-ocean flight to eventual sanctuary in South America."

"When are they leaving?"

"That's the question. I can't say. I don't think they really know. They are so prominent, so notorious, so incessantly in demand by the Führer, they have trouble finding time to go to the toilet, let alone to plot their escape from Berlin and a collapsing Germany. Meanwhile, though, their plane awaits —fueled, serviced, maintained by an expert mechanical group and attended by the Reich's most skilled pilot, copilot, and navigator."

Tarbell stirred, leaning forward in his chair. "These cover business firms—is Fuglein Kompanie one of these?"

The general gave him a quick glance from under lowered brows. "Oh. You've heard of that, have you?"

"I have."

"Well, yes. Fuglein is a moving-van firm. It has been set up by Hans Berger, formerly of Luftwaffe Intelligence, as managing director, and by Albert Linck, an HJ accountant, as business manager and comptroller. It is only one of a number that are operating or soon will be. Actually, Bormann's political structure is divided geographically. Kurt Bednar, SS Brigadeführer, will be political chief for the cover firms in

Oberbayern and the Alps; Alex Heide will head up things in Niederbayern—he's currently a Gebietsführer in the Reichs-jugendführung; the Schwäbische Alp is under Klaus Berg-mann, now an Amtchef in the RJF; Schwaben and Ober-schwaben are SS Sturmbannführer Gustav Singer's; Robert Kohl, Oberbannführer in the HJ, is responsible for the Allgäu; and Karl-Heinz Enzminger, former bureau chief in the Sicherheitsdienst, will lead the Schwarzwald. Farther north, in the Pfalz, the Odenwald, Hesse, and so on, people like Horst Matzdorf, Dieter Kugel, Wolfram Gutermann, and like luminaries will serve similarly. I have a complete roster for the Amis at Home Plate."

"Who is Gautzsch?" Stachel asked.

"He is Bormann's liaison man, his errand boy. By rank, an SS Brigadeführer. By profession, a brutal bastard."

"And he passed on Bormann's orders to you?"

"Yes," the general said. "The reason I'm in on all this is that Bormann, constantly under Hitler's thumb, finds it increas-ingly difficult to leave Berlin. Göring is already lumping around Bavaria and the Tyrol in God knows what stupid business, but Göring's value to Hitler is nil, and I think the Führer is simply keeping the fatso drug addict out of his sight. Himmler is Himmler. He's at the Führer's beck and call, yet, like Bormann and Göring, he believes the Führer has outlived his usefulness and, once he dies in the bunker as promised, Germany would do well to have Heinrich Himmler as its postwar leader. The net of all this is that somebody has had to supervise the secret airstrip, to ready the FW-200, to plan the logistics and keep the lid on so that Hitler won't learn of Bormann's plot to thwart his fight-to-the-last-breath decree. Bormann selected me to do the job, mainly because Hitler trusts me and would believe me when I told him I should be transferred to Munich, ostensibly to oversee the establish-ment of Tyrolean camps, where Hitler Jugend youngsters could be trained as replacements for Wehrmacht personnel lost in combat. But I emphasize—all this is a red herring. The

215

real plot rests in Bormann's flight to South America, after which I am to do what I can—with the assistance of the people at Fuglein—to tease Eisenhower with the Werewolf fiction. Long-range, Bormann plans to use me in his eventual Fuglein-arranged Nazi government."

"But what Bormann, et al, didn't realize," Stachel put in, "was that you have had enough and are ready to desert to the Americans."

"That's so. And to get my amnesty, to safely forward the Bormann plan to American hands, before Bormann can put it into effect, I will use an American B-17—one of the Luftwaffe's black outriders—that has been stationed at the airstrip near Nebelburg for some months. The major problem was to find an aircrew I could trust absolutely. You've seen how suspicious everybody is of everybody else in Germany today; if I were to set up a German crew to fly an American bomber for my personal use, word would be sure to reach Bormann eventually, and he'd see what I was up to. So then, what safer, more skilled crew than an American B-17 crew? But American B-17 pilots and copilots who speak German like Germans are very, very hard to come by. I suggested to Home Plate, therefore, that Bruno Stachel be trained for the job. He is well known for his enmity of the Nazis, and, as an American secret agent, he would be most careful to play things according to directions."

They fell into still another silence.

After a time, Stachel said, "Let me go over this. You have been asked by Bormann to set up a German plane that can carry him, Göring, and Himmler to South America, from where they will direct postwar Nazi machinations, conducted in various German geographical areas by hand picked party people operating legitimate businesses under new, false identities. But you want out, and you will deliver the scheme to Home Plate as payment for your personal amnesty. And you have persuaded Home Plate to send Nightstick over here to serve as your personal chauffeurs in an Ami plane, so that the Amis won't shoot you down en route to sanctuary in England."

"That's about it, Stachel. Yes."

Tarbell chuckled. "God. The trouble these bastards go to to keep in business."

"All right," Stachel said, staring at Lemmerhof as if the general were an especially loathsome insect, "I will fly you to Harrington as specified, so be sure your exhibits are ready." He glanced at Tarbell. "You will not be going, Amos. I want you to become a mole and set up a watch on Bormann's business enterprises. I suggest you start with Fuglein. Mole down, watch the firm, its people, its affiliates, so on. Go to the Hotel Ritter, across the street. Tell them you're a friend of Albert Knabe. Ask for Ludwig Auer. I think he'll help you. He's a disgruntled, crippled war veteran. And, when the Ami armies pass through Munich, overrun you, report to Home Plate."

General von Lemmerhof stood up, his face pale, his lower lip trembling. "You can't do that, Stachel. You can't leave your copilot here. You can't fly a B-17 single-handed. It's dangerous. Why do you think we went to such lengths to replace your Randelmann with this man here—this Folger?"

"I can fly anything single-handed, General. Besides, I'll have Frau Heidemann to assist me."

The general was visibly upset, a fact which Stachel noted carefully as still another confirmation of the truth he'd discerned.

* * *

Later, in the garden, Tarbell joined Stachel and Elfi, who were seated on a bench in the gazebo.

"Any bugs here?" he said in English.

"No," Stachel said. "It's too early in the season for bug-type bugs. And there are no other-type bugs. I've looked."

"All the same, let's stay with English. I feel safer."

"Very well. Excuse us, Fräulein Nagele. Our academic

friend wishes to practice his English. What is it, Amos?"

"Well, as team commander, it's your privilege to appoint me to mole duty on the Fuglein thing, and I'll do it, of course. But there's something you ought to know before you go tootling off in the wild blue with Lemmerhof."

"What's that?"

"Gautzsch came here today. I listened in. He knows all about our being here—you, Elfi, me. Which means Lemmerhof hasn't tried to fool Bormann at all. Bormann knows we're here. And so Bormann must know Lemmerhof plans to fink to the Americans."

"Of course, Amos. Gautzsch has been following us in his black Mercedes since we got here. Bormann knows. And that's why I must play this thing to the end. Besides, what other choice do we have?"

35

THEY LEFT MUNICH by 0300 hours because Lemmerhof wanted to be airborne by midmorning. He had alerted the B-17 ground crew at Nebelburg by a special field phone line that connected the cellar workroom of the Bogenhausen house with the maintenance chief, who lived in a shepherd's hut no more than fifty meters from the B-17's hidden tie-down pad. Navigation charts, with proper courses and heading changes, would be brought to the plane at takeoff—along with the best-available weather data from the Luftwaffe station at Riem—because Lemmerhof had not wanted to leave such telltale documents in the pilot's map pocket, where they might be found by unfriendlies. Stachel thought this was poppycock, of course, because Lemmerhof and his cardboard Werewolf operation—with all of its little zigs and zags, including an Ami bomber set aside for personal use—had long ago been cased by the ubiquitous Gautzsch. But even sillier, in Stachel's opinion, was Lemmerhof's insistence that they fly in daylight; the general was convinced —adamant as concrete—that Ami interceptors would be likely to shoot arbitrarily at an unidentified incoming plane in darkness, while a B-17, even if suspicious, could be easily spotted and allowed probational passage if seen in sunlight.

"Sorry, Stachel, it's a quirk of mine, this unwillingness to fly at night, unseeing and unseen," the general said. "That's the why of the B-17 in the first place. And you must indulge me, since I'm more valuable to Home Plate than you are."

"That's not true, General. I'm more valuable. Nobody goes anywhere unless I'm not only functioning but also willing to function. Wouldn't you say?"

Elfi, tense and irritable, snapped, "There you go again —two man-size children, bickering."

No one said much after that, choosing to keep with his thoughts and watch Hansen's driving. Checkpoints and roadblocks were no obstacle this night: The combination of a general-grade officer and a Grosser Mercedes with chauffeur and a Brigadeführer aide was simply more than the traffic-control and security forces cared to challenge seriously. Most of the vexations and delay came from highway detours, but even these were easier to negotiate, what with the special assistance given the impressive entourage and its haughty vehicle.

Stachel was thinking mostly of Tarbell, now alone and vulnerable beyond description or comprehension. In the time of their association there had been much change in the wiry, balding American—a transformation from the cynicism and querulousness of a chronic German-hater to the quiet watchfulness of a compassionate and empathetic human being.

Tarbell, in his plunge into the German devastation, had seemed to learn what Stachel himself had learned so painfully during the earlier Nazi years: A determined minority of rascals can usurp the history of a nation where the majority of its people are physically and spiritually underfed. For all his superior, disdainful mannerisms, Tarbell had begun —especially and noticeably so since seeing the Germany of faceless ruins, of starving and hopeless millions—to recognize the apolitical, nonpartisan nature of human misery. Blood is blood, agony is agony, dying is dying among daddies and mommies and kiddies and grandparents and aunts and cousins and neighbors and the little old lady down the street, even when it's all been caused by a handful of rascals they've put in charge.

Stachel sighed. The world was going to need all of the Amos Tarbells it could find in the years ahead.

In that uncanny way of hers, Elfi seemed to catch his thought. She echoed his sigh and, staring ahead at the road, said, "Bruno, what is to become of the Fatherland?"

"I don't know."

"Why are the politicians so single-minded? So unbendable? Why do they insist on continuing the ruin? What makes them so arrogantly sure—even when they've brought the roof down on their own heads—that the world will be better off if it conforms to what they think?"

"I don't know."

Von Lemmerhof coughed dryly and said, "It was the betrayal of 1918—the Versailles Treaty—the oppression of the Fatherland's enemies—"

Elfi shouted. It was a kind of explosion, Stachel thought. As if a bomb had been ticking in her.

"Oh, to hell with you and your rotten, goddamn, whining excuses, you miserable, potbellied son of a bitch!"

The subsequent interval was filled with silent strain. Then, despite himself, Stachel laughed outright.

"You are quite a woman, Fräulein Nagele," he managed. "Or have I told you that before?"

"And stop that Fräulein Nagele nonsense, too, damn you. My name is Elfrieda Stachel, and don't you forget it."

"It seems to lack something. It's so, well, stodgy."

"It lacks nothing." She folded her arms and continued to stare unblinkingly ahead, her face set and pale.

* * *

It wasn't until they had cleared Kufstein and were in the climb toward the Wildem Kaiser Valley that Lemmerhof stirred in the back seat, sighed, and said in a peculiarly hollow voice, "You people think you are so good, so superior, because you have washed your hands, divorced yourselves from the so-called German question. Well, you have little cause to raise your noses. I've looked into your backgrounds, and you are not without blemishes of your own. You, Stachel—a killer, a manipulator, a user, a wastrel. You, Frau Heidemann—a poseur, a hypocritical religionist, an alcoholic. You both are as self-serving as I am. Even as Hitler is, for that matter. We—all of us—are alike. With you, it was the drink and the escapades and dirty tricks and holier-than-thou condemnations of the weaknesses in others. With me it's been the search for creature comfort and power over men. With others it's some other story of selfishness. Our whole goddamned nation has done precisely what we've done— hunger for the good, do the bad; aspire to greatness and settle for shame. Like us, the Fatherland has resented the preposterous double standard of world morality—the piety of bigots, hypocrites, and self-righteous graspers. Like us, Germany has built its own ego by deflating the ego of others. Like us, everybody in the world busies himself with the sins of others so he can forget his own. So don't look down your noses at me, my friends. Don't give me your little lectures on propriety. We are doomed—you, Stachel; you, Frau Heidemann;

I—and we are soon to enter hell together. We will leave the hell we made for the hell that waits."

They rode on in silence.

At one point, Hansen said, "Do you mind if I smoke, Herr General?"

"Ask Frau Heidemann," Lemmerhof rasped. "She's the arbiter of moral and behavioral questions in our little group."

*　*　*

The sky was clear and an especially deep blue after sunrise, and the smell of damp, awakening green things was heavy on the mild breeze. April had begun, and there would be much cold and rain ahead, even snow, but spring was moving, and Stachel, still weighed down by Lemmerhof's bitter soliloquy, thought briefly of how fitting it was that Germany was dying at a time when the world was coming alive again.

The B-17 was the G model, same as that on which he and Tarbell had spent so much time together. It sat on a pad of clover under a netting designed to simulate a sheep-dotted hillside; its flanks streamed with dew, its olive-drab surfaces glinted dully in the filtered daylight, and it looked, as Tarbell had looked when they'd said their good-byes, alone and poignant in an unspecific way.

Hansen pulled the car alongside and stepped out to open the door for Lemmerhof. As the general emerged, the Feldwebel in charge of the mechanical crew called attention, and the little group sprang into heel-clicking ramrods.

"As you were," the general ordered, pulling on his gloves. To the Feldwebel he said, "Is the aircraft ready for immediate departure, Steiger?"

"Yes, Herr General."

"Give the charts and headings to the Standartenführer here. Also the checklist. And weather reports."

"Yes, Herr General." Feldwebel Steiger handed Stachel a briefcase. "The course data are in a sealed envelope inside,

Standartenführer. The weather details will be here momentarily."

"Very well," Stachel said. "I'll be making my walk-around inspection meantime. And I'll want to examine the interior, the loading."

The Feldwebel sent a nervous glance at Lemmerhof. "Well, sir, the bomb bay has been sealed. It has been converted into a cargo hold and then, except for the catwalk, sealed off. Unauthorized personnel are forbidden in the cargo and rear areas of the airplane. Orders of General von Lemmerhof."

"Unauthorized? The pilot of this tub is unauthorized?"

Lemmerhof put in, "It's not important, Stachel. You can fly the airplane without knowing what's in cargo."

"I can. But I choose not to. As pilot, I'm airplane commander. I want to see what's aboard that machine. I'll want to know what to worry about if we run into turbulence that starts shifting weights, centers of gravity. A heavily loaded B-17 is no piece of cake, even with a full crew. For an unassisted pilot, it can be very difficult if it wants to be."

"What makes you think it's heavily loaded, Stachel?"

"You wouldn't have sealed an empty bomb bay."

"This is all academic. The cargo compartments have been welded shut. So carry on. There are flight suits and appropriate equipment waiting for you in the cockpit. I'll be in the rear passenger compartment and will give you your instructions on the intercom."

"Instructions? What instructions? I'm the pilot. I decide what movements the airplane makes."

"Indulge me, Stachel. Indulge me. Meanwhile, I'd like you to return my medal—my Tin Cravat, as you so negligently call it."

"Sorry, General. I left it on my bureau when we left this morning."

*   *   *

Elfi looked like a child in a snowsuit, sitting in the copilot seat in her sheep-lined coveralls and helmet. She was trying very hard for nonchalance, but he could see that she was nervous and ill at ease in this most masculine of places. After completing the prestart setting of valves and switches, he handed her the checklist. "Here you are, Madam Copilot. Perhaps you will be so kind as to help me start up this frigging bucket of bolts."

She smiled tightly, nodding. "I'll do what I can."

"Incidentally, you'll notice that the parachutes have been removed from their stowage behind our seats."

"So that we won't try to abandon the plane, right?" She paused, thinking. "Where did they get an Ami plane in such good shape?"

"Who knows? Forced landing. A desertion. Who knows?"

He spread the chart and examined the course laid out there: west by northwest to Ravensburg, northwest to Strasbourg, then straight across France to the channel and on into Harrington. Simple. Straightforward. Nothing cute, as Polly Loomis would say. The altimeter setting for Nebelburg was clipped to the chart, as were quick-reference headings, and, for emergencies, Luftwaffe recognition code for the day, just as if there were truly a Luftwaffe alive and well enough to worry about a lone B-17 flying low and fast across the cellar of the Fatherland on a course for home.

"Start the engines, Stachel," the general said in his earphones.

Stachel glanced at Elfi and gave her a wink. "Ready?"

"Any time you say."

He unlocked the controls and checked his seat adjustment and phone. "Read the starting checklist to me," he said.

"It's in English."

"Read phonetically. I'll understand."

"Alarm bell."

"Checked."

"Wheel chocks."

He glanced outside and saw Feldwebel Steiger standing by with the pull ropes. "Checked."

"Fire guard."

"Doesn't apply."

"Master switches."

"On."

"Battery switches and inverters."

"On and checked."

"Parking brakes, hydraulics."

"On and checked."

"Booster pumps, pressure."

"On and checked."

They worked their way down the list and eventually the engines were bucketing and snorting and throwing blue clouds, with the great propellers thrashing the air and whirling up tornadoes of grass and spray from the night's pools of dew. Stachel set the trim tabs, exercised turbos and props, turned off the generators, and ran up the engines one at a time, with throttles at twenty-eight inches manifold pressure. He checked left and right magnetos, then both, watching the nacelles for excessive vibration. When all appeared normal, he reduced throttle to 1,000 rpm, and sat, waiting for Feldwebel Steiger and his crew to remove the camouflage from his taxiway.

He flipped the interphone switch and said, "Hello, Elfrieda Stachel."

She touched her earphone in reflex, then gave him a wan smile. "Hello, Bruno Stachel."

"You look charming in all your furs."

"I'm sorry it took us so long. Getting together, I mean. The general was right, the things he said in the car on our way to Nebelburg. I'm a fraud, Bruno. And my fraud has caught up with me. All those years, when I was trying to be so good, when I was posing as good, you were lost to me. Now that I'm openly a tramp, here we are. Together as we've never been. It's crazy."

"War changes everybody. It has made you worse, perhaps; maybe it has made me better. And we've met in the middle somewhere. Now we're where we were always meant to be. Who knows?"

"Whatever. I only care that I had you. Even for a time."

* * *

There was a jarring explosion, then the thumping and crackling of machine guns and rifles. An enormous, rolling cloud, boiling with flame and debris, surged skyward from the hangar area across the meadow.

"My God," Elfi gasped, "what's that?"

"It's the beginning of the ending, you might say. About now I expect to hear from General von Lemmerhof, in our caboose."

"All right, Stachel," the general's voice crackled, "begin your taxi. Take us over there by the fire."

Stachel glanced at Elfi and pointed to the right side of the panel. "Unlock the parking brake, will you?"

Then he shot a look toward the ground crew and nodded at Steiger, signaling removal of the chocks; in the same instant he checked the hydraulic pressure to be sure it read six hundred pounds. Then, with inboard engines idling, he walked the ship off its pad with a surge of power to the outer engines. He rolled slowly, no faster than Steiger and his men, who walked alongside, obviously torn between their fascination with the conflagration down the field and their duty, which was to attend the aircraft. Since he had a straight path downwind, he kept the tail wheel locked, using only a touch of brake to correct for minor deviations.

The fire was very intense now, and as they approached, Stachel could see the FW-200 collapsing in the interior incandescense of the flaming hangar. Lying in a scattered row, like lumps of rags, were a dozen mechanics and three Luftwaffe flight officers, and standing over the bodies was a squad of SS troopers and a brace of Obersturmführers, young-faced and looking pleased with themselves.

"Oh, Lord," Elfi said. "What is going *on*?"

"The liquidation of all those who have any knowledge of this B-17 aircraft we're riding in," Stachel said matter-of-factly. "The plan is for us to vanish without trace—from Hitler's, Himmler's, and Göring's points of view, that is."

"You mean Lemmerhof has had all those men executed? Simply because they—"

"You've got it, as the Amis say. But, my dear Elfrieda, unless I miss my guess, you haven't seen anything yet, as the Amis also like to say."

"But why did he burn that other big plane?"

"Because he wants the others—Göring, Himmler—to stay in Germany and die like the heroes they are. He is not about to have them floating around the world after his rather spectacular treason."

He saw motion out of the corner of his eye, and, turning, he made out a black Mercedes, coming at high speed from the direction of the barracks area. The car jounced over the clover field, yawing, to make a skidding turn around the right wing and then a halt just starboard of the main entrance door. Straining, Stachel tried to see who had left the car, but he was unsuccessful. *No matter,* he thought. *I know who it is.*

Von Lemmerhof's voice came over the line again. "We've taken aboard two passengers, Stachel, a fact you might need in handling the airplane. Meanwhile maintain your position. I'm stepping out for a moment to thank my helpers. You may take off as soon as I return aboard."

"All right."

There was an interval of waiting, and he and Elfi sat, wordless, watching the blaze and the SS troopers, smoking cigarettes and laughing. After a time, General von Lemmerhof and Hansen appeared from under the wing to saunter over to the troops. One of the Obersturmführers called attention, and the squad fell in, stiff and severe, in two ranks of six men each. The general returned the officers' stiff-armed salute, gave the troopers at ease, and began to shake hands with each.

"And now," Stachel said, "is where we say good-bye to our timorous and self-deluding friend, General von Lemmerhof."

He was still speaking when the machine gun opened up, out of sight below the right wing. Von Lemmerhof, for all his bulk, virtually bounced into the air, spinning. The troopers and their officers went down as if they had been scythed —helmets rolling, guns clattering—some to roll, half rise, then fall back again. There was a pause, apparently for the gunner to engage a fresh magazine, after which the bodies were sprayed again and a final silence ensued.

"Oh, God." Elfi's voice was faint in the phones.

The door to the bomb-bay catwalk was flung open and Gautzsch, huge in his flight gear, moved in to take a stance on the flight engineer's deck behind their seats. He handed Stachel a sheaf of papers.

"Good morning," he boomed over the idling engines' sound. "Those are your new headings, Stachel. You will now take off and fly us to the beautiful Mediterranean coast of North Africa."

36

STACHEL SHOOK HIS HEAD. "No."

"What do you mean, Stachel? Fly the airplane."

"Not until you bring us parachutes. I'm not flying anywhere, through Ami-controlled skies, over mountains and seas, without a parachute in the cabin for me and my wife. And that's that."

Gautzsch produced a Walther pistol and held it to Stachel's chin. "Fly the airplane."

"Perhaps you are ready to fly the airplane, eh, Gautzsch?"

The big man's eyes showed semblance of thought. The pistol barrel moved to Elfi's chin.

"Fly," he commanded, glaring into Stachel's eyes.

Elfi smiled. "Stay right where you are, Bruno. Even if he shoots me."

"If he shoots you, my dear Elfrieda, he is guaranteed to go nowhere. I'll collapse the landing gear."

Gautzsch sneered, then disappeared through the doorway.

"I take it Gautzsch has been planning to go to Africa all along," Elfi said.

"He and Bormann. Bormann is at this very moment relaxing in the rear compartment, with nothing to do but take mental inventory of the boxes of gold bullion tucked into our welded bomb bay. Gold he will use to build a new career for himself in South America, while Adolf and Hermann and Heinrich, his erstwhile pals, enjoy martyrdom in Berlin or wherever."

"It's been Bormann behind it all, then."

"Right you are. This whole thing, from the phony Werewolf to Fuglein and the other bogus business firms, has been a scheme of Bormann's, calculated to get Bormann out of a dying Reich with a fortune in gold. Poor Lemmerhof's mistake was in thinking Bormann really intended to take him along. His other mistake, I suppose, was when he followed Bormann's suggestion that it would be a nice gesture to get off the plane and say good-bye to all the fellows."

"I feel sick."

"Well, wait until Gautzsch returns. Then throw up on him, eh?"

"Why don't you collapse the landing gear now?" she said.

"It can't be done on this model of the B-17. The gear won't function while the airplane's weight is on its wheels. But even if I could collapse the gear, it would only get us killed where we sit, and Bormann and Gautzsch would find another way. Believe me, those types always find another way."

"I see."

Gautzsch, wearing a parachute harness of his own now, returned with a pair of standard B-17 clip-on chest chutes and harness, and, waving the P.38, said, "Put on the harness. I'll stow the chute packs on the floor here. One move toward them without my permission and you will be shot. And believe me, I don't want to shoot you, I want you simply to get us where we're going with as little fuss as possible."

After he and Elfi had struggled into their harnesses, Stachel said, "Is His Majesty in the rear ready to take off?"

"He was ready five minutes ago," Gautzsch said nastily.

"Then sit on the jump seat there and stay out of my way. I'll be very busy for a time."

Stachel applied power gradually, walking the throttles forward and setting the friction lock against creeping. The airplane began to move into the wind.

"Keep your eye on those dials there, Elfi," he said. "Manifold pressure, rpm, temperature and pressure gauges. If you see any pronounced fluctuations, let me know."

The B-17 was running fast now, its wheels kissing the grass, lifting, kissing again. At 110 mph he eased back on the control column and the airplane flew itself away from the ground, its engines racketing.

"Raise the landing gear, Elfi. The third switch from the right, there on the pedestal. That's it. Good. Now look out the window and see if the right wheel goes up fully. I'll check the left wheel."

At 140 mph he reduced power to a manifold pressure of thirty-five and dropped the rpm to 2,300. Reaching, he adjusted the cowl flaps, then settled back to climb the ship out of the Kufstein notch and over the Bavarian farmlands, rolling and green and dotted with tiny white houses.

"Very nice," Gautzsch said through his phone jack. "You must have done this kind of thing before."

Stachel ignored him, concentrating on the new headings and shooting occasional glances at the sky around and ahead.

*   *   *

Elfi was thinking of Otto, her first husband. She had discovered that Otto liked airplanes as much as he liked her the day he had induced her to take her first flight. She had always had a fear of heights, even suffered vertigo, and so she had declined to go up with him out of a common-sense desire to avoid making a fool of herself. Otto had assured her, in his world's-leading-expert way, that vertigo rarely occured in airplanes, inferring that she was not really being a good wife, since a good wife shares her husband's enthusiasms. So she had agreed to go up in the rickety biplane out of wifely duty.

Oddly enough, he had been right. As the airplane rose, with her in the front seat and Otto piloting in the rear seat it seemed as if the plane were standing still and the ground had fallen away, slowly and majestically. She had just begun to enjoy the sensation—completely free of vertigo when he had looped the loop, or whatever they called it in those days. When they finally returned to the airport, she was a wreck, tear-stained, rumpled, and, climbing from the cockpit, she had been sick all over herself. Otto had tried to help her, of course, but she had slapped him across the mouth and run for the car. She hadn't spoken to him for days.

Watching Stachel now, golden in the sunlight, younger-looking and more alive than she'd ever seen him, she knew that, for all his terrible past, for all his masculine willfulness and arrogant self-centeredness, he would never have been able to abuse her as Otto had on that dreadful day. Stachel had managed to live, to thrive, to ascend, because he was a son of a bitch; but he was a sweet son of a bitch, with a surprising capacity for empathy and tenderness.

And she loved him more than anything or anyone else.

He glanced at her once, and smiled—a beautiful, reassuring smile, with his blue eyes twinkling with an inner elation.

Gautzsch, leaning forward, said, "You haven't picked up the southwesterly heading, Stachel. Why?"

"In a moment. I want to get over this overcast that's forming."

"I should think you'd want to stay below it, where we'd blend with the ground. Up here we'll stick out like a fly on a baby's ass."

"What's the matter, Gautzsch?" Stachel taunted. "You are anxious to keep your rendezvous with the submarine?"

"How do you know about that?"

"I'm a good guesser. You and Bormann can't fly too far in this old tub. Africa, sure. But across an ocean? No. A submarine is more in order, I'd guess."

They flew for a time, gaining altitude, and Elfi let her gaze drift across the sky and the delicate clouds below them. The sunlight was brilliant, and she could feel its warmth on her face, even in all the clamor and trembling and humidity of the cockpit enclosure. There was a darkness suddenly, a motion to the right of her, then another to the left, beyond Bruno's side window.

"Bruno—there are planes around us. Flying with us."

"I know, Amis. P-51 Mustangs." He flipped a switch and the headphones took on a new sound, a hollowness, like that to be heard in a seashell.

A strong voice came in to chatter in English.

"What is he saying, Stachel?" Gautzsch demanded tensely.

"He's saying hello. He's asking me if I'm lost."

"What are you going to do? No tricks now. I warn you."

Stachel shrugged. "I don't know. I'll have to think about it."

"Well, you can't just ignore the bastard."

"Shut up, Gautzsch, I'm thinking."

*   *   *

Stachel peered at the lead fighter plane sitting abeam his left wing tip, rising and falling gracefully in the air currents.

The amiable voice crackled again. "Hi, big boy. What's a-matta-you? You ain't talking. No radio, maybe? Say something to yore liddle buddy. Like a recognition signal, for instance. Yore liddle buddy don't want to think you're a great big bad guy in disguise, now do he?"

Stachel looked over his shoulder at Gautzsch, looming nervously in the crew chief's area. "The lady is now going to bail out, Gautzsch. Clip on your parachute, Elfi."

Gautzsch rasped, "Hold it now—"

Elfi, gazing at Stachel, said, "I'm not going anywhere without you."

"I'm going someplace you might not like."

"We'll see."

"Don't make me waste this grand gesture. After all the years, it's the only one I've ever come up with."

"I love you."

"I know that."

"Call me darling. Just once, Bruno."

"And ruin my image? Don't be silly."

"I love you."

"All right, Elfi, darling, hang on. I'll take you where you've never been before."

Gautzsch roared, "What are you talking about? What's going on here—"

Stachel flipped the radio on liaison channel and, in laborious, precise tones, said, "Goodt day, mein honorable colleagues. Ve are a friendt. Blease forgiff za radio difficulty."

* * *

There was a terrible rattling sound, and she saw the instruments turn magically to junk, and she threw a wild look at Bruno. He was laughing, his strong, even teeth white, his eyes crinkled, and she began to laugh with him, holding his hand, and the earth tilted, passing from beneath the plane up and around and over her head, and the sun glare turned from brilliance to shadow to brilliance in the roaring and whistling.

"I love you!" she shouted soundlessly into the sound. "I love you!"

He was laughing, and she saw his lips form the words.

𝕏

THE DAY WAS moist and heavy with the redolence of a thousand miles of Gulf Coast. Noon had not yet come and already the field shimmered under a brassy sky, and the headquarters flag hung sodden in the September heat. She wished for a breeze; even the slightest stir might have helped. The band, a wad of tinsel in the hard blue shadows of the post exchange, finished its tuneless march with a crash and a thud. She kept her eyes on the undeviating Texas horizon, searching for a feather of dust or some other signal that the sky had not died. But even the cotton-batten clouds seemed to be immobilized, and she watched these for a time, breathing deeply and listening to the shouts and clacks and alkaline squeakings of soldiers on parade in the sun.

At last the blessed dismissal order came, and the formations dissolved to flee for the shade, where the visitors milled about, waving paper fans stenciled "Compliments of Magley Funeral Home" and looking benignly superior for having the good sense to be civilians.

He found her at the rim of the crowd.

"Hello, Polly," he said without enthusiasm, as usual.

"Congratulations on your Distinguished Service Medal, Amos. I'm glad you've been recognized for a really fine piece of work."

"I didn't think you'd come all the way to Texas to say that. The phone's more your style."

"You are a hero. You deserve special attention." She gave him a close examination, and she decided that he looked absolutely marvelous in his tan summer uniform with all its ribbons and glittering brass and the new medal, dangling brilliantly on his left breast. "Any place we can get a tall cool one—to celebrate your medal and the end of the war?"

He took her by the arm and walked her down Pershing Drive to the traffic circle, where the Officers' Club sulked behind its barricade of dusty plantings. In the lounge, after settling in the cool shadows and sampling their drinks, she rested against the cushions and gave him her best smile. "You look altogether smashing," she said.

"It's taken awhile to come back," he said. "I'm still not connected on all circuits. My leg's stiff, my jaw still hurts. But I guess it was worth it."

"All of Washington is talking about you and how you busted up the Nazi business plot. They had a great idea going there, but you got there first."

"I was lucky." He shrugged. "And Stachel got me pointed right."

A stillness settled over them, and she felt a pang.

Tarbell drained his glass and studied the ice remaining there. He said, "Did you ever find out what happened?"

"Only what the air corps reported."

"And what was that?"

"Some fighters—I forget the unit, but it doesn't really matter anyhow—said an unidentified lone B-17 climbed out of the clouds and flew right at them, as if its pilot wanted them to see him. They requested the day's recognition signal. There was no answer for a time, then a voice came over the radio. It was a very heavy German accent, they said. No code word, a German accent, and the fly-boys assumed it was one of those Black Maria types the Nazis were fond of using. Per standing orders, they shot it down."

"Nobody got out?"

"They saw no parachutes. The bomber was falling steeply, burning, and disappeared in the cloud layer below."

Tarbell sighed. "Well, it's too bad."

"Yes."

"You lost Lemmerhof, too. And the Werewolf thing."

She turned her glass in her hand, studying its lights in the dim reflection of the sunlight beyond the shaded windows.

"I lost more than that. I lost Bormann. Stachel was to have flown him to an airstrip in North Africa, where he'd board an American submarine. We were going to interrogate him in Puerto Rico, then drop him off in South America."

She saw Tarbell's astonishment, the quick anger in his eyes. "You what? You were playing footsies with that—that *creep*?"

"He was what Nightstick was all about. Lemmerhof and the Werewolf thing were simply a dust cloud, set up by Bormann. The pseudo-activity in the Alps was, first, to make Hitler think Lemmerhof was building a base for the training of Hitler Jugend Wehrmacht replacements, and, second, to make Eisenhower think the Nazis were indeed setting up the Werewolf operation he feared."

Tarbell gave her a long unblinking stare. "So what was Bormann really up to?"

Polly's eyes met his for a moment, then turned away. "Bormann knew the Americans had traffic with a message-drop in Bern—an outpost in Switzerland that provided a kind of secret, nonpartisan point of conversation between Berlin and Washington. Through the message-drop, code name Max, Bormann contacted OSS operations. I happened to be on duty in Bern that day, began the talks, and gave Bormann the code name Wiseguy. Bormann, or Wiseguy, promised us his complete intelligence file on the Soviets—and they were the best and most extensive in the world, buddy-boy—if we could manage to fly him secretly out of Germany and into South America with a load of Nazi gold."

"But he's supposed to have stayed in Berlin, in the Führerbunker, all along. He never left there. And he's supposed to have died there at the end. The B-17 incident was almost a month earlier."

" 'Supposed to' is the operative phrase there, Amos. That's one part of Bormann's plan that went well. History is only what we see and hear and read, and not always—even rarely, I'd say—what really goes on. Berlin and the Führerbunker were madhouses in the final weeks. Comings and goings, orders and counterorders. Heroes and finks. Everybody aware that Hitler was doomed. Everybody watching out for number one. Bormann was ready for conditions like that. Since the war began he's had a double. And a dummy file on his double. Including dental records. This for when, or if, Germany lost the war and his double's body was found in a, well, convenient place and a coroner's dental ID report was required by somebody. Bormann's double *was* killed in Berlin, and someday somebody will find the teeth. But Bormann's somewhere else, presumably under a pile of B-17 tin somewhere in Southern Germany. Or at least that's what we must assume."

Tarbell stared out the window at the line of barracks, shimmering and somnolent in the Saturday heat. "You never told Stachel about Bormann, this Wiseguy thing?"

"I've never even told the President of the United States. Lemmerhof and the Werewolf were for Roosevelt, Truman, and Eisenhower and all the other practicing Nice-Nellies and the self-congratulating histories they'll write someday about how they broke up the Werewolf before it got off the ground. Bormann, though, was exclusively for me and my boss, Huey Vought. We decided that if the Washington politicians got wind of Bormann's overture, the case would turn into a three-ring circus. So we told no one. Bormann's personal files and behind-the-scenes counsel would make Huey and me the hottest Soviet specialists in the business. We could have written our own tickets, because the Soviets are already our biggest threat and will get even worse in the years ahead.

What Bormann knew about the Soviets and their intelligence apparatus could make Reinhardt Gehlen, our so-called prize Nazi intelligence catch, look like one of the Katzenjammer Kids."

Tarbell coughed. "You knew Bormann would kill Stachel and Elfi as soon as that B-17 landed, didn't you?"

"C'est la frigging guerre, as the French say." She shrugged in the Gallic manner.

"You put Elfi on that mission just to get her killed?"

"Not really. Bormann wanted some sure way he could control Stachel if Stachel got out of line. Holding Mrs. Heidemann hostage would have done it. Don't you agree?"

Tarbell gave her a wary glance. "Why are you letting me in on all this 'real' history?" he said sardonically.

"I've got to start a program to get a nice spot in the new CIA they're setting up. Huey Vought has returned to private industry, in a kind of massive pout, now that he can't be the master spy, thanks to Bormann's, ah, demise. Which leaves me sort of one of the pack. My record's OK, but I need a dash of glamor—something to attract a sponsor among the Nice-Nellies. I thought maybe you and I could buddy up. With my brains and your heroism, we might suggest a good thing to some big shot, don't you think?" She gave him the best smile again.

Tarbell gazed out the window again, his eyes narrowed against the glare. After an interval, he reached into a pocket and withdrew a lumpy envelope. "The day he left Munich —the last time I saw him—Stachel gave me two things. One was a slip of paper carrying the name of a little girl I was supposed to take a box of candy to. The other was this. I wasn't going to give it to you," he said quietly, "because I thought it was in bad taste. But there's really no reason not to, I guess. It was something he asked me to do. And he never was known for his good taste."

She took the envelope and ran a nail under the seal, and a

large Iron Cross with silver piping thumped onto the checkered tablecloth.

"What's this?" she said, amused.

"A Tin Cravat. Stachel borrowed it from Lemmerhof to wear on a reconnaissance. Before we split up, he gave it to me to give to you. He said to tell you that you've earned it."

She laughed and shook her head in mock indignation. "Honestly, now," she chortled too brightly, "isn't that just like him? What a character. He was always one for the flamboyant thumb to nose. I'll miss him." There was a catch in her voice.

Tarbell stood up and walked to the door, where he turned and gave her a distant preoccupied stare. "He's out there somewhere," he said. "He'll turn up. He and Elfi."

Well, she thought, watching him walk stiffly into the sunny world outside, *to hell with you, Amos.*

She sat alone in the beer and tobacco and ammonia smells, getting hold of herself. She wished she had a cigarette, but Gordon, who said he simply couldn't enjoy a roll in the hay with someone who smelled like a pool hall, was in an incredibly good spot at State now, and it was important to please him, and so she hadn't had a single puff in three weeks. It was killing her, sure enough, but Gordon was said to have all kinds of pull among the Nice-Nellies.

Well, back to the old grind.